A
little
Murder
in the
Biggest
little
City

A Little Murder in the Biggest Little City

A novel of fiction by
JAMES TURNAGE

iUniverse, Inc.
Bloomington

A Little Murder in the Biggest Little City

iUniverse books may be ordered through booksellers or by contacting:

iUniverse
1663 Liberty Drive
Bloomington, IN 47403
www.iuniverse.com
1-800-Authors (1-800-288-4677)

Because of the dynamic nature of the Internet, any web addresses or links contained in this book may have changed since publication and may no longer be valid. The views expressed in this work are solely those of the author and do not necessarily reflect the views of the publisher, and the publisher hereby disclaims any responsibility for them.

Any people depicted in stock imagery provided by Thinkstock are models, and such images are being used for illustrative purposes only.
Certain stock imagery © Thinkstock.

ISBN: 978-1-4759-5145-5 (sc)
ISBN: 978-1-4759-5146-2 (ebk)

Library of Congress Control Number: 2012917626

Printed in the United States of America

iUniverse rev. date: 09/25/2012

Prologue

When Larry Columbo woke up on Friday morning, he didn't feel so good. His head hurt, he was nauseous, and every muscle in his body ached. It wasn't unusual for him to feel this way. His job as General Manager of a casino offered him the duty and opportunity to drink more than his share, and sometimes to ingest damaging quantities of a certain white powder, or swallow pills to enhance his good feeling. In truth, he expected all the actual work to be done by his subordinates. His life was one big party.

But today was worse. He had diarrhea and vomiting, and they were becoming more frequent. He decided a little "hair of the dog" might help. He went to the refrigerator and found a beer. He opened it and gulped down over half the bottle. It didn't seem to help. Within a minute, his head was once again poised over the toilet bowl.

Operating the largest casino in Reno, Nevada, for over fifteen years had offered him many perks. He and his family also owned a successful casino next door, and all this fame, fortune, and respectability in the community, gave him access to just about anything he desired in his materially oriented life. He had enough money to buy anything his heart desired, and any woman "little Larry" lusted after. His family had amassed enough clout with the city council to ensure that anything they sought would be given to them. They even had enough power to influence the local police whenever necessary.

But on this Friday, he was no better off than many of the homeless men who spent their nights downtown looking for a few dollars to get drunk enough to forget their pasts. And he was definitely getting worse. What was he drinking last night? He had taken some pills, but didn't remember what they were. He remembered snorting a few lines. Oh well, this would pass, and by tonight he would again be in a party mood. Maybe going back to bed for a while was a good idea.

He laid down on his custom made bed with its silk sheets. He looked at the mirror above, and was frightened by what he saw. His face was contorted, and his fingers appeared crooked. He was sweating profusely, and his body began to cramp. He couldn't control his arms or legs. When the cramping eased for a second, he began to heave, but nothing came out at first. With the second attack, the retching produced a bloody residue. He wasn't frightened, he was scared to death. He tried to reach for the phone, but his body wouldn't move in that direction. The cramping got worse, and the blood was flowing freely from his mouth and nose. In less than fifteen minutes his body stopped convulsing. He had died in his own bed, alone, his silk sheets soaked with blood.

Chapter 1

In the early fall of 1985, Michael Whitten decided to take a vacation. He would take it alone. He had learned from experience how much he disliked traveling companions, so his destination would be determined only by the amount of money he was able to spend, and, of course, what entertainment he was seeking. He was twenty-six years old, and the things he cared about in life were minimal.

He had no way of knowing it, but his decision to take a vacation, combined with his destination of choice would lead to not only changes in his life, but would affect the lives of many others. He was not a man who was happy with his life. But, he wasn't unhappy either. It was what is was. He controlled his fate. He had no close friends, and this was by choice. Therefore he had no one to confide in. There was no one else to discuss the cause and effect of his actions. His deeds would result in unsolved events that lasted for years.

Michael had been born in Los Angeles. He was an only child whose father had abandoned him and his mother when he was eight years old. He had never known why, but that's just the way things happen sometimes. She consequently decided that alcohol was her only friend, so, in the true sense of the word, she abandoned Michael too. When she came home from work, she retreated to her bedroom, and seldom left except to get ice from the freezer. Other than feeding him, and making sure he had clothes to wear at home and school, she paid no attention to him. He had raised himself. He became used to it, he was comfortable with it, and therefore did not seek out friendships in his childhood or his adult life. He watched TV most of the time he was not at school. He liked sports, but didn't especially like the idea of being on a team. He would shoot baskets by himself, or throw a baseball against a wall and retrieve it. When he got older, he found an interest in tennis, but all he ever did was hit the ball against the backboard.

He had lived his entire life in the Los Angeles area. He loved the sun, sand and surf, the sunrises and sunsets. Michael never felt the need to share the beauty of the sea with anyone. He relished the solitude when he sat on the beach at sunset, watching the ocean sizzle as the sun disappeared into the cool water on the horizon. He loved anything he could do in the water, body surfing, and boogey boarding, and with the warm weather virtually year round, he took advantage of the situation whenever possible.

Though it was the opposite of being in the warm sand and surf, he had also developed an interest in skiing. Mammoth Mountain was about three and a half hours away from home, and was said to have some of the best skiing in the west. It offered everything from beginner runs to helicopter skiing in the back bowls. He made several trips there, and enjoyed it immensely. The same lift that would take an expert skier to their runs, would take a beginner, like Michael, to the same area where he could ski less difficult terrain.

He had also made several trips to Las Vegas, and found that gambling was a great pastime. It was just over four hours from home, so he could go whenever the urge came. It was a city that truly never slept. He could do anything he wanted at any hour of the day or night. He spent little time in his room when he was there. He even won some money on several occasions. He stayed mostly at one hotel, because he felt lucky there, and, because he was a frequent customer, and one of his wins was for several thousand dollars, he was given "comps". These consisted of room discounts, and free meals. Vegas made him feel special, even important.

He never had the desire to travel to many of the western states, though he always knew this area would be his home. As far as he could tell, only California offered it all. No other state had everything to offer from great beaches to great snow skiing, even desert life, if that was what tripped your trigger. He had no desire to live in, or even visit areas that had tornadoes, hurricanes, extreme cold, or extreme heat. Considering his likes and dislikes, he finally decided to vacation in Reno, Nevada. He read that, although Reno had all four distinct seasons, the winters averaged 42 degrees in the daytime, and the summers only reached 90 degrees or maybe a few degrees higher, and only during the month of July. Reno had gambling, of course, but also had great ski resorts in the Lake Tahoe area, within minutes, not hours, of Reno. There was Squaw Valley, Heavenly Valley, and many others fairly adjacent to the city. He knew it was too early for the resorts to be open, but his purpose was to explore them before the winter crowds, and return in January or February for a ski vacation.

He went to a travel agency where he received brochures from the hotels and ski resorts. The casinos weren't like Las Vegas, but there were still many selections. From them he found a reasonable place to stay. If the brochure was truthful, it would fit his needs nicely. He called the travel agent and discovered the resort he was considering offered a package including air fare. It was four days and three nights and was quite reasonable. It was a perfect fit for his bank account,

His flight arrived at Reno Tahoe International Airport in early October. Reno advertised itself as the "biggest little city in the world". Michael found it a fair description. The view he had from his window seat told him it was a densely populated area, but to drive from one end of the city to the other, north to south, would probably take no more than 10 to 12 minutes. There appeared to be a downtown area near the university, and a couple of shopping malls south of them, but only a few miles away. The hotel/casino where he was staying was about ten minutes away from the airport, or less, depending on traffic. He was dropped off at the main entrance. The hotel desk was just inside. He checked in right away and went to his room. His choice of accommodations was as advertised. His room was typical, and the casino, though quite small compared to his favorites in Las Vegas, offered the same games and amenities he was accustomed to.

His first day was spent resting in his room, gambling at the blackjack tables and slot machines, and later studying maps of the ski areas. The table limits were much lower than those in Las Vegas. There were many two and three dollar "21" tables, and twenty five cent slot machines as far as the eye could see. He thought of himself as a "cheap" gambler, these games appealed to him. The bell captain was a wealth of information in regards to the ski areas, and the easiest way to get to them. For his second day, he decided to rent a car and explore the slopes.

The day started out partly cloudy, and just under fifty degrees. The forecast was for light rain in the afternoon. He drove his rented Ford Fiesta south on interstate 395 towards Carson City, the capital of Nevada. He passed by Washoe Lake, which was in an area called Washoe Valley. From the signs he saw, it was apparently a very windy area much of the year. He reached highway 50, just south of Carson City, and turned west towards South Lake Tahoe. It was a beautiful drive, climbing through evergreen forest. When he passed the summit, it wasn't long before a view of Lake Tahoe itself appeared. As advertised, it was big, blue, and beautiful. It was a huge lake, appearing as though a gigantic volcanic crater had been filled with water. If there were no mountains on the west side of the lake, it would give the impression it was an ocean. The forest never ended, and soon the casino area of South Lake Tahoe appeared ahead. The whole drive from Reno to the resorts took less than two hours.

He parked in one of the casino lots, and walked down Lake Tahoe Boulevard. He marveled at the large and modern casinos located amidst such a beautiful forest. The mountains behind them reached for the sky. It was one of the most beautiful areas he had ever seen. He walked into, and inspected every casino. They were big, impressive, but not very busy. He thought about it, and realized that when the ski season began in earnest, they would probably be much busier.

He stopped at an outdoor hamburger stand and was pleased with his choice. The hamburger was thick and juicy, and the chocolate shake much better than the fast food joints. As he was finishing his lunch, a light rain began to fall. He continued his walk, and saw where a chairlift to Heavenly Valley ski area began almost at the boulevard. He bought more maps and found there were ten or twelve ski areas not very far from each other. He also discovered one whose proximity made it belong more to Reno than it did to Lake Tahoe. Mount Rose ski area, which boasted the highest altitude in the area, was apparently only forty-five minutes from Reno.

It was now mid-afternoon. He consulted his maps and found that if he left South Shore, and turned off highway 50 onto highway 28 heading north, he would intersect Mount Rose Highway, number 431. It headed east, would pass the Mount Rose ski area, and eventually intersect with 395 back to Reno.

Highway 28 was an even more beautiful drive. It wound around the lake itself, which was on his left, tree covered mountains to his right. The lake was both beautiful and forbidding, with its wind swept crests, and the color changing from blue to grey. When he reached the turnoff to Mount Rose Highway, and had traveled less than thirty minutes, he was soon to learn his first lesson about the Reno area and the Sierra Nevada mountains.

Exiting highway 28 onto 431, the drive was a steady incline until he reached the top. Mount Rose Ski Resort is just east of the 431 summit. As he got to the eastern side of the mountain, barely past the Mount Rose ski area, it began to snow. It was light at first, but the wind began to make it swirl and caused a decrease in visibility. Then, it began to snow harder. As he rounded a curve, he saw an older model Volkswagen van on its side. Emergency vehicles had already arrived. It had obviously slid out of control on the switchback. Michael slowed his speed and let out a deep breath. The snow was piling up. It was not very deep, but deep enough to create very slick driving conditions on a road that was all curves and switchbacks. He hadn't thought it necessary to rent a four wheel drive vehicle. He might have been wrong. He was on the side of the mountain that descended into Reno. The road was only wet when he reached highway 395 in Reno. By then, at an altitude of just over 4000 feet above sea level, snow had once again turned to a light rain.

He returned the rental car and walked back to his hotel. When he arrived, he went immediately to the mini-bar and took a brandy, poured it into the plastic, imitation crystal glass provided by the hotel, and drank all of it in two gulps. The suddenness of a winter like storm had surprised and scared him. A lesson learned. Welcome to northern Nevada.

The next day was sunny and 73 degrees in Reno. He walked the streets, did a little gambling, and, from the top of one of the casinos, enjoyed the view in all four directions. The area around the casinos was heavily occupied by older homes and businesses. But to the north he could see lots of new construction. It seemed to him that a very desirable little city was experiencing a growth spurt.

One of the larger casinos had a huge race and sports book. The National Football League season had begun about a month before, so the book was fairly busy. He enjoyed watching a game from time to time, but didn't follow the teams close enough to believe he could bet on the games. But, when he saw a stack of parlay cards, picked one up, and studied it, he understood the betting frenzy. For only a five dollar bet, it was possible to win thousands of dollars. Because the bet was not only on a simple win or loss by a team, decisions had to be made regarding how many points that win or loss would be, it was very difficult to make choices. He moved on.

The following day he went to the courthouse, just south of the downtown casinos. It contained a small museum, and some of the area's history. He saw pictures of Reno's early days, which were also the early days of legalized gambling in the United States.

Besides the gambling, he had enjoyed the food which was reasonably priced, soaked in the overall feel of the city, and became aware of the variety Reno had to offer. To the west was Sacramento, and farther to the west San Francisco. To the south was Carson City and Lake Tahoe. To the north was a rural and rustic area to be explored all the way to the Oregon border. To the east was a colorful and mysterious desert. Even the downtown area itself was fascinating. There were several very small "mom and pop" casinos, and a few larger ones with lots of neon. In the afternoons some offered local entertainment, and in the evenings celebrity headliners performed in the larger casinos that had hundreds of hotel rooms, similar to Las Vegas.

On the plane trip home, he made a decision. There was only one thing that he would miss if he ever moved away from Los Angeles, and that was the ocean. But Reno did have Lake Tahoe. Michael was going to move to Reno. It was a place he felt was built for him, a city where he fit. He would miss the ocean, but San Francisco and the northern coast of California were only 3 and ½ hours away. It offered everything else he wanted, the great skiing, the gambling, and, because of the tourism, an ever changing population. He had always been a loner, and in Reno he could be a part of something or nothing, his choice.

Chapter 2

Back home in Los Angeles, he had a job. It was not a career, that was certain. He had no family there, his mother had died tragically when he was not quite eighteen years old. He had dropped out of college after less than two semesters. He needed money, and that meant working a full time job, maybe even two. He had worked in a supermarket as a checker, as a waiter in a medium class restaurant, and presently as a baggage handler for an airline at LAX. He shouldn't have trouble finding a job in Reno. He wasn't into material things, so his financial needs were not great.

He began making plans. He would liquidate everything he owned but the necessities. He didn't have much, he had rented his apartment furnished. He didn't buy a lot of "things", he had no use for possessions, and he never entertained guests. The lease on his apartment would be up in June. He decided to give his notice to the airline in mid May. He would settle down in Reno before the ski season began, and start a new life.

He was so excited about his choice, time seemed to stand still, until about a month before the move. He panicked, there was still much to do. Because of his experience on Mount Rose Highway, he decided it was a necessity to have a vehicle that had four wheel drive. He searched for one in a city that preferred sports cars and convertibles. The most severe weather condition the people in the greater Los Angeles area experienced was a heavy rain, accompanied by thirty mile an hour winds. He finally found a three year old, light blue, Subaru Legacy. Its price was almost equal to his trade in, a Chevy Malibu. It was all wheel drive, which was actually better in all driving conditions than four wheel drive. He decided to take nothing with him but the few "treasures" he actually considered to have personal value. That wasn't much. There was a TV, a VCR, a collection of videocassettes to go with it, clothing, and a small microwave oven. There was also a box filled with some kitchen utensils, glasses, cups, silverware, and a few books.

On July 2nd, 1986, he left southern California behind, and moved to Reno.

It was a nice drive, past Mammoth Mountain, straight up 395, giving him ever changing scenery. He was in no hurry, so he seldom reached speeds above 55 miles per hour. He stopped to eat when he felt like it, and left the road to explore some scenic stops along the way. The air outside was warm, and there was a constant smell of pine trees. He enjoyed the quiet of the open highway. He didn't even turn on the radio. The only sound was air rushing through the open windows. He had feelings of hope for a future filled with opportunities, and peace. He arrived in Reno about ten and a half hours later.

He hadn't made plans for living quarters in advance, but his previous walks in Reno had given him a solution. There were many motels in downtown Reno that rented rooms by the week. That would do just fine until he could make more permanent arrangements. The first motel he drove into was across the street from the place he had stayed on his vacation. It was a 50's style building with twelve units, badly in need of painting. He talked to the manager, inspected a sparsely furnished room, and found everything he needed in working order. The rent was reasonable. He had found a home, for now.

He discovered apartment rent in Reno was about half what it was in LA, but so was the pay for the jobs he previously had. Northern Nevada was funded primarily by the casinos, and warehousing. Finding a place to live would be easy, but the one qualification they all shared was that the applicant be employed. That should not be a problem.

First he went to the airport. It was so small, it offered little possibility of employment, mainly because the airlines paid better than most jobs in Reno. Their scale was based on a union agreement reached in conjunction with the larger cities on its routes. Very seldom did anyone quit, so few jobs were ever available. The supermarkets were hiring, but at entry level, and that meant "box boy" at a pay of five dollars and fifty cents an hour. Not enough to support even his meager living expenses. So he applied at restaurants. In 1986, there were few restaurants outside of the casinos. Michael applied to all of them, casino, and non-casino.

He finally got a job at the steakhouse in the "It's a Circus" casino. Calling it a steakhouse was a gross overstatement. It was barely better than a coffee shop. Worse yet, the guests were not in any way of the affluent variety. The casino catered to families. True to its name, it offered continuous circus acts, as well as the largest arcade in northern Nevada. The tips were usually less than ten percent of a bill that was most often under sixty dollars for two adults and two children. That, and a base pay of minimum wage was not going to cut it.

He worked there for six months, basically because he had no other choice. Then came a night when his life was forever changed.

His boss called him aside and informed him that two of the casino's executives were sitting in his section, and that he should take care of whatever requests they made immediately.

As he went to their booth, he quickly glanced at their name tags. Paul was the Casino Manager, and Al was the General Manager. They were average looking businessmen, probably in their early fifties. He introduced himself, and told them that if they needed anything, just call Michael. They were very polite, and seemed to appreciate his attention. He took their orders, and quickly delivered them to the kitchen with a "priority" label across the ticket.

While they waited, he was sure to keep their glasses filled with iced tea. Every time he went to the table he overheard them talking about work, and little else. "It's a Circus" was part of a major corporation, and the responsibility of making a small operation profitable, such as this particular one in Reno, was very challenging.

Their order was ready in less than twenty minutes. When he delivered their meals of prime rib and baked potato, he asked if he could do anything else for them. Al, the General Manager, asked him, "how do you like your job?"

Michael responded, "it's fine".

Al said, "not much room for advancement, is there?"

Michael couldn't think of much to say except, "I guess not".

Al suggested, "why don't you come to work for Paul in the casino? We'll start you out as a change person, so you can familiarize yourself with the operation, and from there, where you go is up to you."

Michael had never liked the food service industry, felt he couldn't make less money, and quickly responded, "thank you, I'd love to give it a try".

Al told him to go to personnel in a couple of days, all the paperwork would be ready. The remainder of his evening consisted of serving only five more tables. That was just as well, he couldn't stop thinking about what had just happened.

That evening when he returned to his motel room, he wasn't quite sure what he was getting into. As a customer in Las Vegas he had, of course, noticed the people walking around making change. But, as with most customers, he had no idea what their responsibilities were, the pay, the hours, or anything else.

Two days later an employee from human resources took him to the slot office to meet the manager. His name was Virgil, and he seemed very pleasant. Virgil informed him he would begin the next night at ten in the evening. His shift would last until six in the morning. He would get a half hour for lunch. As it had been for the waiters in the restaurants, food was free in the employee's cafeteria. Any other breaks would be based on how busy the casino was. He would receive minimum wage and tips at first. Later, he would receive medical benefits and a small raise. After three months he could apply for a departmental promotion.

His first shift was on a Wednesday night. He dressed in the locker room and went to meet his supervisor, Chuck.

He was taken up to the casino floor to a locked cabinet where there were rolls of coin from nickels to dollars. The total "bank" was six hundred dollars, and it had to balance at the end of each shift, or he was responsible for the difference. In the cabinet was also a belt with several pouches, obviously for the rolls of coin, and a wallet chained to the pouch for the bills he would exchange. He put it on, and his supervisor showed him how much and where to put the rolls of coin. When it was full, it weighed about sixty pounds. When Michael was shown how large an area he had to cover on his "graveyard" shift, he knew his back would be aching at the end of the night.

He was fairly busy until about two in the morning. He sold 9 rolls of dollars, 2 rolls of half dollars, 23 rolls of quarters, and 35 rolls of nickels. Then the customer count dropped by about eighty percent. The night became very long. While everyone else was sleeping, he was walking around carrying sixty extra pounds of weight. He was told to keep moving and be visible to any customers who might need him. His feet were aching terribly.

At 5:45 in the morning, he had to count his bank. Now the worst happened. Somehow he was seven dollars and twenty-five cents short, and he was responsible. It would come out of his meager check. And he hadn't received a single tip. This wasn't going to work. He was beginning to think that the entire move to Reno was another big mistake. His entire life was one screw up after another. He had rectified most of them, and, there was a definite pattern, but none of it was his fault.

The next night, while changing in the locker room, he struck up a conversation with one of the blackjack dealers. He started lamenting about the hard work of carrying change, and the little money he was rewarded with. The dealer, Rick, told him, "you should become a dealer. We make pretty good tips, and get a twenty minute break every hour. The heaviest thing you'll carry is a double deck of playing cards". Rick then told him about a local casino that had its own school. The fees were reasonable, and they would put him to work in their casino when he finished. It was considered a "break-in" casino where most of the dealers stayed for a year or two until they perfected their trade, and could get a better job.

That was his last night walking around with sixty pounds strapped to his waist. When he woke up the next morning, he called human resources and quit.

CHAPTER 3

That very day he decided to apply to the dealer's school. When he walked through the door, he saw six "21" tables, a dice table, and a roulette wheel. There were people he guessed were students at each one of them. One of the instructors walked up to him and asked if he needed assistance. Michael told him that he wanted to join the school, and he was immediately taken to an office to meet the school's director.

In the office, they discussed Michael's goals. Michael had many questions, and he received concise and rapid answers. He was told that the average student spent two weeks training, and was sent for an audition at the casino. Once a dealer was hired, he would have a job for as long as he or she wanted it as long as he was honest, and adhered to all the rules. This could work. The charge for their training was only one hundred dollars per game. At the time they taught only the three major games, blackjack, or "21", craps, (dice), and roulette. The school's director told Michael that he could get a job with just a good knowledge of blackjack. Two days later, he began his training.

The job of a blackjack dealer looks simple, and for the most part, it is. You must be able to count to 21 quickly, have the ability to pay correctly, and control your customers and the game. You must also learn to "cut checks", protect your game, the cards and the money, and communicate with the "pit boss" concerning any irregularities. The trainees took turns dealing behind an actual "21" table, but without the real chips. Then they sat in front of the dealer and played the game. Basically, it was "on the job training", which is the only instruction that would give them the ability to start work quickly.

Michael was taken to a "21" game. The instructor, Mary, explained the layout of the game. She showed him how the chips in the tray in front of the dealer were set up. They were in denominations of 1 dollar, 5 dollar, and 25 dollar rows. The largest chips, the 25 dollar tokens, were in the middle. They were green in color, divided into stacks of 20. There were two stacks, the total value being 1000 dollars. Next, to the right and left, were two rows of 5 dollar chips. They were red in color, also in stacks of 20. The eight stacks totaled 800 dollars. Last were two rows, right and left, of 1 dollar chips. They were light blue, and they were also in stacks of 20, the 4 stacks totaling 80 dollars. She showed him how they were "cut", and the proper procedure for doing so. He practiced by himself for about 2 hours. Mary returned, and showed him how to shuffle a single deck of cards properly. He practiced that for about ½ hour. She returned again, and showed him how to "pitch", or deliver the cards, to the players, from left to right, and then how to "scoop" them up, or collect them from right to left. Throughout the rest of the day he was shown how to deal the game, "pick and pay", and protect the game. At first it was a little overwhelming, but, by the end of the day he mentally understood what it was to be a dealer. To become physically proficient would take some time and practice.

As the school was about to close for the day, he was told that on the evening of the next day, he would be taken to their casino, the Nevada Gold, to audition for the shift supervisor. It seemed too soon. His experience as a customer certainly had not prepared him to be someone on the other side of the table. And he hadn't been shown anything about denominations above 25 dollars, or how to adjust to cash play, as well as many other situations Michael knew could exist.

He concentrated very hard as he practiced the next day. He was very nervous, and very unsure of himself. By the end of the day, he felt a little better about things, and so what if he failed the audition, he would get another chance. He was told to arrive at the casino no later than 5:15. About 6 o'clock, a half an hour after the swing shift supervisor came on duty, he was taken to a game where a dealer had five players on a two dollar table. The dealer stood to Michael's side as he moved in place to take over the game. He was very nervous until he had dealt for about fifteen minutes, and the dealer said, "wow, you can actually count!" Apparently there were a lot worse than him coming out of the school. He still didn't possess much confidence, but he realized he just might be able to do this.

He wasn't very good at "pitching" the cards yet, and his shuffle needed some work, but he began to gain a little confidence. Another dealer came and relieved his overseer. Then in another hour, a new dealer relieved her. When he was finally "pushed off" the game, he had been there for about two hours and fifteen minutes. They told him at the school that unless there was a very unusual situation, dealers got a twenty minute break every hour. The shift supervisor, Billy, came over to him. He said, "the reason I left you there so long is because I thought you might like a little practice. If you want to, you'll start tomorrow night". He was going to be a dealer, and he thought he might like it. The biggest part of the job was customer service. He could fake anything for an hour at time. Then on his breaks he could go somewhere and be alone.

The next night he showed up for his new career at 7:30. His shift was 8 p.m. to 4 a.m., the later hours going to the newest employees. The more senior dealers worked from 6 to 2. Billy took Michael to the third floor of the casino. He was introduced to the pit boss, a quite rotund gentleman by the name of Steve. He reminded Michael of one of his favorite old comedians, Oliver Hardy. Billy left and Steve explained to him the procedures as to the coming and going in and out of the "pit", and pushing on and being pushed off a game. This level of the casino offered one dollar blackjack, and even a fifty cent-game designed for "break-ins", meaning Michael. It also offered twenty-five cent roulette, and twenty-five cent craps.

The fifty-cent game had two decks, and was dealt face up. He didn't have to pitch cards, and it was very easy to count with all the cards, except the dealer's, exposed. Michael got a twenty minute break every hour, as promised, and, although he was tired by midnight, he realized it was only the stress of doing something for the first time, and something unusual. Plus, a great deal of interaction with the players is required on a "21" game. People were exhausting.

The 6 to 2 dealers who had their last break at 20 minutes to 2, were assigned the duty of dividing up the tips or "tokes". When they finished, they handed them out to the dealers as they were off shift. For the "late shifters", tokes were delivered to each dealer's table in a small envelope. The Nevada Gold was a "split joint", meaning everyone shared in the tips equally. Some casinos were "keep your own", meaning what you made was yours, and yours alone.

Michael had a break at 20 minutes to 3. He opened the envelope, and was thrilled to discover thirty five dollars. That was ten dollars more than he averaged as a waiter. This was going to be a good thing. The money was better, and the work was pretty easy.

He was on the third floor for about three weeks, learning more, and becoming more comfortable with his job every day. That didn't mean that some of the same people he saw every day were not irritating. People were what they were. One man in particular caused his stomach to roll every time he came into view. He was mean, no, nasty, to every person he came in contact with. That included the dealers, the cocktail waitresses, and the other customers. His name, or more correctly nickname, was "one armed Louie". Michael could not understand why the casino tolerated this miserable human being. He was hated by everyone. In the break room he learned that there were several more regulars that were hated as much as Louie. He just hadn't had the privilege of meeting them yet.

The next week he was scheduled on the main floor, on two dollar games. He was moving up in the world.

Just after he had been dealing about three months, Billy, several pit bosses and assistant managers began to encourage him to learn other games, especially craps. They offered him the opportunity to attend the school at any time and be trained on the dice table. He would not be charged a fee. Management felt it was good for the casino to have as many good dealers as possible available for the most difficult game the casino offered.

Just after he got hired at the Nevada Gold, Michael had found a small studio apartment within walking distance of the casino. It was really just one room, with a kitchenette built in, and not much of an improvement from the motel. He shared a bathroom, but he could afford little else at the moment. Most of the other residents were single men. Michael thought of it as a "halfway house". When he arrived "home" at about 4:20 that morning, he stayed awake for several hours considering what had been offered to him. Becoming a craps dealer appealed to his ego, after all, they were considered the elite dealers in every casino. But what made him consider it even more, was the chance to go to another casino where the tokes were 2, 3 or even 4 times better. He received a lot of information from other dealers about the inner workings of casinos. As a male, if you didn't deal dice, it was very difficult to get a really good job. He finally fell asleep about the time most people were leaving for their mundane 9 to 5 jobs. Once more, he dreamed of a better life.

A couple of days later, Michael arrived at the dealer school at three in the afternoon, several hours before his shift at the Nevada Gold. The dice instructor, Peter, had been told he would most likely have a new student. Peter gave Michael one end of the craps table, and two stacks of old roulette chips. He showed him how to cut the chips properly. He told him, "dice dealers have to cut into many different numbers of chips, and must look professional doing so. And, they do it with both hands, unlike a "21" dealer". For two and a half hours that is all he was allowed to do.

The next day when Michael arrived, he was given the same task, but with certain drills. He had to learn to "drop cut" chips in the order of 5,4,3,2,1, and then backwards, 1 through 5. Again, that was all he did that day. Peter sent him home with two 20 dollar stacks of chips, so he could practice on a bath towel covered table.

With his next days off from the casino, Michael took a break from everything. It was now September. Winter would soon be coming to Reno. He had been told that south of Reno, and a little south of Carson City, there were areas where the trees changed color similar to New England. It was a Tuesday, and although there was no snow on the ground yet, the air was very cold. The wind coming over the Sierras brought the mountain air down to the valley floor. Michael had been directed to an area called Hope Valley. As promised, the Aspens were just beginning to change color. It was spectacular. The trees were full of color. Shades of yellow, gold, and red covered much of the meadows and hillsides. It wasn't a sunset on the Pacific, but it was a beautiful sight.

Thursday, his first day back to work, and just two months before Thanksgiving, he went to the dealer's school before his shift. This time he was not left alone to "cut checks". Peter went through all areas of the table, explaining what would win, and what would lose. The only area not covered this day was the middle of the table where the "proposition", or "prop" bets were made. These bets were risky, and required knowledge, but were outside of the realm of the basic part of the game.

Peter explained that there were 36 combinations on a pair of dice. The number that was most frequently rolled, at least according to the laws of probability, was "7". Six combinations were possible. There were less combinations for every other number. The less combinations, the higher the odds and the bigger the payoff.

Michael had started a notebook. He didn't know it then, but by the time he finished his training, it would grow to 52 pages, front and back. He found the physical challenge of being a craps dealer harder than the mathematical part. He watched the better dealers at his casino, and anywhere else he happened to be. He was obsessive. He had to be the best, and work at the best casinos.

CHAPTER 4

Michael spent more and more time trying to learn the game. If he wasn't at the school, he was studying his notes, practicing cutting checks, or observing games at other casinos. After a couple of months, attending the school every day it was open, came the day he was placed on a real game. The scheduler thought he was being kind to him. He was assigned to the one dollar game. It was very easy, compared to the twenty five cent game. The "quarter" game was always busy with "locals". These regular players were not kind, and never tipped the dealers, no matter how hard they worked. When the night was done, Michael realized he would learn nothing standing on a game that had no business. He asked the scheduler to put him on the busiest quarter game, so he could learn as quickly as possible.

The next night he was on "dice 1", or as the more experienced dice dealers called it, "the game from hell." It was packed with the "regulars", who, for the most part were the "scum of the earth". With every roll of the dice, they all shouted out their demands at once. He had been instructed to take them in order beginning from the middle of the table, focusing on each one when his turn came. Easier said than done. Because the game was so inexpensive, (a ten dollar buy in could keep a player at a table for and hour or more), there were "come" bets, "place" bets, and prop bets with every roll of the dice. Everyone played "the odds". All bets had to be repeated and acknowledged. Michael looked very forward to his breaks.

He began to smoke cigarettes, relishing the solitude of the sidewalk outside the casino, and the feeling of smoke filling his lungs. He wanted isolation from these "bottom feeders", these dregs of society. But, because he had to, he held it inside. His anger simmered, sometimes it flamed. He could not let it out, not now.

Michael worked hard on his game. He tried to ignore the unpleasantness of the players on the table. The months passed, and once again Thanksgiving came. The employee cafeteria served a turkey dinner, and that was the extent of Michael's holiday celebration. He had been invited to one of the married dealer's apartment for dinner, but he preferred to be alone. Besides, Thanksgiving in Reno is extremely busy. Everywhere, on every game, were Asian Americans from the San Francisco bay area who did not celebrate this American holiday. So, for four days in November, they came to gamble. Michael was very tired. He had acquired a taste for hard liquor, so he went to his room and celebrated with a bottle of scotch and his treasured videos.

Winter came, and with it some good snow in the mountains. Not a lot of it reached the valley floor in Reno, but that was all right. His love of skiing had grown. He had purchased a season pass at the Mount Rose Ski Resort, and took advantage of it every time he had a day off. He was becoming a better skier. He loved the rush of gliding on the snow at great speed. The danger of the sport never was a consideration. There wasn't much in life that gave him a thrill. He knew he would never be a "world class" skier, but it was about the only thing in his life that put a smile on his face, though no one else ever saw it. He rode the chair lifts alone. He skied alone.

During the next several months, he became more comfortable dealing this demanding game of craps, which, because of the players, seemed to be more a farce than an actual gambling venue. No one ever seemed to win any "real" money, and what they did win would most likely be lost the next night.

As the dice game became easier, his contempt for the regulars grew. His superior abilities deserved a better class of players. "Henry the Hawk", "German Frank", "Loser Jim", "Crooked Neck Rick", and "Fat Larry" were five of the worst. He began to go to bars at other casinos on his breaks and order a double scotch on the rocks. It became his refuge, and he loved the acquired taste. It's slightly burning feeling as he swallowed it, the smoky taste and unique aroma, helped him wash away the seriously malignant feelings growing inside, or so he imagined. With each week he required more and more of the amber liquid to keep his emotions in check.

When he had been at Nevada Gold for over a year, he knew he had to make a change or go "postal". Besides, tokes still averaged only 36 dollars a night, and he needed more money. He had accomplished something he was told he couldn't do. He had learned all three of the major games, and learned them well, in only a year. He had also learned baccarat, a sit down game that was easy, and had some fairly large "action", but it was not a game that was in all of the Reno casinos. Its popularity was immense in Europe and Asia, much less so in Nevada.

There was a new, small casino planning to open in a couple of months called the "Reno Queen". It was to be decorated like the riverboats on the Mississippi, and promised an atmosphere of pure fun. They advertised their willingness to hire only the best dealers with the highest customer service abilities. Michael decided he would apply for a job. He needed to save his sanity, *and* increase his income. His quality of life had to improve, and soon.

A month after he applied for a dealer position at the Reno Queen, he received a telephone call. The man's name was Ali, and he wanted him to come to the same office building where he had applied for the "Queen", and have a personal interview. He was pumped! He actually might get away from the losers he was dealing to every day. And, unfortunately, his wish that they would meet an early end to their miserable existence was not working.

When he arrived at the interview, he had become a bit insecure. He had learned that the new casino management had made an effort to observe every applicant in their present position. That meant that they had assuredly witnessed a great number of craps dealers who had much more experience and expertise than did he. And, they had watched him and how he handled the miserable people he had to deal to.

By the time he was called into the office, his hopeful attitude had all but "left the building". His desperation to get away from the Nevada Gold had made his attitude more negative about everything in his life. It had probably cost him this job.

A smiling face, and an extended hand came from behind the desk. A dark haired man with brown skin around five feet six inches tall, weighing maybe one hundred and fifty pounds introduced himself as Ali, the man who had called him. They exchanged pleasantries, and then Ali got down to business. Michael thought, here it comes, "thanks for applying, we wish you the best, but we must hire the most qualified, the most experienced dealers". Instead Ali began to tell him what the new casino's environment would be, and what they would expect from their employees. He stressed customer service, and just plain fun. He told Michael that he had observed him personally on the most difficult dice game he had ever witnessed, and found his self control, and attitude, to be at an extremely high level. He had proven that even when he was mistreated, unfairly verbally attacked by one of the lesser players, he did not retaliate and offend the rest of the players on the table. What he didn't know was that if Michael hadn't held his true feelings inside, someone would have been physically damaged, or worse, and he wouldn't be here now. Doing nothing was all he could have done.

He couldn't believe what he was hearing. He was going to open a new casino! He would not lose his mind dealing a mind numbing game to the low life that had nothing else to do with their miserable lives, and surrounded him every day. But, he wouldn't forget them, especially the worst who seemed to intentionally make his, and every other dealer's life, very unhappy. The interview lasted only about ten more minutes. Ali told him he would be contacted soon by someone from the Reno Queen, and that construction was right on schedule. He was going to be a free man. The knot in his stomach might actually loosen. He might be able to sleep peacefully tonight.

It became even more difficult to go to work at the Nevada Gold every night. A little over a week after his interview, Michael was called to attend a meeting inside the almost finished Reno Queen. He witnessed a cheerful and bright casino, unlike the dimly lit cave in which he now worked. He met his shift supervisor, Bob, and Bob's assistant, Lydia, as well as the other dealers and pit bosses. He would be working "day shift", ten in the morning until six in the evening. The dealers were given their uniforms. These consisted of a vertically red and white striped shirt with a red "riverboat gambler's" tie, blue slacks and a blue vest. Bob told them that his goal was to make the casino a lot of money, and his dealers as well. Sounded good to Michael. Based on the forecast as to the day they would open the doors to the public, Michael gave his notice that night to the Nevada Gold.

Three weeks and four days after his interview with Ali, at 12 noon on a Friday, the Reno Queen opened its doors. Michael was to deal "21" that day, the best and most experienced dice dealers were on the two games the casino operated. He had worked with large crowds at Nevada Gold, but there was no possible way he could have been prepared for the grand opening of a new casino, especially one with such limited floor space. No one could move without literally pushing their way through the crowd. Every seat on every table was taken, others standing behind, waiting for someone to leave. Within the first hour, the air was filled with smoke, drinks had been spilled, and the noise level increased to a deafening level. When Michael was pushed out for a break, it took him almost 5 of his 20 minutes just to get to the break room. Everyone was glad that they would be relieved at six o'clock.

When they were relieved, everyone met in the break room to split their tokes. They had only worked six hours, the casino opening two hours late, so they didn't know what to expect. There were forty two of them on opening day, and they each took home 122 dollars. The hard work was worth it.

For the first week, there was a fairly steady flow of customers, the curiosity of the first new casino opened in Reno in several years created a large crowd of "lookie-loo's", and lots of actual gamblers. His schedule had two more days of dealing cards, and two days on the dice table. He would get Wednesday and Thursday off.

Management had definitely picked excellent dice dealers. When the game was not busy, Michael was given personal instruction by the other dealers. He was taught not only better mechanics, but how to handle players. And that meant getting them to "toke" you. As the Nevada Gold had been, the Reno Queen was a "split joint". It was smaller in size and number of dealers, and the table limits were higher, so tokes were much better. The first week's toke average was just over 80 dollars a day, not counting their amazing opening day.

That night Michael celebrated. He had several doubles, and then, on unsteady legs, walked down to the adult book store, just south of the downtown area. He had been there only once before, and found it gave him a slightly perverted pleasure. He went into a room, and sat in front of a plate glass window. He put quarters in the little machine on the wall. In a few seconds the curtain lifted, and a scantily clad girl appeared. She danced just for him, in a very provocative manner. When the quarters began to run out, the curtain would start to come down. More quarters equaled more time. He stayed there for over a half an hour.

Then he walked home, but his mood had darkened, and he didn't know why.

True to his word, Bob worked hard at helping them make money. He didn't want to lose one member of a good crew. Soon, management became unhappy with this. In their view, the dealers were making too much money. The casino should have made more, tokes were just money lost. Three weeks after the opening, Bob was removed, and Lydia was given his position.

The tokes declined almost immediately, as management had hoped. It was evident, even to someone like Michael who was fairly new to the industry, that Lydia did not have the knowledge, nor managerial ability to run a shift. She was simply, but aptly put, a "kiss ass". She would do anything to further her status. Her position in her former casino was "dual rate" That meant that she was both a part time dealer, and a part time pit boss. Not enough experience to be allowed to be in charge of a casino's entire operation. In addition, she was so obvious in her favoritism towards a few of the female dealers, that it became the prime subject of conversation among the crap dealers. It was crystal clear that one of the problems with opening a new casino, was the simple fact that things would change. It would be unusual for the overall situation to improve. Logically, it had to go in the wrong direction.

On what he thought would be a usually slow Tuesday, Michael was not feeling well, mentally or physically. He got to work very early, and put his name on the EO, or "early out" list. Usually, even when it was slow, only one or two got to leave, management required that a specific number of table games must stay open. He was glad his was the first name. EO's were given around one o'clock. Fortunately, he was dealing "21" on that day, dice dealers almost never got an EO. It was extremely slow, and an EO was sure to be given. Lydia's best friend, Sharon, was second on the list. A dealer had called in sick, so only one EO would be given. Strangely, Sharon became very ill and was given the opportunity to go home. Michael protested that he was just as ill. His request was denied. He almost walked off the job. With the decline in tokes, and an unpleasant working environment, there just didn't seem to be any reason to stay. But he did, at least for another week.

In his time off, Michael found himself retreating more and more to his small apartment. He had no desire to be around other people. He spent his time drinking and watching his favorite videos over and over again. His blood boiled, why was this type of thing happening to him again? He thought this move to Reno would change his life. His sleep was restless. His childhood haunted him over and over again, his father's constant mental and physical abuse, and his mother's feigned ignorance. His infrequent personal relationships had all ended badly. He wouldn't make those mistakes again. He always felt as though the world was against him, and now he knew he was right.

For the entire next week, Michael was more sullen than usual. He was very quiet, whether dealing cards or dice. Two of his dice shifts had been taken away. He spoke to no one in the break room. He began to spend several of his breaks at a local bar two blocks away. Old habits were returning. He seethed with an anger that created violent thoughts. He realized he actually hated Lydia.

The following Sunday he did get an EO. As he was about to leave, Ali, who was the casino manager, asked if he could have a word with him. Michael went down to his office, and they freely exchanged thoughts about what was changing within the property. Michael was honest. He didn't "pull any punches" as to his feelings about Lydia. Ali seemed to understand, stating the fact that new casinos go through some changes within the first six months. When Michael left to go home, he felt good about the exchange.

On the ensuing Tuesday, just before the start of the shift, Ali called an impromptu meeting. He simply stated, "I want you all to know, Lydia has my full backing in every situation". Michael had been used. He was on a "21" game. He received a break after forty minutes. He walked out of the Reno Queen, and never looked back. He left in anger. He felt, and truly was, betrayed. He would have his revenge, somehow, someway.

Two nights later, after who knows how many double Scotches, and half a pack of cigarettes, Michael followed Lydia when she left work. He wasn't sure why. She went to one of the older and larger casinos in Reno called the Stagecoach. She sat at a bar in the rear of the casino. The bartender brought her white wine, without her asking for it. She played the poker machines, drinking glass after glass of wine while chain smoking. All the while she talked to no one, lost in the machine and her thoughts. After about an hour and a half, Michael left, walked home, and thought about everything that was happening in his life, and who was to blame for it.

CHAPTER 5

He knew he was always welcome back at the Nevada Gold. About a week after he left the Queen, he went to see Billy, and was told he could start the next night on swing shift.

Michael was grateful, most of the management at the Nevada Gold had treated him well. The one realization he took away from the Reno Queen, was that he had to make more money. Besides, having to deal to those dice players again was not going to be pleasant, it would be horrific. And with the experience he now had, they assuredly wouldn't be happy to see him again either. They could no longer manipulate or intimidate him. The regulars loved to harass the break-ins, and if it wasn't for the support of some of the upper management, they would have been run completely out of the casino by most of the pit bosses.

During his first night back, Michael began to notice some changes in the working environment. There was a tension, and uneasiness that wasn't there before. It is not unusual to have changes in casino management, but those that had taken place at the Nevada Gold, in a short period of time, were obviously not good.

There was a new casino General Manager. He was not from Reno. He had come from the Midwest where gaming was getting a strong foothold, and aiding its economy. He had an MBA, and that impressed the owners. But this little, local casino should not have been run by a "pencil pusher". It had always maintained an aggressive and positive approach to being successful. It still believed in gaming as a profitable venture. In fact, per capita, at one time, it was the biggest money making casino in the world. Annually, they planned losses in the food and beverage department to ensure customers came to their casino to gamble. They offered a 99 cent breakfast, and 50 cent beer daily. The owners never wanted a hotel, it was simply lost revenue. The Nevada Gold was a gambling joint. They could feed off of the others who had thousands of rooms. Slots, table games, the race and sports book, and Keno guaranteed a great income for the property since the early 1960's.

It didn't take Michael long to realize that the new General Manager, whose name was Art, was a fool, no, a complete idiot. He knew nothing about gaming in Nevada, had no people skills, and was driving away the customers with his "new and improved" ideas. He raised food and drink prices, increased the table limits, and took away slot machines that used coin, replacing them with the new "ticket in, ticket out" machines used in the new "Indian" casinos in California and Oregon. Worse yet, he had promoted some of the most incompetent and ambitious people, who, when Michael left, were in much lower positions. These self-proclaimed superstars were ruining both business and morale. Somehow, no one seemed to notice. That seemed odd to Michael, because the philosophy of the Nevada Gold had always been that if something was working, why change it?

When Michael had left, a man named Rollie was running the casino's sad little poker room. Thanks to his friend, Art, he had now become an assistant shift supervisor. He loved his power, and abused it with every opportunity. He was on graveyard, but because Michael worked the late swing shift, he had to deal with him for a few hours every night. Tension between them was obvious. It had begun when Michael worked there previously. Rollie considered himself an intellectual, and a great asset to the casino. Michael considered him an egotist who lacked the intelligence of a blade of grass. And the way Rollie treated those who were not among his little clique was despicable. Rollie saw to it that when Michael's dice game closed, he was put on the worst games in the casino. He made sure that mistakes were made by the pit boss assigning breaks, assuring Michael would be skipped or completely forgotten. If his name was on the EO list, Rollie crossed it off.

Michael was now in a trap he had made for himself. He felt his skills as a craps dealer were still somewhat inferior to those who worked in the better casinos. Dealing to players who played much larger sums of money required knowledge he did not possess. He had to have a job, so he would have to remain at the Nevada Gold while he became more proficient on the dice table. The biggest obstacle he would encounter was suppressing his temper. Once again, and much to his dismay, none of his "favorite" players had passed away while he was gone. The pit bosses who sat on the dice tables knew Michael very well by now. He was given a lot of freedom when dealing with the regulars. But there were limits. A few of the shift managers and their assistants, such as Rollie, insisted the dealers treat them with a respect which was, in Michael's opinion, totally unwarranted.

But Michael did have a goal, and without it he would have gone completely out of his mind. He would become one of the better dealers in Reno. Then he would be able to audition at a casino that had respectable customers who also knew how to take care of their dealers financially.

Every night was a struggle. Thank God there were bars in every casino. Michael never missed a chance to down a double scotch on his breaks. Strangely, he never seemed to get drunk. He figured the growing anger and pressure inside of him was burning up the alcohol. He hadn't even thought about skiing in a long time. Sometimes he gambled a little on the video poker machines, but most of his free time was spent in his room, watching videos, and drinking cheap scotch. He associated with few of his fellow dealers. Those he did talk to had stopped inviting him to anything outside of the casino, he always declined.

The days, weeks, and months went by slowly. The only positive side to his predicament was that dealing a twenty five cent game developed his physical skills quickly. He had much to learn about games where the money played consisted of a much larger denomination. He began to frequent a couple of the casinos where he might seek employment. Their dice crews were excellent, and by watching them in action, he could learn much about higher limit crap games.

Michael struggled through more than a year at the Nevada Gold. He finally thought he was ready for bigger things. Before his shift started on a Wednesday, he walked down to the most famous casino in the world. Its fame was not achieved because of its size, it was because during

WWII there were signs advertising it everywhere soldiers went. The signs would read "the Goldmine or Bust", and then would give the mileage to its front doors.

Michael walked into the Goldmine, and asked if the shift manager was available. Day shift would be finished in about an hour, but he was still there. In a few minutes, an Asian American man of about 35 years of age, maybe 5 feet 9 inches tall, walked up to Michael and introduced himself. He said, "Hi, my name is Alex. I'm the day shift manager. How can I help you?" Michael introduced himself, and asked him if he could get an audition on the craps game. Alex said he was always looking for good dice dealers, and that if he could come back around one in the afternoon the following day, he would be happy to give him an audition. Michael was very excited. He had watched this crew and made up his mind that this is where he wanted to be. Besides, the dealers here kept their own tokes. The dice game split between the four dealers, and had one "21" game that was part of their crew. There was a great opportunity here for some real money!

That night at the Nevada Gold was a "piece of cake". Knowing he was going to get his chance tomorrow enabled him to ignore the regulars, concentrate on his game, and fine tune it for the following day. When he got home, he slept well for the first time in months.

He awoke the next morning about eleven. He showered and shaved, went through his notebook, and, around noon, went out for a light breakfast. He got to the Goldmine about 12:45. Alex saw him right away. He told him that there was a decent little game in progress, and when the dealer on break came back, he should push into the "stick" position, that is, the dealer who is on the outside of the game who retrieves the dice after each roll. He also "books", or accepts the proposition bets, the mostly one roll bets that are risky, but pay well.

Although Michael was a loner, and mostly anti-social, when he was working he could be charming. He had watched many dealers, and learned to copy the mannerisms and verbiage of the best of them. Not one of these players would ever know how he really felt about them. He needed their toke money. He also knew that his ability to give outstanding customer service was extremely important as was the actual dealing of the game in regards to getting a job at a good casino.

He did well, he had memorized every payoff, and even corrected one "base" dealer as he was about to pay a complicated bet. He had a better angle from his position to see how the chips were stacked. After 20 minutes, he moved inside. His hands moved quickly, and he did not falter as he paid every bet accurately. Twenty minutes more, and he was pushed off the game. Alex met him, and told him he liked what he saw. One of the dealers on day shift wanted to transfer to swing. Michael could take his place. He would start the following Monday.

Michael was elated, to put it mildly. He had a few hours before his shift started at the Nevada Gold, so he went to a bar at the edge of downtown to have a celebratory drink. One led to two, two to six. Barely able to walk, Michael went to a pay phone and called in sick.

He stumbled back to his room about nine thirty that evening. He kicked off his shoes and passed out on the bed.

The next morning he awoke with the king of all hangovers. His head was throbbing, and nausea was the only other feeling he had. He vomited several times. He tried to think about the night before. The only thing he clearly remembered was ordering his first drink to celebrate his new job. When the nausea became only a mild discomfort, he brushed his teeth, washed his face, and decided to go out for some coffee.

Michael walked to a small casino that was known by locals to have great coffee, and decent food. He ordered coffee and dry toast. It took four cups to help him eat the toast. When he finished, he had one more cup, bought a local newspaper, and walked back to his room. On the way, his thoughts traveled to the fact that he was feeling very happy about giving his notice at the Nevada Gold that night. Only three more shifts, and he was truly going to start a better life.

The first thing he did when he reached his room was to pour himself a glass of water. He added two Alka-Seltzer to it. He drank it down, sat down in the only comfortable chair he had, and did nothing for about half an hour. Finally, fully awake and a lot more coherent, he picked up the newspaper. On the front page was a story that captured his attention immediately. The headline read, "Reno Queen Shift Supervisor Found Dead". The article went on to say that she was found in the parking lot of the Stagecoach casino next to her car. She was apparently a mugging victim. She had suffered fatal head trauma, delivered with great force from a rounded object. The police were still looking for the murder weapon, and had no information at this time as to who the perpetrator might be.

Michael was surprised, but not in shock. He certainly didn't feel sad. She was a very bad person, and everyone was better off without her. He hated her now, just as much as he did when she was alive. Good riddance. He turned a few pages of the newspaper, and read the comics.

He arrived at work that evening about 45 minutes early. He wanted to be sure and talk to Billy before his shift. He found him easily in "pit 1" on the phone. He waited for the phone call to end. He told Billy what had happened, and his shift boss understood. He congratulated Michael, told him he appreciated all his work, and again made him aware that he could come back anytime. Then he said, "oh, by the way, I know you worked at the Reno Queen for a short time. Did you see the paper today?" All Michael said was, "yes, I did". He thanked Billy and walked away.

He went to the scheduler and put his name on the EO list. He decided he would do this the next two nights as well. The less he had to put up with the dice game, the better.

Just after midnight, he got his EO. He decided not to go to one of the bars. He didn't want another hangover. He went to his room, had a drink and a half while he watched videos, and went to sleep. He didn't have a restful sleep. He saw Lydia's face over and over again. She looked terrified. He could even hear her short scream. What he couldn't see was the smile on his face. At 4 a.m., he woke up with a jolt. He got up, poured a glass of water, and within minutes forgot his dream, and went back to sleep. He didn't dream for the rest of the night.

The next two nights, his last two shifts at the Nevada Gold, were very busy, so he didn't get his EO. That was all right, two nights he could endure. On his very last night he was on good old dice 1. One of the members of his crew was a very nice young Hispanic gentleman, just out of school, who Michael actually liked. When they pushed onto the game at 8 p.m., the game was packed with the worst of the worst. Because Michael didn't care, and because he wanted to let all these regular losers know how he felt, he made an announcement before he allowed the first roll of the dice. He said, "Okay, listen up. Juan is a nice guy, and this is my last night putting up with all of you. If I see any of you assholes giving him a hard time, I'm going to jump over this table and kick your ass". The pit boss sitting as the box man, a veteran of many years, was laughing so hard he had to get up and take a walk. The regulars started to go "oohh", and say things like "he thinks he's tough". To which Michael replied, "I'm not fucking kidding". It was a rather tame night. Soon, but not soon enough, it was over.

Chapter 6

Michael was so anxious that he woke up just after 6 o'clock on Monday morning. He had four hours until his shift started. He went through his morning routine, then decided to take a walk and have some breakfast. He went to the same little casino he had gone to the morning of his horrendous hangover. It was two doors down from the Nevada Gold. As he was entering the building, he saw his old buddy one armed Louie enter his former place of torture. Seeing Louie made him think about Rollie, who was still working inside. The graveyard shifts would still be working for a couple of hours. He could feel his blood pressure rise, remembering the last year, and how much he hated every minute of it. Their time would come.

After breakfast, he still had a couple of hours to kill. He decided to do a little research. The downtown library opened at 8 a.m., and was just two blocks away. He went upstairs to the botanicals section. He wasn't interested only in the plants, he was also interested in the pesticides used to control them. Finally finding the books he was looking for, he sat down and studied them closely. He got lost in his reading, and forgot about the time. When he looked up at the clock, it was just after nine. He quickly put the books away, and hurried home to get ready for his first shift at the Goldmine.

After punching in at the time clock, and drinking a cup of coffee bolstered by the nicotine of a cigarette, Michael went upstairs to meet his dice crew. Alex was there and shook his hand. Then he was introduced to Randy, Chris, and Stu, who were the other three dealers on this Monday. They had ten minutes before they opened the dice game, which had been closed on graveyard. They decided who would have which breaks, and moved into position to begin their day.

About 10:30 a single player walked up to the table. He was tall and gaunt, with thinning blond hair worn too long. He threw down a thousand dollars on the table. Chris leaned over to Michael and told him that his name was Carl, and he was a poker dealer at the Goldmine. The worst news was that he seldom tipped unless he got very drunk. He played a decent game, 25 and 30 dollar bets on each number, but nothing to warrant a thousand dollar buy in. He obviously had too much to drink before he came to the table, so after about 20 minutes the box man walked up and talked to him. He said, "we don't want to take your money. Why don't you go home and sleep for a couple of hours?" Carl threw his chips on the table and said, "color me up". The box man told him he had 1100 dollars. He took his money and threw in four 25 dollar chips saying, "for the boys".

Not very long after that, a nice little game developed, and lasted throughout the day.

At 6 p.m. swing shift pushed them off the game. They took their tokes and met the "21" dealer who was splitting with them. Each of the 5 took 108 dollars home. Nice first day.

Michael was given Wednesdays and Thursdays off. He spent a lot of time in the library. He discovered that many of the items he was researching were easy to find, available, and legal to purchase. He was in no hurry to put his plans to work. He wanted to be absolutely positive he knew what he was doing. He copied dozens of pages.

His job at the Goldmine was going well, with the exception of one of his fellow dice dealers, Barry, who, for some reason, took a complete dislike to Michael, and was very obvious about it. He constantly criticized Michael, and harassed him at every opportunity. He apparently thought he was being humorous. What he was really doing was putting himself on an ever growing list.

After he was there three months, he decided it was time to find a decent place to live. He didn't want to move too far away, he enjoyed being able to walk to work, and there was plenty of cheap food downtown. He didn't cook. He starting checking the want ads and soon found a small apartment just north of downtown, near the university. He went to look at it, and decided it would be perfect for him. It even had a carport so he wouldn't have to scrape off snow and ice in the winter. It had a bedroom, kitchen, and living room. The building was in good repair. The furnishings were simple, and in decent condition. The best part was that it was only 200 dollars more a month than he was now paying. Life was good.

With the exception of having to put up with Barry a couple of days a week, he finally liked his job. The money was good, and most of the players knew how to play dice well enough, that dealing to them was almost fun.

The months flew by. He liked his new apartment. It had just enough room for his needs, and he didn't have to share a bathroom.

During his first winter at the Goldmine, he went skiing a couple of times, once to Mt. Rose, and once to a resort on Lake Tahoe's north shore called "Northstar". The winter snowfall was very heavy that year, and all the resorts were busy. That made for a better winter at the Goldmine. There were lots of people in the casino every day.

Michael worked on his list. He decided some of the names could be crossed off, not worthy of any effort, and some were moved to the top and put in bold print. He only thought about it in the evenings, during the day his mood was generally good, but after a few scotches when he got home, he was invaded by memories of being mistreated, and his mood darkened. His only real pastime was watching his videos. The weeks and months ran together. It wasn't as though time was "flying by", it just seemed to be one very long day.

After he had been at the Goldmine for a couple of years, he began to notice subtle changes. When a piece of equipment was broken, or just not working properly, it didn't get fixed, unless it was an absolute necessity. Also, midweek business seemed to be less and less. The dice dealers were scheduled to deal "21" one, or two days a week, almost never on the weekends. Sometimes these were very good "money" days. That was pretty standard for a casino where the dealers kept their own tokes. Now, more and more frequently, only a few dealers had very good days.

During an eight hour shift there might be only a couple of players who were tipping very well. The best of the clientele was definitely going somewhere else.

Michael was getting worried. His great job seemed to be not so great now, and his problems with Barry had gotten worse over time. Both men were open about their hatred for each other. It was so obvious that one day Alex took them down to his office individually and talked to them about it. If they wanted to keep their jobs, their relationship had to become less noticeable to those around them, and non-existent to the customers.

A surprising decision by management guaranteed at least a part of their day would be less profitable. The restaurant would no longer be open for breakfast. Their other casino across the street would be taking care of the Goldmine's customers. Michael realized that all the changes added up to management's attempt to move the Goldmine's business to "McDougal's", where "breakfast was now being served". He might have to look for another job. But, first there were things to do.

As several months passed it was apparent business was definitely declining. Every day before work, Michael decided to go to breakfast at the Nevada Gold. While there, he would find Rollie so he could watch his routine. He found out where he had his morning coffee, where he would spend his last hour every day, and confirm his days off. Like most compulsive, obsessive people, Rollie was a creature of habit. It was easy to know where he might be at any time in that hour.

Precisely at the beginning of his last hour, he would go to the poker room, and pour himself a cup of coffee. He would carry it to the desk where the players signed up for games, and purchased chips. He would stand and talk to the poker supervisor. If he was called away, which was fairly likely, he would leave his coffee on the desk and proceed to the area where he was needed. He would usually be gone about ten minutes. He made it too easy.

Michael knew he had to make a change. A new and very large casino had been built between It's a Circus, and a casino named the Diablo. It was called "Legend". He thought about applying, but he wanted to get away from downtown. He heard from a co-worker that the "Pot of Gold" casino in Sparks, was hiring. They had built a new tower which was to open a week before New Year's Eve. Sparks and Reno literally run together. Unless you lived in the area, you wouldn't know which of the cities you were in. He decided to apply.

A few days after he put in his application, he was called for an audition. He told them he was working day shift, and that was just fine, they were looking mostly for swing shift employees. The audition was set up for the following Friday at 7:30 in the evening. Michael had reached the level of expertise he had sought, and auditions were merely a formality.

A couple of days later, while he was having breakfast, he read an article in the paper that he found personally quite interesting. One of the assistant shift supervisors at the Nevada Gold, a Rolland Thomas, had been found dead in his apartment. He hadn't shown up for his shift for two days, and had not called anyone at the casino. The police were sent to investigate, and found him on his kitchen floor. He had apparently had some sort of seizure, and had fallen and expired, laying in a pool of blood he had expunged through his mouth and nose. An autopsy would be performed to determine the cause of death. Michael thought to himself, "oh well, shit happens".

The following Thursday, the day before his audition at the Pot of Gold, there was another article Michael found of interest. A local resident, who was well known in the casinos as a regular patron, was the victim of a hit and run involving an unknown vehicle. He had been crossing Center Street downtown, in the middle of the street, probably somewhere between the hours of eight and nine in the morning. He was thrown about thirty feet, and was dead before the EMT'S arrived. There was only one witness. She was an 82 year old woman who thought it was a blue car. The name was being withheld, while the authorities attempted to find relatives. He did have one distinguishing physical characteristic, he only had one arm. A sad story, but he should have used the crosswalk.

CHAPTER 7

When he entered the Pot of Gold for his audition, Michael was very confident. His only feeling was the anxiety of having to wait until they were ready to watch him. He was placed first on the "stick", as he had been at the Goldmine. This was standard procedure, all three positions on the dice table had big responsibilities. When he was pushed inside, he only dealt for ten to twelve minutes when the regular dealer pushed him off. The swing shift manager took him out of the pit. He introduced himself as "Jake", and said he was prepared to offer him a job. Michael accepted, but asked if he could give a full two weeks notice at the Goldmine. Jake told him that would not be a problem, the new tower wasn't expected to open for about three weeks. They decided he would start the day after Christmas so he could familiarize himself with the casino, and get to know the other dealers.

The next morning, as he started his shift at the Goldmine, he was trying to decide when to give his notice. He had never planned to make it two weeks, but he needed the time for other business. He was on a mission to let Barry know how much he despised him, and that he would never forget what an asshole he had been. First, he decided he would give a very short notice. In the past, dealers who had given two, or even one weeks notice, were told they could leave the next day. He wanted to control the situation. He knew that he couldn't have his confrontation with Barry until he gave notice.

He now had Sunday and Monday off, so on a Thursday morning he told his scheduler and shift boss, that Saturday would be his last day. They were unable to find a replacement for him, as he knew would be the situation, so he would be able to work his last three days. They weren't happy with him. He had been scheduled to deal "21" on Friday. He would find out at the end of the day his schedule suddenly changed, he would be on the dice game.

When his shift began that day, as was usually the case, they opened a closed game, and stood without players for more than an hour. During that time, when he and Barry were both inside, he had his chance. He said, "Barry, you are a complete asshole. You've been lucky I needed this job, or I would have kicked your ass a long time ago. Saturday is my last day. But you haven't seen the last of me. I will remember how you've treated me, and never think I won't". Barry didn't quite know what to say, and had a very confused look on his face. About ten minutes later three players walked up to the table. They remained busy the rest of the day.

When their shift was over, and they went to divide their tokes, Barry simply walked up to Michael and said, "fuck you". Michael just smiled.

Michael had known little about Barry outside of work, he didn't want to. But now he had to. Barry had Monday and Tuesday off, so they would be working together his last two days.

Friday was fairly busy, and they could do nothing but ignore each other. When tokes were split at the end of the day, all was quiet. Michael pretended to go the opposite way Barry went, but had actually circled around some slot machines and followed him out the door. Barry walked straight to his car, which was in a lot about three blocks away. The Goldmine did not have employee parking. Now, at least, Michael knew where he parked.

His last day at the Goldmine, a Saturday, was a good day. The dice table was still open as his crew relieved the graveyard crew. They stayed busy all day, as did their "21" dealer. When they split at shift's end, they each had 222 dollars. Michael questioned himself if he had done the right thing. He made a decision not to follow Barry again today. Time was on his side, and he had lots of patience. Besides, he was in too good of a mood.

The casinos in Reno experience their biggest lull in business between the end of the Thanksgiving weekend and a day or two before New Years, depending on which day of the week it happens to fall. So when Michael started at the Pot of Gold on December 26th, he didn't expect it to be very busy, it wasn't. His new shift manager, Jake, took him to the main pit, introduced him to the pit boss, Fran, and asked her to show him the "21" procedures. She took him to a closed table, and went through the process for single deck, double deck, and "shoe" games, which had 6 decks. Then she walked him over to a live game, and had him deal for about 20 minutes. Jake then took Michael to the dice pit, which at the moment only had one of its four games open, and was standing dead. He was introduced to the dice supervisor, Glenn, and met three of the dice dealers. One of them, Tom, was the next to go on break, so Jake asked him if he would show Michael the break room, the toke room, and where their schedules were posted. Tom was very personable, stood about six feet tall, maybe one hundred and eighty pounds with curly blonde hair and mustache. Michael thought he might have met a dealer he could tolerate.

Almost all casinos are twice as large below the main floor level. This was the case with the Pot of Gold. There were offices, wardrobe, the coin room, a room with cases of beer stacked to the ceiling, and almost as much whiskey and other hard liquors, electrical rooms, heating and air conditioning control rooms, and storage of many types. The dealer's schedule was posted next to the wardrobe room. Tom showed him this first. New schedules were posted weekly on Thursday, and took effect the following Monday. Next they went to the break room which was actually upstairs from the main floor through a door almost hidden from public view. It was a pleasant room. There were flowers on the table, and the food area was clean and neatly arranged. The casinos downtown made little effort to establish a pleasant environment for their employee's breaks. The toke room was downstairs from the break room, across from a bar. Tom explained that the 6 to 2 dealers would wait at that bar for tokes to be distributed, and, as did the Nevada Gold, tokes for dealers who worked later shifts would be delivered to their tables.

They returned to the dice pit and found there were now three men playing. Jake had Michael push in on the stick position, and told Tom he could take another break. A nice, easy little game for his first night. He thought he was going to enjoy this job.

New Year's Eve was only five days away. The grand opening of the new tower was to happen on December 30th, which was on a Friday. The Pot of Gold was very large, and the plan was to have every game on the casino floor open by 8 o'clock that night. The actual celebration was to begin at nine.

Michael was scheduled at eight. He was on a "21" game located near the elevators to the new tower. There were dozens of customers already surrounding the tables, anxious for them to open up. This area was going to be a five dollar minimum, while the rest of the casino began at ten. Management wanted to make sure everyone saw the new tower, and the new restaurant. Cheaper table limits would undoubtedly bring more customers to that end of the floor.

And, boy did it work. Michael looked forward to his breaks more than ever before, at least since the grand opening of the Reno Queen. There were spots for seven players on each table, and seven players he had all night until just after three in the morning. Some people actually went to bed! He hoped his shift would end at four, as he was scheduled, but that didn't happen. They were not going to be allowed to leave until all the games in that pit were closed. It was just after five when the first table lost its last player, and was locked up. Michael finally got to go home around 6:15.

He went right home, had one scotch and one cigarette to wind down, and fell into a dreamless sleep. It was now New Year's Eve, and he was scheduled from 6 at night until 6 in the morning.

Tokes were not divided that morning. Even those on the toke committee worked abnormal hours. The three of them decided to come in at five in the afternoon, divide the tokes, and give them out as everyone came in at six. There were many who worked overtime, and the division would take some time.

When Michael arrived at the Pot of Gold around 5:30, he waited with everyone else in the break room until they were told their money was ready. Before that even happened, they had heard through the grapevine that for 8 hours the amount was 180 dollars. Swing shift dealers totaled a number of over 80. That was 22 dollars and 50 cents an hour. Michael had worked 10 and ¼ hours, so he would be receiving 230 dollars. And he still had New Year's Eve to look forward to.

Michael was scheduled for the same pit that night. That was fine with him. It was quiet compared to the main area of the casino which was only about 50 feet from the lounge where a very loud band was playing. He was still tired from the night before, and he cherished the idea of some relative solitude compared to the pits in the "middle of the action". But things change. An hour and a half after he opened his table at six, he was pushed out and told to go and see the scheduler, George. George told him that one of the 8 p.m. dice dealers had been taken to the hospital with an undisclosed health problem. He was needed on that crew. Good news, bad news.

Dice dealers generally hate to deal anything other than the game they had worked at so hard to master. That was the way Michael felt, except tonight. He was drained, and the noise in the dice pit was already deafening, and it was early. He was seldom nervous, but tonight was different.

His crew pushed out a very tired day shift crew that had started two hours earlier than their normal shift. The game was crowded. After three or four minutes, Michael settled into the game. New Years is known in the business as "amateur night", and this night was no exception. Invited, "high rollers", would be on the 25 dollar minimum table. Michael's table had only a 5 dollar minimum. Of the eight players on his end of the table, only one knew how to play the game. Four of them were only playing the "field" where bets are self made by the player, and win or lose with every roll of the dice. Dealers call it a "sucker bet", because the odds are so heavily against the player. That doesn't mean no one ever wins, luck is luck. But with the numbers 5, 6, 7, and 8 not in the field, 20 of the 36 combinations on a pair of dice are eliminated. The other three players knew enough to make one or two bets.

The night stayed busy, and time moved quickly. At midnight, the people from the marketing department handed out hats and noisemakers. Eleven fifty nine p.m., plus fifty seconds, at the end of the traditional ten second countdown, all hell broke loose. For about three minutes, everyone, except those working, made as much noise as humanly possible. For almost five full minutes, no one was playing. Then, just as if someone had thrown a switch, everything returned to normal.

Because it's a stand-up game, and because money can be lost or won very quickly on the dice game, by three in the morning his game had no players. The earliest crew was still on their game, so Michael's game was closed to allow the first dealers to come in that night an opportunity to go home. The graveyard crew, which had come in at 2 a.m., pushed Michael's crew out just after five. Exhausted, he limped to his car and drove home.

As they had the day before, the toke committee came in at five the next evening, New Year's Day, and divided the tokes. Michael was scheduled a 6 to 2 shift on this day. After the Eve is over, everything slowed down. When he opened his toke envelope, he had 385 dollars, or 35 dollars an hour. His energy returned.

Business doesn't completely drop off after New Years in the Reno casinos. There are still the skiers, and in the first part of the year is "Martin Luther King" day, and then the Superbowl. The Superbowl is as busy as any other holiday, and there is more money spent than on New Years. With the addition of the new tower, the Pot of Gold now had about 2000 rooms. Unlike downtown, this was important, there was no other casino nearby whose customers would help fill the gaming tables. In slower times marketing also sought conventions. Some of these groups were good tippers, and some were not. As did most dealers, Michael cared little how many rooms were occupied, as long as the customers were good tokers.

Tom and Michael spent a lot of time together. He had worked at the casino for over four years, and gave Michael some insight into the casino's management and some of its regular players. He told him which pit bosses he could trust, and those he couldn't. Michael began to realize that the old adage about casinos was entirely true. "They're all toilets, some are just cleaner than others."

The owner of the Pot of Gold was a small and greedy man. His name was Jerold. In the community, outside of the casinos, he portrayed himself as a generous man, a benefactor in the community. The truth was the exact opposite. When the conventions arrived, he would give a speech to welcome them in the convention center. Contained in his speech were the words, "you don't have to tip my employees, I pay them very well". No one who worked on the casino floor ever received a raise. Minimum wage was the standard. Ownership had created a separation of the "haves" and "have-nots" within the casino.

Michael was now on a dice game almost every night. Not counting the holidays, his first month's average was 95 dollars a day. He was glad he had made the change, especially because he was hearing rumors that the Goldmine might close.

He didn't give a damn about the possibility of his old casino closing. He felt no connection or loyalty to it. But he did have unfinished business with Barry, and if it closed before he could find out certain information, that might not happen. Now that he was working evenings and Barry was on days, it was going to be difficult to follow him after work. His only opportunity would be on his days off.

Having his days free, he had become one of the regulars at the library. He had amassed about thirty pages of notes obtained from his research. There was a wealth of information, and it was all for free. His unusual interests had produced a great amount of knowledge pertaining to insecticides, botanicals, the dangers of common household cleaners, and "over the counter" medicines. He was a little surprised by the simple fact that so many every day items could be so dangerous. For example, when certain over the counter medicines were mixed with each other, they could cause serious illness, and in some cases death. Household cleaners could cause the same disastrous results. He had learned a great deal about the human anatomy. It was enlightening how fragile the body was, and it didn't matter how big or how small the person. A few anatomy books, and a couple of publications about the martial arts had given him surprising information. A quick and sharp blow with an object, or even a trained hand to a precise area, could cause unconsciousness or even death. There were several areas in the head and neck area which were extremely vulnerable.

He even researched the mechanical aspects of the automobile, heating, and air conditioning. Although modern cars and trucks are complicated, they could be disabled quite easily. All things mechanical had weaknesses. Modern heating systems, with all their safety features still contained vulnerable areas.

In late February, he went to the Goldmine on his first day off, a Thursday. It looked the same inside, with the exception of having even fewer customers. He walked towards the pit, but stayed out of sight behind a slot machine. There was Barry on the dice game. He assumed that he still had Monday and Tuesday off. Satisfied, Michael left.

The next day he returned to the Goldmine at 5:45, fifteen minutes before the end of day shift. He watched Barry get pushed off his game and move to the area where they divided tokes. Michael left and drove to the parking lot Barry used. He quickly checked the lot to make sure his car was there. Confirming that it was, he parked his own car behind the lot in position to see Barry when he arrived. Barry got in his car and drove away. Michael followed. He headed for the freeway, 80 east, and got into the north bound lane, and accelerated to merge with the flow of traffic.

He merged onto northbound 395 until he reached the Panther Valley exit. He turned right at the bottom of the off ramp, and was obviously headed for the area where there were manufactured homes. Michael did not enter the residential area. Instead, he parked his car and ran inside the complex, hoping to see where Barry's car was headed. He couldn't see it anywhere. He ran to the back of the area, and up a small hill. He saw it. The car was parked in front of a home off to his right. Michael went back to his car and drove home.

At the end of February, business at the Pot of Gold was a little slow. The hotel was not even half full, except on weekends. It was still a good job. Lots of dealers took EO's, especially the married women who had children. So the tokes did not drop as much as they could have. He was still averaging about 80 dollars a day.

Tom had become someone Michael felt he could trust, but he knew it would be an "at work" relationship only. He began to talk about how he had come to live in Reno, his first job as a waiter, and his experiences at the Nevada Gold and the Reno Queen. Tom had only dealt in two casinos, and both had great reputations for treating their employees fairly well, as well as having a good customer base. He was very surprised that so many of the casinos in the downtown area seemed to have so little value for their hardworking men and women on the casino floor. Michael told him about the horror of dealing a "quarter crap game". Tom said he had heard stories about it, but never believed it could be quite that bad. Michael described some of the worst people he had known, both players, and co-workers. Tom laughed as he was told how badly Michael was treated by these people. Michael didn't laugh, he just became quiet.

Nothing much changed at the Pot of Gold until the Memorial Day weekend. For the Reno area, this signifies the beginning of summer, and results in more hotel rooms being filled daily. There had been two small conventions, one in March and one in April. Each lasted only 4 days. One was a convention of teachers, and they did not toke well, most of them not at all. The other was a pharmaceutical convention, which consisted of younger people, and they toked slightly better than average.

Michael heard disturbing news. Business was so poor at the Goldmine that it was certain to close after Labor Day. It was time to get to work. He didn't want to be too late.

It was mid June, and the Reno Rodeo was in all its glory. These cowboys were a lot of work, a lot of noise, and toked no one but the cocktail waitress, and she was lucky to get a quarter for four beers. Barry got off work at six, and headed for his car as usual. It had been a very busy day and he was tired. All he wanted to do was get home, put his feet up, and have a nice, cold, beer of his own. He put the keys in, started up his five year old Nissan Sentra, pulled out of the lot, and headed for the freeway. As he entered the on ramp, he remembered that his wife wasn't going to be home until later. She was taking a summer class at TMCC, Truckee Meadows Community College. The subject was "Interior Design". They were planning to buy a small home in a new development, and she wanted to decorate it herself.

As 395 began a gradual incline towards the Panther Valley exit, the Sentra began to stutter. He was losing power. He thought he might have blown a head gasket. When he reached his exit, he went down the off ramp and turned right. He immediately pulled off the road to a small side street. He got out of his car, opened the hood, and expected to see a little steam, or fluid dripping under the car. There was nothing. He thought he would be able to make it home. He closed the hood, turned around to get back in the car, and saw something flash in front of his face. It was the last thing he ever saw.

The story about Barry's demise was not on the first page of the Reno Gazette Journal the next day. It was on page three. The reporter wrote, "Barry Sorgen, a dealer at a downtown casino, was found dead less than a mile from his home yesterday. He apparently had car trouble, and while attempting to discover the problem, fell and hit his head on a rock, or other sharp object, causing a cerebral hemorrhage. It is believed he died instantly. An autopsy will be performed."

CHAPTER 8

Changes were beginning to happen at the Pot of Gold. And, as usual, they weren't for the better. Rumor said that ownership had miscalculated the effects of the expansion. It had been estimated that 70 to 80 percent of the new 1000 rooms would be filled year round. What they failed to consider was that other casinos south of the downtown area had been expanding. Unlike the Pot of Gold, they were in close proximity to the Reno/Sparks Convention Center, which had tripled in size the last year, enabling Reno to have much larger conventions than in the past. In addition, these two casinos were providing lavish amenities for their guests, including world class spas, and richly decorated restaurants. There had been no improvements to the existing services at the Pot of Gold. They had simply created more rooms and a new restaurant. Even the new restaurant was a failure. It was in the back corner of the casino, just past the new tower elevators.

At concept it was to have been on the top floor of the new tower, offering dramatic views of the Reno/Sparks area. Located where it was now would require customers to seek it out in order to find it. In addition, the menu was limited, and the quality of the food was reported as less than excellent.

As ownership always seems to, the blame for the lack of sufficient business was placed on the employees who worked on the casino floor, and middle management, even though some of them had been in their positions 20 years or longer, and were responsible for the property staying very successful thanks to the rapport established between them and the customers. The owners, especially the "man himself", Jerold Ibarra, considered themselves blameless for anything that might be negative regarding the property. In their own minds, they were infallible. The truth was, not a single principal payment to the bank that funded the expansion had been paid. Jerold had lost the 100% ownership he had inherited from his father-in-law. He was now equal partners with the bank.

Of course the work force knew otherwise. Michael and his fellow dealers, who actually worked with the customers daily, and heard their complaints and suggestions, were never consulted as to positive changes which would rejuvenate the business. How would they know what was really going on? They were just workers, not all-knowing executives.

The change Michael liked the least was the firing of the "Table Games Manager", who was now Jake. The result, to say the least, was disastrous. Management did not replace him immediately. They, for God knows what reason, placed the Marketing Director in charge of the pit. He knew nothing about anything, including marketing.

Events throughout Michael's entire gaming career in Reno convinced him that the majority of management was ignorant when it came to good business practices. They were totally unaware of how to keep their customers happy. One casino he had worked in that had the best understanding of the industry, was the Nevada Gold. For all the negative things that he experienced, he had to admit that they had at least one very wise and competent director. He was in charge of the slot machine play. His name was Brad. Brad's philosophy was, "if it ain't broke, don't fix it". He didn't move slot machines if they were making money for the casino. He didn't replace employees who worked hard and supported his plan. When most casinos hired new management in any department, they made changes. In most cases, these changes were only done to justify their employment. They made no sense, created no new customers, and often displeased their customer base.

For once, Michael had no intention of looking for a new job. He didn't want to go back downtown, and the reputation of management in the two successful casinos south of town, was not favorable. He decided to stay, and "ride out" the changes. He would keep his mind occupied with other interests, and not think about his work. It had become a job, and only a job. It would pay the bills.

Michael and Tom worked together four days a week. When they were on different dice crews, they tried to have the same breaks. It wasn't that Michael *had* to talk to someone, he simply enjoyed the chance to release thoughts he held previously only to himself. He was pretty sure Tom believed some of the things he confided in him to be exaggerations, or even his imagination.

The Pot of Gold finally found a new games manager. His name was Tony. He seemed to be a competent man, who was of the old school. That meant that his dice dealers were once again considered the elite, the best the casino had to offer. And, by this time, Michael considered himself one of the best the Reno area had to offer. There was only one problem with him, he was too good at his job, which meant he wouldn't be around long. He was also a bit of a misogynist, believing all dealers should be male. Although Michael understood the latter, this was the end of the 1990's, and women had to be tolerated. After all, they did make money on the "21" games, but other than that, all they did was bitch about the money, and how difficult their job was. They should have to deal a real game just once.

For whatever reason, Tony liked Michael. He was put on the main crew, always working 6 to 2. That also meant that his game would have the higher limits. On weekends and holidays, his game would have a 25 dollar minimum.

The second weekend Michael was put on the "main crew", the biggest dice player in Reno showed up on their game. His name was Ed, or as he was known by everyone, "Mr. S". He had a line of credit, as many of the better players did, but his was a whopping 100,000 dollars. The first thing he did was ask that the table minimum be raised to 100 dollars. He didn't like playing with other players who might do something stupid on the game. Customers who didn't know the game well, often made late bets, getting their hands in the way of the roll of the dice, or some other thing that might interrupt the rhythm of the game. The dice manager was more than happy to accommodate him.

He asked for a 50,000 dollar marker. Michael was glad Mr. S didn't start on his end of the table, he wasn't even sure which denomination chips to give him, or how many of each. He didn't know how he played. The dealer on the other end, a Chinese gentleman named Kam, knew him well. He gave him 4 stacks of 25 dollar chips totaling 2000 dollars, 4 stacks of 100 dollar chips totaling 8000 dollars, 2 stacks of 500 dollar chips totaling 20,000 dollars, and one stack of 1000 dollar chips totaling another 20,000 dollars.

As did many other "high rollers", he played a simple game. He played the pass line with full odds, and followed it with two come bets with full odds. If the point was four, ten, six or eight, he would put 100 dollars on the "hard way". That meant the winning roll would have to be two "2's", two "5's", two "3's" or two "4's". The hard 4 or 10 paid seven to one, the hard 6 or 8 paid nine to one. (A come bet is the same as the pass line, but is made after the point is established, and the next roll of the dice decides the number on which that particular bet will be won.) The only other bets he made were bets for the dealers. His bets began with 200 dollars on the pass line, and 200 dollar come bets. If he won a bet, he would increase his basic or "flat" bet, to 300 dollars. He took full odds, that is double the bet on the line. The dealers always had a 25 dollar bet on the pass line, and 50 dollar odds. He would also put a 25 dollar chip on the hard ways for them. Now this was a dice game everyone could love.

Michael was thrilled when his chance came to deal to Mr. S. He had never seen a 1000 dollar chip at the other casinos. He seldom saw a 500 dollar chip.

Mr. S played for about an hour and a half. When the box man "colored him up", he had won just over 12,000 dollars. The dice were inconsistent, or he could have won or lost a hundred thousand. The dealers had over 2800 dollars in their toke box.

After he left, management decided to leave that game at the 100 dollar limit for a while, in case he returned.

Michael's table had no players for the next hour until the limit was lowered back to 25 dollars. Even then, they never had more than six players at a time. One time, when they had no players, Michael found out from the other dealers that they hadn't seen Mr. S for several years. The reason he came back was that he liked the Games Manager, Tony. He followed him wherever he worked.

At the end of the shift, when tokes were distributed, each dealer took home 130 dollars. The dice pit helped, which wasn't always the case.

As long as Michael concentrated on his game, and didn't let his thoughts drift to the dislike he now had for management, everything was fairly good in his life. He did want to visit the Nevada Gold soon. It had been too long since he had seen any of his old "friends".

About a week and a half after Mr. S played at the Pot of Gold, Michael was having a late breakfast at his favorite little hangout downtown. He purchased a newspaper to read while he ate. On page two of the first section was a story that he found very interesting. The investigation into the hit and run that had occurred on Center Street, resulting in the death of a man who had only one arm, had finally produced a suspect. A dealer from the Nevada Gold casino had been arrested and charged with felony manslaughter. Her name was Lori Stanton. She had apparently confided in another dealer whose name was not reported. Her mistake was that the dealer she told her story to, was secretly dating one of the casino managers. She had told him, and he told a friend of his in the Reno Police Department. Traces of paint taken from her six year old Toyota matched the two found on the deceased. They were light blue in color.

CHAPTER 9

Michael had not had a real vacation since he moved to Reno. He had taken a few extra days off to ski, or to take day trips, but he hadn't had a full week to himself for years. He had a week coming at the Pot of Gold, and, because they were one of the casinos that had agreed to give "vacation tokes", he could afford it. He would receive everything that was made while he was gone.

Unfortunately, he hadn't saved enough money to go or do anything very exciting. He decided that didn't matter, he would take a week off as soon as possible. He thought he might go to the Pacific coast for a few days. The weather was getting warm, he missed the ocean and would enjoy walks along the beach. The northern California and southern Oregon coasts were less likely to be crowded with tourists as was the southern California area. Working in noisy, crowded casinos had increased his need for some alone time.

He put in for his vacation to take effect the week after the Fourth of July weekend. Casinos don't usually like to give vacations in the summer, but because the overall business had decreased during the last year, he thought he had a good chance of his time off being approved. It was also a bonus that Tony liked him so much, and gave his approval to the scheduler. He was pretty sure he would be allowed his time off.

He received his written approval for July 9th through July 17th as vacation time. Five days off, and with full pay, plus his regular days off on each end, totaled nine days away from work. More time than he needed.

About 7 o'clock on the morning of July 9th, he packed up his car and headed west on I-80 towards San Francisco. He figured he'd find a small motel somewhere north of the city where he could afford to stay for a few days.

He ended up in Fort Bragg, about three to four hours north of San Francisco, depending on the route. It was just north of Mendocino, and less than two hours away from the Oregon border. It appealed to him mostly because it didn't appear to be a booming area for tourists. He also liked the way the ocean came into Noyo bay, which was surrounded by restaurants and boat houses. From there he could travel north or south on scenic Highway 1, finding secluded beaches, and small restaurants with nice views for his meals.

He found a motel that was reasonably priced, for northern California. Because his only expenditures would be the motel, food, and gas for his car, he could afford the room which would cost him twice as much as a comparable room in Reno. And it did have a view of the ocean, if you put your nose to the window, and stared off to the right. It would do just fine.

He checked in, unpacked, and walked towards the bay to find a place to have a late lunch. There was a small, rustic restaurant that had outdoor seating overlooking the bay. The majority of the lunch crowd was gone. It was 3:30 in the afternoon. He had his choice of seating. He ordered the "daily special", which was red snapper. It was pretty tasty, as was the accompanying salad, which was fresh and crisp, with a Roquefort dressing and Bleu Cheese crumble.

Satisfied, he continued walking around the bay. The daytime temperature was 78 degrees. He enjoyed the sights and smells. He walked for a couple of hours. As the sun slipped lower in the sky, the temperature dropped quickly. He decided he should head back to his motel. He arrived back just before sunset. The thermometer on the outside of the building read 60 degrees. He assumed the temperature would drop into the mid to lower 50's during the night. It was much warmer than Reno during the winter, but, because he was on the ocean, the air was damp. Reno was usually quite dry, so to Michael, 50 degrees near the coast, felt very cold.

The next day he decided to head north on Highway 1. It was a beautiful day. The sun shone over the ocean and reflected itself in long patches of bright light. The cliffs were jagged reaching up to the highway. And on the right was the greenest forest he had ever seen. It wasn't long before he reached MacKerricher State Park. Moss covered rocks jutted right out to the ocean. The mix of green trees, the ocean, and the moss were a gift to his sense of smell. Unlike the beaches in southern California, there was no litter on the beach, only birds and a few sand crabs. What he liked the most was the sound of the surf. There is nothing like it to soothe a troubled mind. He walked around for a couple of hours until he got hungry.

Back at his car, he decided to return south. His maps showed there wasn't much between where he was and the Oregon border. He had passed a small roadside restaurant on his way up. He decided to see if their food was any good.

The restaurant was called the "Greenery". It was a vegetarian only establishment. He had a sandwich made with freshly baked twelve grain bread, aged Swiss cheese, organic tomatoes and romaine lettuce. It was seasoned to perfection, and delicious, although a little over priced. He enjoyed his lunch, and studied his maps while he ate.

After lunch he decided to head back north a few miles and enter the Humboldt Forest. He had always wanted to see the redwoods.

It took him less than an hour to be in the middle of the giants. Pictures couldn't do them justice. The tops seemed to touch the clouds, and many of their bases could have been hollowed out to make a small house. He laid down on the ground and looked up. It felt the exact opposite of when you looked out of the window of an airplane and saw the ground so far below. And the pine smell was unbelievable. He let his senses take in the wonders of nature. There was a peace, a quiet, and the ultimate solitude in this forest. He felt at home here, and, for the short time he was in the grasp of nature, lost all anger, all the hatred that usually filled his soul.

Around 5 p.m., he stopped his walk through the forest. It was time to head back to his motel. He wasn't very hungry, but realized he needed something to eat before he went to sleep.

Returning to the motel, he walked the five blocks down to Noyo Bay, and this time he took a light jacket.

He looked around and saw a building that was obviously a restaurant, lit up in beautiful fashion. It was mostly windows. He decided to go there, and even if the prices were out of his reach, he would at least have a salad, and enjoy the ambience.

It was named "The Light In the Bay". The menu was not as pricey as he feared. He found a seafood platter of shrimp, bay scallops, crab meat, and sea bass was only 28 dollars and 50 cents. It came with a salad and rice Pilaf. He ordered a glass of the house white wine, which was a crisp and pleasant Chablis, and waited patiently for his meal.

He looked over the restaurant and realized the other patrons in the restaurant were all couples. Men and women enjoying each other's company, as well as a fine meal. He was the only one eating alone. This usually didn't bother him. He seldom noticed anyone else at all. Maybe it was what he had experienced during his day trip, maybe it was the wine, but he began to become depressed. His food was tasteless. He left part of it uneaten, and decided to go back to his room. On the way he passed a convenience store, purchased a bottle of scotch, and continued to the motel. Once there, he poured himself a good sized drink, sat in the dark, and became lost in deep and dark thought.

The next morning he decided to cut short his trip to the coast. He checked out of the motel and headed south to Bodega Bay. The Alfred Hitchcock movie "The Birds" was filmed there, and it was on his way home.

It took him just under three hours to travel the distance. He pulled into a restaurant parking lot and went inside. He had an early lunch consisting of a tuna sandwich and iced tea. When he was finished, he went outside and started walking. None of it was familiar. The town had obviously changed a great deal since the movie was made.

He found it a pleasant ocean front community. But he'd had enough of that. He walked back to his car and headed for Highway 116 south, where he would intersect with 80 east. He would be in Reno in about four and a half hours.

Chapter 10

Michael arrived in Reno in a foul mood. Usually long drives gave him peace. Not today. He went to his apartment, grabbed a bottle of scotch, lit up a cigarette, and turned on his videos. He sat there for over three hours. His mood had darkened. He hadn't thought about what he would do when he left the coast early. Now he knew. He went outside and started walking.

A few minutes later, he was at the Nevada Gold. He went right to the crap tables. There were two of them, Henry "the hawk", and "German Frank" on the "game from hell". He stood and stared at them for a long time. What he wanted to do was rip their heads off. It was a good thing he didn't have some sort of weapon, he most likely would have used it. He had to get his thoughts under control, the time wasn't right. He knew he had to walk away, but his feet just didn't want to move. He finally felt his blood pressure lower, and left the casino. He walked west, away from home. He needed to take a long walk, and burn off some anger. He circled around some of the other casinos, and almost an hour later, ended up at his apartment.

It took him a while, but he finally got drunk enough to sleep, and not dream.

Michael slept until ten the next morning. He got up, showered, and headed out to get some coffee and a muffin. He was still trying to remove the hatred he had felt from last night's excursion. While he was eating his muffin, he realized he needed money. He would have to go to the Pot of Gold about 5:30 and get some of his tokes.

When he left for the casino, he knew he would only have two days coming to him. About 5:45, Beverly, the head of the toke committee gave him two envelopes. They totaled 147 dollars. She asked him, "You worked at the Goldmine before here, right?"

He said, "yes, why?"

"Do you remember the story of a dealer named Barry who died in an accident."

Michael said, "yes."

"Well, it turns out that it wasn't an accident after all. Apparently he was murdered." Michael was genuinely surprised. "He was having an affair, and his wife was so upset, she told her brother. The guy was a mechanic, and somehow fixed it so Barry's car would have a problem when he went home from work. He had followed him that day, knowing he wouldn't get all the way home. He came up behind him when he got out of his car and hit him with a hammer and killed him. I guess his wife didn't know what her brother had done, she's not suspected to be a part of it." Michael felt disappointed.

The next day he went to the library. He went through the last few day's newspapers. The article he was looking for was in the paper that came out on the day he left for the coast. The police had started treating Barry's death as a murder after his car was carefully inspected. The fuel injection system had been intentionally damaged. Then they sought a motive. After questioning his co-workers, and discovering he had been seen frequently with a young woman he worked with, they questioned his wife, Ann. Through her they found out that she had tearfully confided in her brother, Travis. When they found out his occupation was an automobile mechanic, they were pretty sure they had their killer. A footprint from a boot was found at the crime scene, matching a pair in his closet, and a hammer was found hanging in his home's garage wiped clean, but not clean enough, he confessed to the crime. Michael thought Travis had done the world a favor. But, it should have been him. He would have found more joy in being the one responsible for Barry's demise.

He still had almost five days left on his vacation. He would use them well. He might have to take another short trip to Sacramento to get a few things he would need. He didn't want to be seen purchasing them in Reno. He knew a couple of places where he could get everything. He would leave first thing tomorrow morning. For the rest of this day, he would try to unwind. He headed north on Highway 445, also known as the Pyramid Highway. In less than an hour he would be at Pyramid Lake. He had never been there, but people he worked with said it would probably please him. It's a desert lake, surrounded by unusual rock formations, and sand.

He found it looked almost exactly as the picture he had formed in his mind. He parked in one of the lots and started walking. He had never seen a body of water that seemed so desolate. He felt as if he was on another planet. Walking for over an hour, he was finally able to clear his head, and not think at all.

When he got back to his car he got in and just sat there. There were several boats and jet skis on the lake. Some were fishing, some were water skiing, and the jet skis were just racing back and forth. He watched them, mindlessly, and lost track of time. Hunger brought him back into focus. He started up the car, headed south. He needed to find something to eat.

He drove for over forty minutes until he got to an area called Spanish Springs. There was a convenience store on the south west corner of a cross street. He stopped there, went inside and purchased a wrapped sandwich, and a "slurpy". He went back to his car and ate the sandwich, drank part of the "slurpy", and headed back to Reno. He drove straight home, parked his car, and locked himself in for the rest of the night.

Chapter 11

He left for Sacramento the next morning around eight. He planned to stop in Truckee, California and have breakfast at the best place in the entire area, the "Squeeze Inn", which was only open for breakfast and lunch. Every day of the year would find it busy. It had been in Truckee for as long as most people could remember. It was a long building, but very narrow, (hence, the name), located within a group of restaurants and small specialty shops. Its popularity was based on its choice of over 60 omelets and 30 sandwiches, as well as hamburgers and Mexican food, all delicious, all large. Each was named after people and places in the surrounding area. The names weren't official, they were what the locals called them.

He arrived in Truckee about 8:45, found a metered space to park his car about three doors down from the "Squeeze", and went inside. The waitress brought him coffee and water while he decided what to order. He requested the "Buckin' Buster", which contained sausage, spinach, mushrooms, and a variety of cheeses. He had a choice of biscuit or toast, and cheese or mushroom sauce. The biscuit and cheese sauce would do nicely.

When his food arrived, he ate with his head down, and never looked up until he was finished. He paid his check, left the waitress a five dollar tip, went to his car, and headed for Sacramento.

He reached his destination in just over two hours. He spent almost forty minutes, total, in two shops deciding on his purchases. He paid for the last of them, went back to his car, and was back in Reno in under three hours. For the next couple of nights, he would be busy planning how he would cross off things on his list.

On Thursday, July 17th, the day before he was to return to work, he went to the Pot of Gold to check his schedule. He would be on the 6 o'clock dice game Friday through Tuesday, his normal schedule. While he was there, he picked up the other four days of his tokes which totaled 384 dollars. Business had been good while he was gone.

The next morning he went to a late breakfast, as had become his custom. On his way home, he bought a newspaper. He opened it when he got home, he couldn't wait any longer. The lead story on the front page was about the plans for "Hot August Nights", an annual Reno event centered around old cars, and rock and roll music from the 50's and 60's. When he finally reached page 3, he found interest in an article titled, "Five Reno Casino Regulars Found Dead". He read, "Five long time Reno residents, and patrons of downtown casinos, were discovered dead in their residences. They were found over a period of three days, and all had a similar cause of death. Although individually they were seen in several casinos, they all spent the majority of their time in the Nevada Gold. An investigation has been launched, beginning with general autopsies of all five. Although all five men were above the age of sixty, and had health problems, a criminal investigation is under way. Names will be released after notification has been given to any remaining relatives."

Arriving back at work that evening, it was evident that the Pot of Gold had not ceased in its desire to change the status quo. They decided to adopt a downtown Reno program of giving out "player's club cards". If a customer would give their name, address, phone number, and other minor information, they could receive a card that would earn them "points" for their slot and table game play, which would get them "comps" and other free or discounted rates in the casino. Marketing thought this was a great idea. Of course, they hadn't asked their regular customers, who now would have to obtain "points" on their cards to receive the same privileges they had received before the new plan was instituted. Slowly, many of the better players began to disappear. The dealers heard "through the grapevine" that they were seen at the two casinos in south Reno, the "Shangri La", and "Peyton Place".

Michael liked working at the Pot of Gold. Unless there were many more drastic changes, he would stay there for a very long time. Besides, unlike the other places he worked, he had no problems with his fellow dealers, and tolerated most of the pit bosses.

About a week after he returned to work, there was a follow-up article about the five casino patrons who were found deceased in their homes. All had died within three days of each other, and all had some sort of internal physical breakdown which caused massive internal bleeding. Police seldom believe in coincidence, so a complete investigation was underway. One thing they were looking at was surveillance video from the Nevada Gold. Because there were so many ways to cheat the casinos, the camera systems were very good, able to zoom in and see much detail. The recorded tapes were kept for thirty days before they were used again. The police were able to identify all five men playing on the crap tables over a three day span. What they found most interesting was that there was another individual, other than the five, at the tables at the same time they were there. There was no clear view of his face, he kept his head down, but he had longish grey hair, and a full beard. He appeared to be around the same age as those he played next to. What caused them to look at him more closely, was that in one film, from one angle, it appeared he had placed something in a drink, sitting on the ledge, under the lip of the table. Because of this discovery, a full toxicology report was ordered on each of the men. Results were expected within a couple of weeks.

It was about ten days after he came back that he and Tom had a chance to talk. He told Tom about the coast and how he marveled at the redwoods. His soul was filled with a peace, a quiet solitude, he hadn't felt since he left Los Angeles and the Pacific Ocean. They were even more amazing than his walks on the un-cluttered beaches in northern California. Tom asked him if he met anyone to share his experiences with on his travels. Michael responded, "why would I want to?" Tom simply didn't know what to say.

After that conversation, it appeared to Michael that Tom was avoiding him. Oh well, he didn't want any friends anyway. No one understood him.

A couple of weeks later, there was a small article on the 5th page of the newspaper. The toxicology report on the five men who had died showed only one commonality. Aluminum Phosphide, a fumigant, was present in each blood sample. They were searching the casinos for the man in the surveillance films.

For almost two years, there were no severe changes at the Pot of Gold. Then the major "shake-ups" began. The General Manager, who had served the property for almost 30 years, was released. The owner, Jerold Ibarra, had belittled him in the presence of a large group of customers in the buffet, as he was having his lunch, he resigned on the spot. And that was just the beginning. The hotel manager was released, and his replacement was the worst choice imaginable. One of Jerold's sons, Frank, who was well known as a compulsive gambler and alcoholic, was given the position. He had never actually worked in the casino environment, and had never shown an inclination to do so.

These were bad enough for the property as a whole, but then came the worst for Michael. Two of the three shift managers were fired. The only one they kept was the worst. His name was Bill, and he had been placed on the graveyard shift for disciplinary reasons several years ago. The day and swing shift positions were filled by individuals outside of the table games department. Day shift went to a woman out of marketing by the name of Berta, and swing shift was placed in the hands of the slot shift manager, Leroy. It seemed to Michael that they were intentionally destroying what was once a great business.

At first, there were no changes that directly affected Michael. A few weeks later it began. Leroy was given permission to eliminate two entire crap crews on weekends, taking the pit down to two tables. Management closed the old pit at the very front of the casino, and adjacent to the show room. In the main "21" pit, where most of the tokes were made, four "21" games were removed, and replaced with what the dealers called "circus games". These were games based on the same greedy premise as slot machines. The risks were great, but the payoff was high. The problem with these games for the dealers, was that unless there happened to be a large payoff, very few tokes were made by the dealers.

Instead of hiring a new general manager, or promoting someone from the gaming department, the position was given to the "risk management director", or in other words, the casino's resident attorney. His entire focus was to eliminate monthly expenditure's, and that would begin with the staff. He made it obvious that he wanted to get rid of long time employees, who had amassed greater benefits, as well as a somewhat higher pay level. He began by giving everyone split days off. Michael was given Tuesday's and Thursday's off. All dealers were given three days off every other week.

Then one day, as Michael was checking his schedule, there was a notice posted that all dealers would have three days off every week, and were required to be available for a shift on their scheduled days off if business warranted it. If management was trying to "piss off" the dealers, they were succeeding. Michael decided that if they called him on his day off he would tell them, "fine, I'll come in, but I have to tell you that I had 5 or 6 glasses of wine with lunch, and I'm a little drunk". Bullshit was best countered with more bullshit.

A few weeks later, on a slow night, his old boss, Jake, walked up to Michael's table. They exchanged pleasantries, and then Jake said, "I think you would make a good pit boss. If you're tired of dealing, come see me at the Shangri La, I'm now the games manager there. At least think about it". Michael was getting tired and bored with being a dealer, especially now that so many of the better, more challenging players had deserted the property. The good thing about being a pit boss was the consistent paycheck. The bad thing was he would make less money overall. A lot to think about.

He watched what the pit bosses did more closely the next few days. He noticed that they didn't seem to do much. They were allowed to drink coffee if they wanted it. They got a 20 to 30 minute break every 2 hours. It was a hell of a lot easier than what he did every night. He also liked the idea of having a little power. He just might do it. Besides, things weren't going to get any better at the Pot of Gold.

The next Wednesday, his day off, Michael called Jake at the Shangri La. Jake told him to come to the casino about two in the afternoon.

He had never had any reason to go to the Shangri La before. He arrived about 1:30, not sure about parking or where Jake's office might be. The casino was brightly lit, colorful, and had a cheerful aura. It had a tropical theme. There was a large fish tank behind the hotel desk. A waterfall was next to the escalators going up to the second level. Imitation palm trees were everywhere. Lots of neon was used wherever possible.

He asked one of the pit bosses where Jake's office was. He was directed to the second floor. He didn't want to be too early, so he walked around, inspected the pits, the restaurants, and other gaming areas such as Keno, the race and sports book, and the poker room. About 1:50, he got on the escalator. He found the door marked "Games Manager", which was open. He went inside and saw Jake doing paperwork at his desk. He looked up and saw Michael, smiled, stood, and came around the desk to shake his hand. He told Michael to take a seat, and Jake returned to his desk chair.

James Turnage

Jake said; "You're here, so I assume you have decided to make a change."

Michael said; "Yes, I believe I have, but I have a few questions. What will my relationship be with my shift manager? Where does my authority begin and end? Will I get raises, and when?"

Jake responded; "Vanessa Stryker will be your shift manager. She is very bright, and appears to be very fair. I have only known her for a couple of months, but I think she will be what we are looking for to handle a very busy swing shift. Your authority will be based on your good judgment, and therefore supported by Vanessa. Raises are based on performance. Reviews given quarterly."

Michael's response to all this was; "Can I have a couple of days to make a decision?"

Jake said; "Yes, but only a couple, I have to complete my swing shift staff by the end of the week".

When Michael left his meeting with Jake, he was a bit uneasy. Two nights later, when he was at work, the choice became clear. Tony wasn't at work. During his shift he discovered Tony had been removed from his position, while he was on his days off. He had disagreed with the changes being made. There would be no new games manager, the position had been eliminated. Leroy would be in charge of all decisions regarding gaming on swing shift.

And decisions he made. Lots of them, and not many of them for the good. Checking his next week's schedule, Michael found several changes. First, he changed the hours. The majority of swing shift would come in at seven instead of six. Then he changed the "high limit" "21" dealers. Instead of the best dealers, who the regular customers were familiar with, he put dealers on the game who were simply the fastest. To him, more hands an hour a dealer produced was more important than keeping long time players in house. Then he broke up the crap crews. He mixed the dealers on the games, and took away consistent hours. Michael was now on the 7 p.m. crews some nights, and the 8 p.m. on other nights. He even had one 9 p.m. shift on a Saturday night. Leroy was making his decision about Michael's future for him.

The morning after he saw his new schedule, he called Jake. He told him that he would be very happy to work for him again. Now, he had to go and buy at least three suits.

He found a discount store that had decent quality suits, ties, and dress shirts at a reasonable price. He purchased a black, grey, and medium beige suit, four shirts and five ties. He figured he could mix and match between his purchases, and would have enough for now to begin his new job.

Chapter 12

After giving a short notice to the Pot of Gold, he began his new job a week later. Jake introduced him to the swing shift supervisor, Vanessa. She was a woman in her late 40's to early 50's, with short red hair. She was attractive and well dressed, and seemed pleased to meet Michael. She promised him he would be trained well before taking over his new position. That was the first lie she told him. The second was, "we work as a team here, if you ever need help, I'm always available".

Michael was extremely naïve regarding the treatment and responsibilities of a middle management position in the casinos. The little training he actually received was not by Vanessa, but from another pit boss. His job didn't seem too difficult, but the accountability was enormous for the pay he was to receive. After a few days, he was given a section of a pit to supervise by himself.

The beginning of swing shift was extremely hectic. Every table is counted at the end of each shift. Swing shift is the busiest. All the chips in the trays must be divided properly, so the value can be established quickly. All cards must be changed as the new shift comes in. While all this is going on, there are players who are "cashing out", and the supervisor must confirm the amount. There are players who want "markers", which means they want to use the credit they have previously established. And there are always problems with the dealers which must be handled immediately. There was only one person in each part of the pit to oversee all this. Needless to say, his first night was overwhelming.

One of his most important responsibilities was to calculate a player's win or loss. This was especially important with players who had taken out markers. It would be easy if he or she was the only player on the table, but that was seldom the situation. He knew how to do it, but, as it always is in a casino, that individual situation was not the only thing he was able to concentrate on. Multi-tasking is what made an effective supervisor.

After about four shifts, he was beginning to relax and take control of his job. He learned to prioritize, and focus on what he was doing at each moment. What he was still unhappy about was that his supervisor, Vanessa, was never around when he needed her. She was always in the break room smoking, or socializing with other casino management. In a few days, it got even worse.

Michael had been working there less than a month. He was alone in the high limit pit. There was a small convention from Hawaii in the hotel, and every one of them were "marker players". He was very busy. He had already issued 12 markers. A dealer called him over to witness a "color up" of one of those players. He had been watching the man, and his estimate was pretty close when the dealer cut out the chips. The man had profited 2,300 dollars. While he was next to the dealer, another player called to him from another table, and said he needed a marker. Michael acknowledged him, and said he would be right with him. Apparently, this was not good enough. He complained to one of the casino hosts, (a totally worthless position in the casinos), and the host found Vanessa smoking in the break room. About 30 minutes later, she called Michael into her office.

She had her assistant with her, and she told Michael to have a seat. She said that a credit customer complained that he had been offended when he asked for a marker. He said that Michael said, in a rude manner, "I'll be with you in a minute". Michael explained what had actually happened, but Vanessa took the side of the customer.

When he left her office, Michael realized what Vanessa was really all about. She would do anything to make herself appear valuable and hard working, even at the expense of her subordinates. He was getting insight into why swing shift pit bosses didn't last very long.

After that incident, Michael watched Vanessa very carefully. He found her entirely lacking in positive attributes. She used her charms to hide the fact that she was an ambitious bitch, who lied about everyone else if it helped her achieve her goals. And she knew he was aware of her real character. She began to try and get rid of him. It was very obvious, if only to Michael.

She reminded him of a long forgotten part of his past, a mistake he had corrected when he was twenty-three years old.

—

Her name was Catherine. She was beautiful, with a smile that could melt solid rock. They met at the beach on a summer's day in August. He was sitting alone, at one end of the beach. She walked up and put her towel about ten feet away from his. She just stared out at the ocean for a while, and then, without even an introduction, turned to him and said, "would you put lotion on my back"? He could barely speak, and simply mumbled, "okay". It was a lovely back, from her shoulders to her toes. When he finished, she turned her head and smiled that Catherine smile, and said "thanks". He moved back to his spot. He couldn't stop glancing over at her, while she pretended to ignore him. Over thirty minutes later, she rolled over onto her back, propped herself up on her elbows, and looked Michael over carefully.

Not being anything of a ladies man, Michael became a bit nervous. When he locked eyes with her, his heart rate went off the charts. She had all the attributes that defined the word female. If he was not mistaken, she was interested in him. The words exciting and frightening became synonyms.

She said, "what's your name"?

He said, "Michael".

She said, "I'm Catherine, do you come here often"?

He said, "I love the ocean, I come whenever I can".

Catherine spoke with a confidence that made him uneasy. She asked him, "do you always come here alone"?

Michael responded, "yes".

She inquired, "so you don't have a girlfriend"?

He simply said, "no".

Catherine smiled impishly, sat up, and said, "I find that hard to believe". She got to her feet and walked over to Michael. She reached out and touched his left hand and spoke what would be fatal words, "maybe we could get to know each other better".

And so it had begun. She had given him her phone number on an old receipt from Frederick's of Hollywood, turned and went to her towel. She took what seemed like forever to pick up her belongings and her towel with her backside facing him. She finally stood, turned her face to him, smiled that smile, and said, "I hope you'll call", and walked away.

Michael simply had no idea what had happened. He had very few experiences with the fairer sex in his life. He knew he wanted this woman, but she scared the shit out of him. Even before he left the beach, he knew he would call her. He simply had no choice.

He called her the very next day. He had no idea what to say, but he eventually asked her to have a drink with him in a café on Santa Monica beach around seven in the evening, just before sunset. She said she would meet him there.

The café, "The Tides", was crowded when Michael arrived. He asked the hostess for a table outside so they would have a view of the sunset. She told him it might take a few minutes. That was okay with him, Catherine wasn't due to arrive for about fifteen minutes. But, as he turned around to look over the restaurant, there she was, early. She walked right up to him, gave him a kiss on the cheek, smiled, and said, "hi, I couldn't wait". Michael said, "our table isn't quite ready yet". She told him, "that's all right, I'm not in any hurry now that I'm here with you". Fifteen minutes later the hostess escorted them outside to the patio.

Catherine did most of the talking. She told him she was born in Kansas City, Missouri, but her parents moved to Los Angeles when she was five years old, so she was raised in southern California. She had gone to school in the San Fernando Valley at Van Nuys High School. Her family had moved back to Kansas City after she graduated, but she decided to stay. She was now working in a small boutique in Santa Monica, and taking a few night courses in "Fashion Design" at Santa Monica City College. She lived in a small apartment, close to work and school. She shared the apartment with a roommate who was a full time student at UCLA, by the name of Marsha.

True to his personality, Michael told her only what he felt obliged to about himself. He was born and raised in LA, was now working at a restaurant in Westwood Village near UCLA, and lived alone in an efficiency apartment in West LA.

They ordered white wine, shared an appetizer that had fried clams, fried zucchini sticks, and popcorn shrimp. They added a small Caesar salad. She continued to talk on about work and school as the sun began to set over the ocean. The night was warm, with a gentle sea breeze keeping the air delightfully comfortable. He wasn't listening to much of what she was saying, he couldn't keep his eyes off what was in the thin tank top she wore. She noticed, took a sip of wine, smiled and said, "like what you see"? Michael didn't know what to say. He was sure he blushed, because she began to giggle very quietly. She reached out for his hand, leaned out of her chair, and kissed him gently on the lips, all the while hypnotizing him with those clear blue eyes. Michael stopped blushing, he was sure, because all the blood from his extremities was now centered in an area of his body he hoped no one could see under the table.

They stayed for another twenty minutes, and she said, "why don't you follow me to my place, it's close by, and we can listen to some music. I have a cold bottle of wine in the refrigerator, and my roommate's staying over with her boyfriend."

So, away they went. Catherine lived about a half a mile from the ocean. It was a large complex, with no guest parking. She called back to him and told him to park on the street, and that her apartment number was 322, towards the rear of the complex. Michael's first instinct was to drive back to his place, but "little Michael" was now in complete control of his actions. He did as he was told, and briskly walked to the back. Her apartment was in the third of four separate buildings, on the second floor. He climbed the stairs, and saw the lights were on in her apartment. He knocked on the door. She immediately opened it, smiled, grabbed the front of his shirt, and pulled him inside. She had been lighting some candles, so she clicked off the overhead light. She turned the switch on the stereo, and the smooth and sexy tones of Teddy Pendergrass came to life. He was sensually telling her to "rub me down with some hot oils, baby, and I'll do the same thing for you". She sat down on the couch and patted the cushion for Michael to come sit next to her. He did as was commanded. She opened the wine, poured them a glass, and scooted very close to him. He could feel the warmth of her thigh against his. He was doomed. She sat her glass down, took his and did the same, put an arm around him and kissed him so passionately, he lost the ability to breathe. The next thing he knew, they were entwined so tightly, sweat began to trickle down his forehead.

She had to be at work by nine the next morning, so Michael left for home just after seven. She kissed him once more at the door, and said, "see you *very* soon".

She worked days, and Michael nights, and she had classes two nights a week, but they were together whenever time allowed. Michael had no idea what the word "love" meant, he had never received or felt it, even from his mother. There was no doubt that he was "in lust" and confused it for real emotion, feelings that were something more than just physical attraction. She was good at everything, making Michael feel wanted and special for the first time in his life.

This went on for nearly two months. Whenever possible, they were at his or her apartment. One night, after they were physically satisfied, she turned to him and suggested, "what would you think about us getting our own apartment?" Michael didn't know what to say. After his mother passed away, he had never lived with anyone else. He preferred to be alone. On the other hand, he supposed this is what couples did when they were in love. He told her, "maybe we should look into it."

Less than a week later, Catherine called Michael with some "exciting" news. She had found a place they could afford. It was in Mar Vista, which was still in West LA, just east of Santa Monica. It was a one bedroom, with a fairly large living room and kitchen, and had a carport for one of their cars. What Michael didn't know, yet, was that she had found this place before she had talked to him about sharing an apartment.

The next day they had off together, they went to look at it. It seemed adequate to Michael, and between them they had almost enough furniture to satisfy their needs. Anything they didn't have, they would get from thrift stores. Catherine said, "let's do it", and so they did.

Michael realized there would be advantages in living together, such as, no driving back and forth all the time, shared expenses, and being able to have sex whenever and wherever they wanted, no roommates involved. Signing the rental agreement, he signed both their fates.

They moved into the apartment two weeks later. At first everything was fine. Because of their schedules, they weren't together much of the time. Bathroom use was not a problem, and they both ate their meals whenever they could, at home or fast food joints.

Another couple of months passed. Things were going pretty well. He enjoyed the physicality of living with someone, and for the most part, he was happy when they were together. He was still having an issue sharing the apartment with someone when often all he wanted was "alone time" The frequent sex made up for it.

One Sunday afternoon, when Catherine and Michael were both off, she posed a question which made Michael's heart stop beating, literally. She wanted to get married, something Michael had never even thought about. She was well prepared, giving reason after reason why it made sense. For example, when one of them got a job with medical benefits, the other could be on the policy as well. They would each have the right to make decisions for the other if for some reason he or she was not able to do it for themselves. Financially, they would have more purchasing power, and so on. This time Michael told her he had to think about such a big decision. He would need at least a few days.

For the next three days, that was all he thought about. For the first time in his life, he was truly frightened. He tried to focus on all the positive reasons Catherine had given him, but fear trumped them. He knew if he decided to agree with her, there would be a lot of change, and for a man who had always resisted change, didn't *want* change, that would be the most difficult part. The truth was that he was addicted to this woman, or at least to her body. He didn't want to lose her. This was the first time in his life he had a relationship with another human being. Sure, there were times he resented her being in his home, but he conquered those feelings with the anticipation of the physical pleasure that was sure to come.

Finally he made his decision. Marriage wouldn't be that much different from what they were now doing, and Catherine's reasons for wanting to get married did make sense. He would say yes to her proposal.

The morning of the fourth day after she brought the subject up, he leaned over her before they even got out of bed, and said, "will you marry me"? She screamed with excitement, rolled on top of him, and one thing led to another.

They decided not to wait very long. Michael had no one he wished to be with them when the ceremony took place, and Catherine decided she would tell her family after the fact because it would be difficult for them to come half way across the United States on a rather short notice. They made plans for a civil ceremony in two weeks. Each wanted to take a couple of extra days off so they could take a short vacation which would serve as their honeymoon. They agreed to find a reasonable hotel in San Diego for a few days.

Two weeks later, on a Thursday at two in the afternoon, an assistant justice of the peace at Santa Monica City Hall, pronounced them, "Mr. and Mrs. Michael Whitten. They left right from the courthouse for their hotel on the north beaches of San Diego.

San Diego is very different from LA. There was more beach with less condos reaching out to the shore. It was slower paced, and to Michael and Catherine, it was like another country. They swam, walked on the beach, ate seafood every meal, and drank lots of rum drinks with those little umbrellas shading the ice. And, of course, they had sex morning, noon, and night. Three days flew by, and it was time to go back home and to work.

For both of them, their first day back was a Monday. She was back at the boutique hustling customers for a commission, and he being overly attentive to his diners so he received better tips for serving over-priced food.

The first couple of weeks of their marriage were not dissimilar to when they were just living together. But, then Michael began to notice a few subtle changes. Her side of the closet was growing, pushing his clothes into a lesser space. There were things he didn't recognize in the living room, and new appliances in the kitchen. Although he was not very observant, she seemed to have a number of new earrings and bracelets. She began to stay later at work, even on his days off. When she went to her classes, she didn't return home right away when they ended. When Michael wanted to have sex, she frequently said she was too tired. She wanted new furniture, and hinted that they should move to a nicer apartment in a better section of LA. The biggest change was that she thought Michael should get a better job. A job with a chance for promotion and one that offered medical and dental benefits. Change had come.

As far as the job was concerned, Michael did not enjoy food service. There was an advertisement in the local paper for a supermarket chain with openings in his area. It offered not only pay increases, but advancement and benefits. He made up his mind to check it out.

About a mile away from their apartment was a "Smart Shopper" market. This was the company who had placed the ad in the paper. Michael decided to apply for a position, he could always decline if he changed his mind.

When he told Catherine about this, she made up his mind for him. If he was offered a job, he should take it. It was the best thing to do for them.

He met with the store manager two days later. His name was Walt Grimes. He was about 5 feet 11 inches tall, maybe 50 years old, and about 25 pounds heavier than his frame could carry. He was pleasant, and got right to the main points. What they were looking for were young men to work and train for store managerial positions. If Michael was hired, he would be a "box boy" for about a month, and then be trained as a checker. His pay would therefore increase rapidly, and he would be able to get benefits in only three months, instead of the usual six. Mr. Grimes said he would call him, one way or the other, in a few days.

There was no doubt that his home life was deteriorating rapidly. He would come home from work just before midnight, and the sink would often be full of dirty dishes. There would be an ashtray full of cigarette butts next to her favorite chair. Too many times there was an empty wine bottle next to an empty glass on the same table. And, of course, she was sound asleep in their bed. He felt as though he was losing all the benefits of living with someone. He remembered why he loved living alone. There was no doubt in his mind, he had been used. She was a cunning and selfish female, who would do anything to make her life better, not caring about anyone else, especially her husband. She was like the rest of them.

Exactly three days later, Mr. Grimes called him. He offered him the position they had discussed. Michael decided it was a good idea. He might have a future instead of just a job.

As far as the home front was considered, he felt it was irreparable. He thought about divorce, but growing up in California, he knew how the legal system would give her anything she wanted. He didn't have much, but he could lose everything. He had no proof of infidelity, or any sort of abuse, physical or mental. No, that wouldn't work for him. He would have to find another way, just as he had done with his mother.

He told Catherine about his new job. She was excited, or so it seemed. He told her he thought they should take a few days off before he started at the Smart Shopper. Maybe they could go to Palm Springs for a couple of days and just relax. She replied, "I think that's a great idea. I've always wanted to shop in some of the stores I've heard about there". He just wanted to think about everything. He knew it would be their last trip together.

They left the next week. Michael had made reservations at a hotel that had a large pool, tennis courts, and even a 3 par golf course. The two hour drive was pleasant, though they didn't talk much, which was unusual for her, and great for him. They arrived in mid-afternoon. They checked in, and decided to go down to the pool and cool off from their drive across the desert. They swam, and then laid down on a couple of reclining deck chairs. Both of them were quiet for over half an hour until Michael could no longer resist. He simply said, "I'm not happy. I don't want to live with you anymore. I'm sorry." She just stared, not sure how to respond. Then she shot to her feet, stomped away, and grumbled something Michael did not understand. He didn't move for the next two hours.

He sat there for a while and decided he had made the right decision. If the physical relationship was no longer there, he didn't want to live with her, He was better alone, making his own decisions, his own plans. He finally got up. Sunset was on the horizon. He headed for the hotel's bar. Up to this point in his life, Michael was not much of a drinker. Things change. He asked the bartender for a double screwdriver. He had learned to like the slight, sharp taste vodka added to orange juice. He had another, and then one more. It was now 8:30 in the evening. He decided it was time to face Catherine, who was most likely in their room. He took the elevator to the 9th floor, went to their room, unlocked the door, and went inside. She wasn't there. He was curious, but not worried.

He wasn't sure what to do. Should he look for her or stay in the room? He made up his mind that for a while, at least, he would just watch some television. About 11 p.m. she unlocked the door and entered their room. He didn't say anything, he just stared at her. She looked awful. Her hair was a mess, and she had obviously been crying. She glanced at him quickly, and went into the bathroom. Nearly ten minutes later, she came out. She had fixed her hair and makeup, and was barely wearing a black teddy he had never seen before. She glided over to him, sat on his lap, and kissed him seductively, something she hadn't done in many weeks. She knew Michael's weaknesses, but underestimated his intelligence and his resolve. It wasn't easy. Old feelings, and pleasant memories flooded his senses. He pushed her off his lap. She fell on the floor. She looked at him with an expression of utter disbelief. For the first time in their relationship, she knew she had lost the game. Michael stood, stared at her with clenched fists, and walked out the door.

He returned over three hours later. She was asleep in the bed. He sat in a chair, closed his eyes, and thought about what he had to do next.

The next day he arrived back at their apartment alone. They were not socially involved with any of their neighbors, so he doubted anyone would ask where she was. And if her job called, he would say no more than that she left him, and he didn't know where she went. It felt right. He was happy not to have to share his car or his apartment with anyone ever again. Besides, in a couple of days he would be starting a new job. Life was looking a lot better.

CHAPTER 13

Michael wasn't sure how to handle Vanessa. He supposed he could go to Jake and tell him what she was really like, but he didn't know what sort of relationship Jake and Vanessa had. He could always quit, and find a dealing job somewhere else. But he had developed a real problem He hated her. He hated the way she flirted with men who had power so she could get whatever she wanted. He hated her for her misuse of power, for her verbal abuse, which was always done with a smile. He wouldn't stay there forever, just long enough to take care of her.

Michael knew he could create a few changes that would benefit him. He intentionally fell behind in his work in the high limit pit. He was finally removed from it and placed in a pit that had 5 dollar "21" limits, a couple of "circus" games, and a baccarat table. The only price he paid for this was that he had to work a later shift. No big deal. Of course this meant he would not be able to observe Vanessa's after work habits, except on his days off. He could solve that little problem very easily.

One of the "21" games in his pit was a six deck "shoe" game. On one particular evening, there were only two players, a young couple. About twenty minutes later, a man around forty years old came and joined them. He called Michael over, and asked him if the table limit could be changed to a 25 dollar minimum. And he wanted a two thousand dollar marker. Michael told him he would have to call the shift manager.

Michael was a little surprised when five minutes later Jake came into the pit. He realized that Jake must have seen the customer on one of the monitors in his office. He knew the man as a regular player from other casinos. He raised the limit to 25 dollars immediately, but told the young couple they could still play for 5 dollars. He told Michael to print out the marker, while he had the dealer give him two thousand dollars worthof chips.

As Jake was leaving, he called Michael over and told him to watch that game as closely as possible. If he needed help with the other games, he was to let Vanessa know right away.

The high roller, who Jake had called "Mr. Coulter", was getting lucky. So was the younger couple, but they never played over 20 dollars a hand, while he occasionally played the table maximum, which was 500 dollars a hand. About an hour later, Mr. Coulter had won over 5000 dollars. Of course Michael had kept Vanessa informed, and he knew they had a camera devoted to that game to make sure it was fair. Card counting was rampant in the casinos, but it was very hard to count down a six deck game. Vanessa sent her assistant into Michael's pit. He said that surveillance, (the people who watch the games from the camera room), said everything looked alright. Michael thought the same thing. Almost four hours later, Mr. Coulter cashed out after paying back his marker. He had won almost 25,000 dollars.

A couple of weeks later, Jake came to see Michael in his pit. After running the game tapes through a computerized program, the head of surveillance informed Jake that Mr. Coulter and the couple on the table with him were a "card counting team". They had worked out a three person system that gave them an edge in the percentage of winning or losing. Michael was surprised, but not amazed. If there is money to be made, someone will find a way to do it, honestly or not. All the casino could do about it was to notify Mr. Coulter and his "crew" that they were never welcome in the casino again, and this information would be given to all Reno and Las Vegas casinos.

Even though none of this was Michael's fault, Vanessa inferred that it was. She intentionally made Michael's job more difficult whenever possible.

On his first day off the very next week, he went to the Shangri La a half an hour before Vanessa was to get off work. He parked his car in the farthest part of the lot the customers used, and waited by the employee's exit. She didn't come out at 1:30 when she was relieved by the graveyard shift manager. He waited, patiently. Just before 2:30 she finally came out the door. He would stay a good distance away from her. All he wanted to do right now was find out what type of car she drove.

He followed her as she left the building, about twenty feet away, moving behind cars so she wouldn't catch a glimpse of him. But she didn't go to the employee's parking lot. She went to the first lot on the side of the casino, and unlocked a two year old red BMW. He should have guessed, the employee parking lot was beneath her. Michael wrote down her license number, and headed back for his own car.

Two days later, he was back at work. Vanessa was off. Vanessa's assistant, Nate, was in charge. Michael had settled into work for a little over a half an hour when Nate came up to him. He showed him a form that had been signed by Vanessa. She had "written him up" for the card counting incident. Michael wasn't pissed off, he was livid. But he held it in, kept his feelings to himself, with the exception of telling Nate it was unfair. There was nothing he could have done. Nate simply held a blank stare. He showed no feelings, he took no one's side in the matter. Michael decided to sign the reprimand. By her signing that paper, she had cemented Michael's decision about her future.

When Vanessa came back to work a couple of days later, she stood two pits away and stared at Michael, As she did, she smiled that wicked smile. He just stared back. If she could have read his mind, she would certainly have lowered the corners of her mouth. She might even have registered fear in her eyes. This had become personal. This one would give him great pleasure. She was even more evil than Catherine. She deserved more attention to detail.

On his next day off he returned to the casino, again about the time Vanessa was supposed to be off. This time she came out right on time. His car was two rows over from hers. He watched her get in, light a cigarette, and drive off. He followed her. She went west on Peckham Lane, all the way to West Macarran, and turned left. About a half mile later she turned right into the Caughlin Ranch area. He followed her for three blocks, she turned right, and then turned left into a driveway four houses down the block. It was one of the smallest houses in the area, but he wasn't surprised, Caughlin Ranch was a high end income area of the city. He was parked at the end of the block. He watched her drive into the garage, and drove home.

His work week went along in ordinary fashion. That was just fine. He had been there just over two months, and didn't plan to be there that much longer. Routine was a good thing.

On Vanessa's next day off, Michael called in sick. Around four in the afternoon, he parked down the block from Vanessa's house. He was looking for a sign to let him know if she was home. Around 4:30, he got what he needed. She went out to check her mail. When she did, she was in a bathrobe and slippers. Either she had slept very late, or she was planning something for the evening and was getting prepared. One trait Michael possessed beyond anything else was patience. He sat low in his car until just before 6 p.m. when a late model Mercedes pulled into her driveway. There was still plenty of daylight, giving Michael the ability to see who it was with the aid of binoculars. He was a little surprised, but not shocked. He knew that Vanessa wasn't that good at hiding who and what she really was. He now realized that he had made a good decision weeks ago. The man going into her house was Jake. It was all very clear now how Vanessa got whatever she wanted, and how she was allowed to write Michael up for something that he was not responsible for in any way. This made it very interesting. Jake had a wife and two young boys, with a third child due in four months. Life could be hell for some people, and very soon.

Back at work, Michael played the game. The next time he saw Vanessa, he stared at her until she felt his energy. When she looked at him, he was wearing a small smile, and made it last more than thirty seconds. She didn't smile back. He would swear he saw her shudder just a little.

For the next couple of weeks they kept their distance from each other. That was fine with him. He had made up his mind to begin a new job search. He wanted to go back to being just a dice dealer. He was more comfortable working behind the tables, and he would make more money. So his search for a job would be based on just two factors, a casino that had good dice play, and the toke average would have to be very good. His choices were narrowed to two, "Peyton Place", which was near to the Shangri-la, and the "Legend", which was located downtown.

A few days later Michael walked the few blocks from his apartment to the Legend. He had only been in there once before, he hadn't really cared for the style, or the overall energy he felt while he was inside. He knew the dealer's made pretty good money, and there were plenty of "high rollers" on the craps tables.

As he walked to the back of the casino, where the dice pit was located, he saw a familiar face. One of the assistant shift managers he had worked with at the Goldmine made eye contact with him. He walked outside of the pit, and shook Michael's hand.

He said, "Michael, good to see you. Where are you working now?"

Michael said, "good to see you too, Ron. I'm at the Shangri La, but I'm going to be leaving there soon."

Ron said, "are you in here looking for a job?"

Michael replied, "I was thinking about it. I live close by, and I wanted to check out the casino."

Ron told him, "I'm the day shift manager, and there would be room for you on the dice crew if you choose to join us."

Michael always considered Ron an intelligent and fair man. By the time he arrived home, he had made up his mind. He would go back and see Ron the next day, and then give his notice at Shangri La.

When he met with Ron the next dy, he asked him if he could start in a couple of weeks. He would only give Jake a week's notice, and would have a week to himself before he started yet another job. Ron simply said, "sure, glad to have you on my team".

When Michael gave his notice, Jake faked surprise. He wasn't very good at it. He was certainly aware of Michael and Vanessa's relationship, but he pretended not to be.

For the next week, Michael only saw Vanessa twice. But he had been observing her. He knew her days off were Monday and Tuesday, and it was Monday when Jake went to her house. It made perfect sense the day had to be the same every week to be consistent with whatever story he had given his wife. Michael's last day was on a Saturday. That meant on Sunday night he had work to do.

Chapter 14

The forecast for the week's weather called for a cold front to come through the area. If anyone lived in Reno for two years or more, they would learn two valuable pieces of information. First, everyone keeps a coat in their car or truck year round. Second, because it is bordered by the Sierra Nevada Mountains on the west, don't blame the weatherman if he forecasts a great day for a picnic, and blowing snow ruins it. Reno is a high desert area. Downtown is over 4200 feet above sea level. Most communities are elevated above the city, reaching heights of nearly 5000 feet. Heaters were coming on in the evenings in everyone's home. It's easy for the air to become chilly after the sun goes down, especially if the wind comes up from the northwest, as it usually does.

　　With a week off, and the weather less than perfect, Michael decided to take a little time to explore the area east of Reno. He left in mid morning on Tuesday following his last Saturday night at Shangri La. Interstate 80 is the east/west highway through Reno. The first city you encounter, going east, is Fernley, Nevada. Fernley grew as Reno grew. It was less than an hour from Reno, depending on the weather, and the houses were much cheaper there. Michael got off I-80 to have lunch. There was a medium sized casino just off the highway called the "Silverado". He parked in the lot and walked inside. He saw very few customers. The coffee shop had less than half of its tables occupied. He decided to sit at the counter. He was a little surprised that the prices were equal to, and in some cases greater than, those in Reno. He ordered a French Dip and French fries, with a coke. When he finished he ordered a piece of apple pie with a scoop of ice cream which the casino claimed to be homemade, and the "best in the west". When he finished, he pretty much agreed with their appraisal.

He went back to his car. The next stop east was Fallon, Nevada. There was a Naval Air Station there. He was curious about Nevada's history of military involvement. He had read that in the city of Hawthorne, which was far southeast of Reno, there existed the largest ammunitions cache in the west. The reason for it being so far inland, was because the military determined during WWII, that an enemy plane could not fly a round trip at that distance. Then, of course, there was the 1950's tests of nuclear weapons at the Nevada Test Site, 65 miles northwest of Las Vegas. Fallon Naval Air Station was now the site of "Top Gun" training.

He was once again on I-80, and following somewhat confusing signs, exited onto highway 50 which went to Fallon. When he arrived, he saw Fallon was a little larger than Fernley, though no more interesting. He stopped at a fast food place to get something to drink. When he got out of his car, he could hear the military jet aircraft which were not very far away. He got directions to the base. It took only ten minutes to arrive at the front gate. When he drove up to the gate, he was told to turn around, absolutely no one but authorized personnel were allowed on base. He was informed that he could not loiter near the base either. He decided to drive back to Reno.

He arrived back in Sparks, just east of Reno, after 5 o'clock. He didn't want to go home just yet. He decided to stop at the Pot of Gold to kill some time and see how good or bad the business had become.

He walked in the front door, which was the old part of the casino, and where the showroom was located. The only person he saw was a change person. He walked past the bar where the dealers waited to get their tokes, and towards the main pit. He saw maybe a dozen people, and four of them were day shift dealers going to the break room.

When he got to the main "21" pit there were only four tables open. A little farther down was the dice game, and the only people there were three of the dealers and a box man. Business was obviously far worse than when he had left. Too bad, at one time it was a nice little job, and a pleasant place to work.

Michael stopped to have a drink at the "dealer's bar" on his way out. The bartender remembered him, but didn't know his name. They engaged in conversation, and he told Michael that the new policies had caused many of the regular players to go elsewhere. Many of the employees had also left in search of more profitable employment. About fifteen minutes later, Michael tipped him and left for home.

He slept in the next morning until after 9:30. He showered and walked down to his favorite coffee shop. He bought a newspaper from the machine outside, and went in to have breakfast.

While he drank his coffee, waiting for his bacon and eggs, he read the paper. On page two was a story he read completely. The swing shift manager at the Shangri La, Vanessa Stryker, had been found dead in her home in Caughlin Ranch. The coroner determined that she was a victim of carbon monoxide poisoning. She was found by a fellow casino worker on Monday evening who became dizzy when entering the house. He pulled his shirt over his nose and mouth, discovered Ms. Stryker unconscious in her bedroom, went back out the front door, and called 911. Name withheld at the person's request. Although the house was less than five years old, the investigators discovered a broken pipe designed to ventilate the toxic gases generated by the home's heating furnace to the exterior of the home. The levels in the home were roughly 500 to 600 parts per million. The normal levels are 0 to 5 parts per million. With the change in the weather, authorities determined the heating system had been turned on to remove the chilly atmosphere in the house. Carbon monoxide is colorless and odorless, virtually undetectable without a carbon monoxide detector. The house did not have one. The detective investigating the case is treating her death as accidental at this time. Michael showed no emotion, and actually had none. He simply felt that the trash had been taken out. Of course he knew that Jake was the "casino worker" who had found her. He wondered what his wife had thought about when she learned that her husband was the person who had entered the residence of a female co-worker and found the body.

When Michael finished his breakfast, he walked south on Virginia Street to the Truckee River. He followed the path alongside to the west. He liked the river, especially the sound of it. It wasn't the Pacific Ocean, but it was somewhat soothing to him. His mind ceased to churn at its usual tumultuous pace, at least for a while.

With several more days left until he started at the Legend, he wasn't sure what he would do. There were several places he had never been in the area. Maybe he would explore some of them. And maybe he would just hibernate in his apartment for a few days.

CHAPTER 15

David Rafferty had less than two years until he could retire with a full pension. He had joined the Reno Police Department right out of college over 33 years ago. He began in traffic patrol, but was promoted very quickly. He became the youngest detective in the department's history. He probably could have gone to Las Vegas, or even Sacramento or San Francisco, and made a lot more money, but he was a "born and bred" Reno boy, and he still loved living in the Reno/Tahoe area. He was a graduate of UNR, The University of Nevada at Reno, a devoted fan of the "Wolf Pack" football and basketball teams, and had never thought about leaving his home.

He arrived at his desk on Tuesday morning about 45 minutes early, as was his custom. He liked to read the newspaper and have a couple of cups of coffee before he began his day. He was reading about one of his own cases, the death of Vanessa Stryker, one of the shift managers at Shangri La. Something in his better than average memory threw up a red flag.

More than five years ago he had worked another case. An assistant shift manager at the Nevada Gold had died in his home. He was called in to investigate the possibility of a homicide, but, at least on the surface, that did not appear to be the case. The deceased had most likely suffered an aneurism or a seizure. A preliminary autopsy was performed, but produced no definitive cause of death. The coroner decided to close the case.

The thing that was troubling him most, was that Ms. Stryker's home was fairly new. It was built under the latest safety codes and requirements. For a gas heater, which was still under warrantee, to have such a severe problem in its early years of operation was extremely unusual. Right now it was just an uneasy feeling in the pit of his stomach, but he had learned in his many years of being in a profession that was often focused on the strange and even bizarre, things happen that are not one hundred percent natural or normal. Often, too often, human hands were involved.

He was also the lead detective when five casino regulars were found within three days. He was certain they were all homicides, committed by the same person. They had a picture of him, but he had never been located.

Rafferty hated little mysteries. The big ones allowed him to sink his teeth into a full blown investigation, and there were always clues or leads to follow. The little ones seldom gave up much information. Hell, most of the time he wasn't sure where to start. This time he knew he had to start with the heater. Who made it? Who sold it? Who installed it? This could take some time.

Chapter 16

A few days before he was to start at the Legend, Michael processed through Human Resources, and suffered through orientation. It took almost four hours. After his paperwork was completed, he was taken on a tour of the hotel and casino. There was lots of floor space, and lots of table games, mostly "21" of course. There were four games in the dice pit, and all four were used on swing shift. Except for holidays and special events, only two were used on day shift. When he was taken to the hotel to see one of the rooms, he was surprised to see how beautiful the lobby was. Crystal chandeliers hung from the ceilings, and there were display cases on beautiful wooden tables displaying antiques from the very early days of Reno, Sparks, Carson City, and Virginia City. The walls were covered in alternating panels of rich wood and a thick fabric of red and gold. However, when he was shown one of the rooms, he was disappointed.

It wasn't much nicer than many he had seen, and not as nice as two of the ones he had stayed in, in Las Vegas.

The orientation portion was merely a reading of the rules and regulations to be followed by all casino employees. It seemed to last forever.

Michael's first day was a Thursday. As it was in most of the casinos, Thursday was the slowest day of the week. Ron had plenty of time to show him around and introduce him to some of the other dealers and pit bosses. Then he was shown the procedures for "21", and taken to the dice pit to see how it was set up.

Even though this was day shift, Michael noticed that the dice game was a five dollar minimum. Many of the casinos had decided on a three dollar table on day shift. The "21" tables started at five dollars, but there were two twenty five dollar games, and even a single one hundred dollar game open. This was a good sign that business was good. And that meant that tokes were good.

In the afternoon, he was put on the dice game. There were never more than four or five players at one time, but it felt good to "get his hands back in the game". On his last break, which was at 5:20, Ron gave him his schedule. He would have to deal "21" two days a week. He would be on the dice game on Saturday, Sunday, and Monday, and have Tuesdays and Wednesdays off.

Michael had only been there a few months when a change came. A former games manager, and friend of the general manager, decided to return to the Legend. The present games manager, Bruce, was going to return to his former job, day shift manager, and Ron would be going to swing. He wasn't sure he liked it, but he couldn't do anything about it.

Three months later, the job was okay, and he was making pretty good money. He knew swing made a lot more, but he was now on the dice game five days a week, after having been there only a few months, and he was sure he wouldn't be in the same situation on swing. Besides, being the "newbie" on the shift, he would be working the later shifts. He didn't mind that too much, but he was happy with his evenings off, at least for now.

He began to gamble almost every evening. He wasn't addicted to it, didn't gamble that much money, but, other than being in his apartment, gambling was the only way for him to be in his own little world. He mostly played the poker machines. They at least gave him the impression he was making decisions as to the outcome of each game. He spent most of his time at It's a Circus. It was close to his apartment, and the cocktail waitresses got to know him well, making sure his scotch glass was never empty. He was a good tipper, and if he won a large sum of money, he was even better. He never stayed long if he was losing, and he never stayed long enough to get too drunk. He would go home, watch a video, and fall asleep.

The day came when the changes were made. The former, and now present games manager, Carl, had taken charge, and he decided to make himself important immediately. Bruce had come to day shift, and would be Carl's puppet. When Michael found out Carl's relationship to the general manager was more than just a friend, he knew that Carl would have complete freedom to make any decision he wanted, good or bad. Carl was considered a Columbo family member.

Generally, in most casinos, day shift has more senior dealers. Swing shift is very hard work, and graveyard is an unhealthy choice for most. Sleep deprivation was the biggest problem. Dealers with more experience are apt to be more friendly with the customers, but they are also slower, especially the "21" dealers. Many long time and frequent customers enjoy the rapport they have with the dealer. But Carl decided the games needed to speed up. His theory, which was shared by many others in his position, was that more hands per hour equaled more money for the casino. He harassed the slowest of the dealers to the point of causing many of them to cry. Then he decided to open as many table games as possible, even if it was a slow day. A dice crew normally has three positions. One was on the outside andwas called the "stick man", and two inside, called "base dealers", to move the chips, and pay or take bets. Carl decided to eliminate the stick position, and use it to deal "21". This meant all four dealers would rotate through the card game and then back to the dice table. The result is a much slower dice game, and much less protection from possible cheating by taking away a pair of eyes. Then he decided to make the game a three dollar game instead of five.

Once again, Michael was becoming unhappy. He began to think about transferring to swing shift.

Within two weeks the tokes started to go down. The average dropped around ten dollars a day. Two weeks later, they had dropped twenty dollars a day. He put in a transfer request. He should have put it in sooner, it would probably take a month or two for the change to be made. It was the beginning of May, and business would not increase dramatically until a couple of weeks after Memorial Day and there would be a need for more swing dealers.

When Michael came to work the Monday after Mother's Day, he overheard a conversation in the employee's cafeteria. Carl had taken his mother to dinner the day before. They went to a casino adjacent to the Legend named Diablo, owned by the general manager's family, the Columbo's. Carl was driving. They went into the parking garage, and were looking for a space when an older pick-up truck came from the other direction and pulled into the space Carl was headed for. Carl got out of his car and confronted the man who was driving. A loud argument ensued. No one was sure exactly what happened after that, but there were rumors of a fight, and that the man in the pick-up was badly injured, and not expected to live.

That evening, Carl was asked to come in for questioning at the police station. The other combatant had lost his fight for life. He claimed self defense. An investigation would take place. Carl was released on his own recognizance, as well as a guarantee from the Columbo family that he would be available whenever the police needed him to be. He was then placed on a paid leave of absence.

Michael had witnessed Carl's quick temper. He had no doubt that he could become violent. As he thought about it, he realized what a foolish man Carl was. Everyone has to be in control of themselves, or else they could pay a very high price. Performing even a single rash action, could jeopardize one's freedom.

During his shift that day, Michael noticed a more relaxed environment. Other than some discussions on their breaks about "the incident", the dealers quietly went about their jobs. Knowing Carl wouldn't be back for even a few days, (or longer, they hoped), made all their jobs much less stressful.

Bruce had temporarily been given two hats. He would be the day shift supervisor, but also perform the duties of games manager. His presence on the casino floor would be less than before, so the dice crews were back to normal, and only the number of "21" games that were actually necessary would be open. Michael hoped that Carl wouldn't be back until he was on swing shift.

CHAPTER 17

Her favorite part of preparing for classes was the research. Most professors took no pleasure in the tedious task of going through old material to find one fact, or one story worthy of the effort. But Hillary Fisk considered it a treasure hunt. At the age of 29, she had been a journalism professor at UNR for nearly five years now, and the passion for her job had grown. Her job was everything. She didn't have a steady boyfriend. She wasn't considered a beautiful woman, pretty would best describe her. She had a very "girlish" figure on a 120 pound frame. She was 5 feet 8 inches tall, with curly auburn hair that hung just past her shoulders. Her lack of a "love life" was her decision. She was just too busy doing what she cared about the most, and relationships have to be a work in progress, lots of time and lots of energy are required if they are to succeed.

When she was researching material that was related to Nevada, or Reno itself, she felt somewhat like a detective. She had been a resident of the state of Oregon until she took the position at UNR, and she loved learning everything she could about her still fairly new home state.

It was easy lecturing her classes using examples of some of the well known writers of the more famous newspapers such as the Wall Street Journal, the New York Times, the Washington Post, the Chicago Tribune, and many others, but she had decided to lecture and critique some of the writers and the stories published by Reno's only newspaper. She would begin ten years back. Even in a little city like Reno, a lot can happen in ten years. There were years of great snow fall, floods, brush fires, new growth, and even the more tawdry such as murders, kidnappings, and thefts of all types. It was going to take some time, but that was alright with her. She didn't have a big social life to worry about. Her main interest was in education.

She found files from the paper in the computer, but she also found them in the library at the university. Although she was interested in ten years, she found they were mixed up a little. She was actually reading files from about thirteen years back. She found stories about a major flood that had happened, and had cut a swath through I-80. She found stories of gubernatorial elections, corruption in the political arena. She learned of changes in ownership and management of casinos. But what caught her interest was a story about a murder of a casino shift manager that had never been solved.

She had worked at the Reno Queen. She was found deceased in a parking lot from a severe head injury. The police had assumed her assailant was a mugger. Considering all the elapsed time, she guessed the case was closed. She went on with her research.

About two hours later, she came across a story about the death of a casino assistant shift manager. This case was closed because it appeared to be from a natural cause. He had worked at the Nevada Gold. She had earlier read about another casino employee death. She left the research area and went to the main part of the library where they kept current copies of the local paper. There it was, "Shangri La Shift Manager Found Dead". She wondered how many casino workers died somewhat unusual deaths? She decided to make it part of a class subject. Each of the three stories she found so far, had been written by a different reporter. This was not unusual for a small market newspaper. Writers who showed real promise often left after a brief time and went to larger market areas for more money and more recognition. She noticed one commonality, the detective in all three cases was a man named David Rafferty. She might have to contact him for details missed in the paper.

Chapter 18

In mid June, Michael was accepted on swing shift. He was put on the 8 o'clock dice crew with Tuesdays and Wednesdays off. It was good to be back working with Ron, and because it was a late shift, he doubted he would see Carl much, if he ever came back to work. The swing dice manager was a small man by the name of Mitch. He seemed alright, although a little lazy. The only person he was immediately suspicious of was the assistant shift manager. His name was Dale. Michael had seen the type before. He was ambitious, overly friendly, which meant he was being deceptive, and it was obvious he would crawl over anyone's back to receive a promotion. He reminded Michael of his old "friend" Rollie, God rest his useless soul.

Swing shift was much busier, to Michael's liking. There were some good dice games on the weekends, and he was quickly regaining his skills. He was a little disappointed in the other dealers. A casino that had good dice action was supposed to have very good dealers who could take care of the customers and quickly analyze the way they played, especially on swing shift. He thought the dealers at the Goldmine, and the Pot of Gold, and even the day shift dealers he had worked with at the Legend, were far better overall. He was soon to discover why.

It didn't take him long to learn that Mitch tried to literally kill the dice games, and favored dealers who preferred not to work. He didn't want players, he didn't want to have to work at all. Michael was a real dealer. Michael's only goal was to make tokes. Without a game, that was obviously not possible. He encouraged players to come to his game, and that made him the enemy to Mitch. The most disappointing part of all this is that Mitch could make Michael's life miserable. Swing shift was like a pit of snakes, you could be bitten from anywhere, anytime.

The great equalizer was that the money was very good. It was rare when they didn't receive over a hundred dollars a night in tokes. The bad news was that he found the majority of the pit bosses and dealers despicable. And he discovered upper management had a reputation for cruelty and depravity he hadn't been aware of on day shift.

Michael just tried to do his job. To punish him for wanting to work, Mitch had him scheduled to deal "21" games whenever it was not absolutely necessary to have him in the dice pit. Michael decided he didn't care. The tokes were the same no matter what a dealer did to get them. Besides, "21" is so much less work than the dice game. He knew that if a dealer who only dealt cards was forced to learn and deal craps, he or she would collapse from exhaustion after one hour on the table. It was long known in the industry that the only "real" dealers were dice dealers.

Dealing in the "21" pit, away from dice, Michael discovered the Legend was full of evil people. It was as if the devil had risen up and created a place where he could wreak havoc on the earth. He saw more and more of Dale, and watched as he revealed his true person. There was a female pit boss with red hair by the name of Peg. She seemed to love to be a part of the group that thrived on the dark side. Every casino job Michael went to was worse than the last. But this one had all the horrible parts in one place. There was need for retribution, and not just for himself, for everyone who worked there who was part of the honest, and hard working staff. He just might have to be their avenging angel.

Chapter 19

David Rafferty decided to begin with the installer of the heating system at the home of Vanessa Stryker. He found him at his place of work, "Reliable Heating and Air Conditioning". His name was Sam Overton. He had worked for the company for thirteen years. Rafferty talked to the owners of the company before he talked to Overton, and was told that he was reliable, knowledgeable, and was considered to be one of their finest employees.

Rafferty and Overton met in a small office that was often used as a management conference room. Overton was about thirty five years old, approximately six feet tall and one hundred and eighty five pounds. He had sandy blonde hair that needed a trim, with no facial hair, tattoos, or piercings. Management told Rafferty that Overton had been married for ten years and had two children, a girl eight years old, and a boy just about to turn five. He appeared pleasant, confident, and committed to his job.

Rafferty began by asking him about the brand and quality of the heater he installed in the Stryker residence. Overton assured him it was one of the top three brands used in new homes, and was quite reliable with a ten year warrantee on parts and labor. The home was in a high end neighborhood, and the general contractor was well known for attention to detail and quality. Rafferty said, "is there any reason you can think of why the ventilation segment of the heater would fail?" Overton replied, "no, none at all. These systems today are about as safe as an Easy Bake Oven." He was sure that there was no logical way carbon monoxide could have leaked into that house. Rafferty believed him, completely. He asked Overton, "if your boss gives permission, would you be willing to check the heater and see if it was tampered with?" Overton said, "sure, I'll see what I can do".

A detective's primary objectives investigating a homicide are discovering motive and opportunity. He was now sure that this was no accident. Now he had to discover who wanted her dead, and why. Sometimes it's easy to find a starting point, but not this time. He would have to find out who her friends and enemies were at the Shangri La, and before. He would have to seek out past personal relationships, family members, and anyone who might have been considered an enemy. A lot of work to do.

Chapter 20

Hillary Fisk was having a great deal of fun preparing for this class. The research was tedious, but rewarding, and she was discovering many things about "casino life". But she needed help. She knew one of her students had a father who was a casino manager. She might have to impose on him and ask if she could have a conversation with his father.

She had only been to two casinos since she moved to Reno, and neither of them was in the downtown area. She lived in south Reno, and both of the casinos she had visited were there as well. One was the Shangri La, where she went once in a while on Friday nights for their seafood buffet. Every few months there was a coupon in the newspaper making the buffet half price. The lines were long, but it was worth it. The other casino was Peyton Place. She had met three other professors for a drink after work in an intimate and quiet lounge. This was the extent of her casino experience.

Her research was not solely about unusual deaths related to casino employees and patrons. Many of the stories written by the reporters were often shoddy, and too often she could find no follow up story. She was fascinated by the number of attempted thefts by both "inside and outside" individuals. The volume of employee fraud far surpassed those by "unknown" persons. She uncovered cases regarding employees who worked in the vault or in the "cage" trying to steal cash. She supposed being around that much money on a daily basis made some at least think of the possibility of taking a little home. She discovered cases involving dealers who had stolen chips, and sometimes even cash, from the very tables they were working on.

She read one particular case that surprised her, and found disturbing.

Management in a downtown casino had become suspicious of a female dealer. She was a good employee, a talented dealer, and had been a games supervisor at her previous employment. She was a single mother of one boy, aged nine years. Over about a three month period, a pattern was detected when she had been dealing on the roulette wheels. Pit bosses keep track of cash transactions of one hundred dollars or more which are deposited into the drop box. Her game's boxes always ended up with a lot less that the pit boss had estimated. These boxes are emptied and counted at the end of every shift. The casino manager had no choice but to call the state Gaming Commission. They sent out two enforcement agents. The roulette wheels at this casino were separate from the rest of the table games, against a wall. One agent was positioned in such a way that he could observe her game. The other was in the surveillance room, his eyes glued to the monitor which was being fed the view from a camera placed over the table. They watched her for less than thirty minutes.

She arrived from her break in a hurry, she was about two minutes late. She threw her purse under the table and relieved the dealer who was upset with her tardiness. Within ten minutes, a player came to her table and laid down a one hundred dollar bill. She followed procedure and called out to the supervisor, "changing one hundred". When the supervisor acknowledged, she gave the customer one hundred dollars in chips. The next thing she would do was to put the money in the slot of the drop box. She didn't. What she did was fake it. Instead, she rolled the bill into a little ball and palmed it. The agent in the camera room clearly saw what she had done. He left the surveillance room, joined the other agent on the floor. They informed the pit boss of their next action. With the pit boss, and a relief dealer behind them, they arrested her and placed her in handcuffs. When they searched her purse, they found nothing. But reviewing the films of the day, they saw that she had palmed chips off the game as she was leaving for her break, and dropped them in her purse. Doing a little leg work, the agents discovered she had been cashing in chips at three other casinos every day she worked.

Calculating what she could have stolen over a period of time, it was estimated that she had pilfered 30 to 40 thousand dollars.

Hillary found it almost unbelievable that anyone would attempt to do what she had just read. She thought about the woman's little boy, and wondered if he had family to take care of him while his mother was in jail. She knew that every dealer had to have a sheriff's work card to receive casino employment. This woman would never be able to get one again in the state of Nevada, and probably nowhere else in the United States. By stealing from a casino, she had given away her career.

The next class day, she made up her mind it was time to add to her knowledge of casinos. As class was ending, she asked the young man, Allen, if he would talk to his father and tell him she was seeking some information. He said he would let her know at the next class. This was a Tuesday, the next class was on Thursday.

As Thursday's class was about to begin, Allen walked up to her with a note. Opening it, she read, "Dear Ms. Fisk, it would be my pleasure to meet with you. If you do not have classes tomorrow, Friday, we could meet after lunch, around 1:30 p.m. in my office". It was signed "Lawrence Hall, Casino Manager, Stagecoach Hotel/Casino". He had written his personal phone number at the bottom. She called him as soon as class was over.

She arrived at the Stagecoach at 1:15 on Friday afternoon. He had told her to come up to the third floor where his office was located. She had fifteen minutes to spare, and since this was only the third casino she had visited, she took a quick look around. Unlike the casinos in south Reno, this property looked quite old. She could almost hear the walls reciting the history of this casino and of Reno itself. The ventilation system was not as efficient as the newer buildings, and therefore the smell of cigarette smoke and stale beer filled the air. She didn't find it annoying, to the contrary it captured her sense of historical curiosity. She fantasized about what this place might have looked and sounded like in the 1950's.

Arriving at Mr. Hall's office, she walked in and introduced herself to his secretary. He was waiting for her as she was led inside. He was a man, about six feet tall, and weighed between 190 and 200 pounds. He had wavy brown hair that was graying at the temples. He wore a dark beige suit, white shirt, with a red patterned tie. He greeted her with a firm handshake and a warm smile. She was seated on a leather couch, and he faced her on an opposing leather chair. She thanked him for giving her his valuable time, and explained what she was working on for her journalism class. He seemed quite interested in her project.

Hillary said, "Mr. Hall", to which he interrupted and said, "Please call me Larry, I don't think we need to be formal".

She said, "Okay, Larry, I have some questions, but I realized, preparing for our meeting this morning, I don't believe I know enough about your industry to ask the *right* ones". She continued, "maybe we could begin by you telling me some of the history of downtown Reno and its casinos from the memory and perspective of someone who has made it his career. And as you are speaking, if you don't mind, I will interrupt with questions to help me be quite clear as to your descriptions. I am very *casino ignorant.*"

Larry said, "that will be fine. I started in the industry as a change person in the early 70's, or, as I like to remember it, *the best of times.* But first, let me give you a brief tour of the casino, so you'll understand better some of my references". Hillary loved the idea.

They left his office and took the elevator four floors down to the basement level. This area was most definitely not glamorous. He showed her storage areas, wardrobe areas, men's and women's locker rooms, the door to the vault, offices for the food and beverage director, slot director, and security. The last place was the employee cafeteria and break room.

They then walked up a single flight of stairs, as did the employees returning from their breaks, to the main casino floor. As they arrived at the top, Hillary concluded that this is just what she needed. Larry was wise. He knew that before she could understand anything else about the workings of a casino, she had to feel, to experience with her own eyes and ears what thousands of casino employees must do every day.

Larry walked her to the middle of the casino floor. It was a large aisle with rows of slot machines to their left, and the table games pit to their right. There appeared to be 20 to 25 card games. She saw two roulette wheels, and three dice games. In the far left corner, partitioned off, was a sign that said "POKER". There were less than two dozen players on all of the games. Larry explained that Friday afternoon would usually not be very busy until about five or six in the evening when the locals got off work, and the tourists began to arrive from California, Oregon, Washington, and even western Canada. He let her just stand there for a few minutes to soak in the feeling. Next he walked with her towards the front doors on Virginia Street. There was an area under a gazebo about twenty feet inside the front doors. There was a stage and a bar with seating for about thirty people. It was too early for the band to be playing, but the bar already had about ten patrons. Across from the bar area, on the opposite wall, was the Keno area. She had no idea what Keno was. Larry explained that it was an old game with its basis coming from China. There are eighty numbered ping pong balls, twenty picked at random each game. The payoffs are based on the amount wagered, and the winning numbers drawn. Maximum win was 50 thousand dollars. The game also had maximum risk, which meant terrible odds. From there they went towards the back of the casino, past the pit. Back here was another bar tucked away in a corner. It had access to the parking lot outside. Hillary asked Larry, "while I've been researching, I read a story about a shift manager who had apparently been sitting at this bar before she left to get into her car. Then she was killed by a mugger". Larry said, "yes, unfortunately, that's true. Reno is not a high crime city, but we have our share of unfortunate incidents".

Next, he took her up a long escalator to the second floor. Here was the casino's coffee shop, open 24 hours a day. There was also another pit and another bar, as well as many more slot machines. Larry explained that this bar and pit only opened later in the evening, and the pit was non-smoking.

The last place he took her was to the seventh floor. There was only one thing to see here, the steakhouse. This was one of Reno's oldest fine dining restaurants. It was called the "Bunkhouse", and was very popular with locals and tourists who knew its existence. It had room for only 50 patrons at one sitting.

Back in his office, Larry asked if she would like some coffee or water. Hillary said water would be nice, so Larry took two bottles out of a mini-frig and opened them, handing one to Hillary.

He then said, "now, how about those questions".

Hillary told him, "the tour was a great idea. I understand much more than I did before. I can see the attraction people experience in the casino environment. So, the questions I have for you now are in more of a personnel nature. Is that alright with you"?

Larry said, "probably, let's see where this leads."

She began, "generally what is the relationship between employees. By that I mean, do the different departments get along well, and does supervision and their dealers, slot personnel, food service and bartenders and cocktail waitresses have a good working relationship"?

Larry responded, "there are no simple or 'black and white' answers to your questions. To answer the first part of your question, almost everyone from all departments have a congenial relationship with each other. Of course there will always be some personality conflicts. The exception might be the poker room. The dealers and players are a 'different breed'. They see gambling differently. They tend to be quieter, more separate from the rest of the property. And as far as the day to day relationship between management and supervision, it depends on the department, and even the shift. Overall, pit bosses and dealers have an understanding. There are often menial clashes, but they both understand each other's responsibilities, and respect each other's duties. Dealers know that supervisors make much less money than they do, because tips are the essential part of a dealer's income, and in most casinos, tips added to even minimum wage exceed that of the supervisors. They also know that it was their choice to, as we call it, 'put on a suit'. Pit personnel on graveyard are usually closer to each other, more of a feeling of family. Day shift is pretty good overall, but, oddly enough, being single or married makes a small separation. Swing shift is full of egos, but they seldom get in the way of their work, they're just too busy. Slot personnel are the least problematic. It's a huge department, with a lot of turnover. They don't make a great deal of money, even though the casino makes more money from that department than any other, by far. Food service is not dissimilar to anyone working in a restaurant outside of the casinos. It is what it is. Good food and good service makes for good tips. That's it in a nutshell. Bartenders and cocktail waitresses and their supervisors are a whole different matter. Supervisors generally make very little money in relation to the difficult job they have. It is not unusual for them to be ostracized by those who they oversee. Bartenders are 98% egotists, and they expect big tips from customers and the cocktail waitresses they serve. The waitresses are a mixed breed, depending on age, and, quite honestly, their experience and appearance. Some work hard, and respect the job they have, and the bartenders who 'take care of them'. Some do little but, as we call it, 'run for the money'. In other words, all they care about is the money they make in tips. They will take extra good care of someone who is a good tipper, and less with those who aren't, or don't tip at all. These types often do not tip their bartenders well either."

Hillary could only say, "wow. You obviously have a difficult job on so many levels".

Larry replied, "that's why I'm a drinker".

Hillary chuckled, and said, "I don't believe I can think of another question at this moment. May I call you if something comes up which I might believe crucial to my curriculum?"

Larry: "Anytime."

They exchanged pleasantries, and Hillary left with her head buzzing with information overload. She did know what her next step would be.

Chapter 21

Michael was not a happy man. He found he had deep and dark feelings for many at the Legend, and for way too many on swing shift. He had been there for over a year and a half, and now understood why many in other casinos nicknamed it the "Leprosy". It was a disease you couldn't kill, but it was killing downtown Reno with its skyways linking three casinos together, and eliminating foot traffic on Virginia Street. Many considered its construction the beginning of the end of downtown Reno.

His feelings for Mitch developed into full blown hatred. Swing shift had over 20 dice dealers, and most of them were treated very badly. Michael's situation worsened when Carl got involved. Although Michael and Carl seldom spoke on day shift, Carl apparently had great respect for Michael's dealing abilities. Carl told Mitch that he didn't want Michael dealing cards, he was to be a dice dealer, and a dice dealer only. Mitch couldn't show it, but he was seething inside. What he did do, was to put him on the worst schedule possible, and with the worst dealers.

He wasn't sure if he could make another change. The money was still very good, and he was running out of places he might be welcome. Anyone who still did not believe the "toilet" adage, should work at this outhouse for a while. He just might have to clean some of it up.

While Mitch was being Mitch, Dale was doing all he could to advance his career. He had become a "mini-Carl". He was treating the dealers with disrespect and animosity. Any time he witnessed a dealer that did not adhere 100% to the rules, he would report them to Carl. He went right over Ron's head, who would certainly have talked to that dealer before taking any sort of disciplinary action. And worse for Michael, Dale and Mitch were close friends. That meant Michael had to watch his back every moment.

Chapter 22

Hillary decided it was time to call detective Rafferty.

She placed the call to the Reno Police Department after her Tuesday class. He wasn't in, so she was transferred to his voicemail. He didn't get back to her that day, but on Wednesday morning while she was in her office, the phone rang about 9:30 in the morning. The voice on the other side of the line said, "good morning, is this Ms. Fisk"? Hillary replied, "yes it is. How may I help you"? "This is detective David Rafferty with the RPD, and I was returning your call. I'm sorry I couldn't get back with you yesterday, I was out of the office and didn't return."

"That's quite all right. Do you have a few minutes so that I might explain why I called you?"

"I have all the time in the world."

"Detective Rafferty, I teach a journalism class here at the University, and I have been researching articles written for the local paper involving crimes related to the casinos. I discovered you were the lead detective on several of those cases, and hoped you might be able to give me your personal perspective."

"I'm unsure if I would be of any assistance, but I would be more than happy to meet with you."

"When would be a convenient day and time?"

"Almost any weekday is good, and my time is somewhat flexible at this point."

"I have a class to teach tomorrow, so maybe Friday? I could buy you lunch for your trouble."

"Sounds great. How about 12:30?"

"Do you have a favorite place?"

"How about the 'Gold and Silver' out on West Fourth Street. It's an older local's place, nothing fancy, but the food is good, and there's plenty of it."

"Fine, and it's close to the University and the police station. I'll see you there. By the way, how will I know you?"

"I'm about six feet tall, grey hair, and I'll be wearing a ten year old grey suit and blue tie."

"Sounds perfect. I'll see you then."

Hillary was pretty excited. She had progressed from her normal research pattern of going to the library, or using the computer, and was, in her own way, doing some detective work.

Chapter 23

When Michael went to work on a Monday evening in April of 2001, something was different. Carl had been back in the casino for about three months, but had been less of a problem. The "incident" had obviously forced him to control his temper. But that was not the change Michael was feeling. The pit was very quiet, and it wasn't until his first break that he understood why. Dale had not come to work. He had literally disappeared. No one had seen him for three days. Nobody seemed to want to talk about it much. He was certainly not well liked, or worse, by many of the dealers. But it was strange. Those who knew him well, were quite confused. He wasn't a heavy drinker, didn't gamble, and had a steady girlfriend, though they lived separately. Therefore, there was no speculation as to why he wasn't where he was supposed to be.

Michael was not concerned in the slightest manner. He felt that one less bad Apple on a disease filled tree was a good thing.

For days there was no word about him. Then a full week after he disappeared, there was some news. He had apparently been seen in Elko, Nevada, a city northeast of Reno, about 290 miles away. He had been seen going into a store that sold hunting and fishing equipment. Less than 24 hours later, this was proven to be an erroneous report.

Then, two days later, nine days after he failed to show up for work at the Legend, a body was found. A hiker, who was out for a morning's walk with his two dogs, found the body of a male human being, buried in a shallow grave, in Hazen. Hazen is a desolate area east of Reno, and about 15 miles east of Fernley. Dental records would be subpoenaed and a DNA test would be performed. The remains had apparently been there over a week, and desert animals had rendered the corpse unidentifiable without forensic testing.

Michael thought this was all interesting, vermin devouring vermin. If it was Dale, he surely wouldn't lose any sleep over the loss of a man who had just enough power to make the lives of many people more difficult than they should have been.

Mitch seemed distraught. Maybe it was because he lost a friend. He kept more to himself than usual. He seemed to be nervous about something. He showed even less concern for his job, and the dice pit in general. Michael wondered if Dale and Mitch had talked about him.

As usual, Michael simply went about his job. Although the dealers he worked with were of a lesser quality, he took care of the customers on his side of the table, and attempted to make as many tokes as possible. All the while, Michael was thinking to himself, "one down, and at least three to go".

Just over a week later, the local paper reported the autopsy on the body found in Hazen had resulted in a positive identity. The remains belonged to an assistant shift manager at the Legend casino by the name of Dale Fitzter. His family had been notified. The cause of death was a broken larynx, resulting in damage to the airway. Asphyxiation was the cause of death.

Michael had sunk into a deep depression, a depression mixed with an ever growing fury. When he was not working, he was a recluse. He stayed in his apartment, drinking and watching his videos. He didn't gamble anymore. The only time he left, other than for work, was to get something to eat. And, even that became more and more junk food he purchased from a fast food joint or a convenience store. He preferred to spend as little time as possible outside his sanctuary.

He had no sleep pattern. When he got off work at four in the morning, he frequently stayed awake for five or six hours. Then he might sleep for a couple, awake again for a couple more. He lost track of time, and had to set an alarm to make sure he would get to work on time. Even his grooming habits were affected. He didn't shower every day, and he only washed his hair when he had to. He was in a darker place.

Chapter 24

When Hillary Fisk walked into the Gold and Silver at 12:25 on Friday afternoon, she immediately spotted detective Rafferty. He was sitting at a table about fifteen feet from the door. She walked towards him, he stood and said, "Ms. Fisk?" She responded, "detective Rafferty?" He said, "please call me David". She, "it's Hillary". They shook hands and sat. Hillary suggested they order first, so their conversation wouldn't be interrupted. David agreed. The waitress came, and she ordered a chef's salad and iced tea, he chose a hamburger, French fries, and coffee.

When the waitress left, Hillary spoke first; "I like this place. It has a 50's diner feel to it. It must be a local's favorite, just far enough away from the casinos that most tourists wouldn't discover it".

David told her, "It's been around since the early 50's, and I don't think it has ever been remodeled".

Hillary said, "before we get to my class research, tell me about yourself".

He told her that he had been in Reno all his life, and he was getting close to retirement. He told her he was married with one grown daughter who had given him two grandchildren, a boy four years old, and a girl just one and a half.

David said, "your turn". Hillary told him about growing up in Oregon, and after getting her Master's degree, she applied to UNR. She was single, an only child, and had fallen in love with northern Nevada after only living in the area five years.

Hillary began telling him the reason for her inquiry by restating what she had told him over the phone: "I came up with this idea for my journalism class to focus on reporters and their articles written in our own newspaper. When I began my research, I became interested in quite a few stories written about the darker side of the casinos. I read about deaths, some which appeared to be from other than natural causes. I read about larceny committed by both persons who worked in the casinos, and those who did not. Some of the articles were well written, some were not, at least in my estimation, and very few had follow up articles giving the reader an end to the story. The common denominator in nearly fifty percent of the more serious cases, was that you were the lead detective. I hoped you might be able to give me some information, some closure to these cases. I want to use these as examples for my class of how a story should contain not only the who, what, where, when, why, and how, but also offer a complete story, not just part of one."

David told her, "I'll be happy to give you any information I can, as long as it doesn't violate any legal restrictions. My memory is pretty good, especially about cases that left me with questions, whether they were closed or are still open".

Hillary checked her notes: "Let's begin chronologically. How about the murder of a shift manager from the Reno Queen, a woman named Lydia Williams. Was it ever solved?"

"No, I'm afraid it never was. The case is still open, technically. If it was a vagrant, or a street person, we may never be able to find a suspect."

"Were you satisfied that it was a mugging, or robbery?"

"Yes and no. On the surface it appeared to be a sad but simple case. But two things still bother me. We never found a murder weapon, and, after interviewing the bartender who served her wine for a couple of hours, he said Ms. Williams told him she lost all the money she had, playing the poker machine. I know that doesn't mean that her attacker knew that, but it didn't appear that the contents of her purse had been disturbed. And one last thing. The damage to her head was so severe, the coroner thought it appeared to him that the person who struck her did it with great anger, as it would be in a crime of passion. Without any evidence, I was told to let it go as a mugging."

"What is your gut feeling?"

"Even with all the time that has passed, I'm still more of the opinion that she was murdered with intent. But, without anything to prove it, the case had to be closed."

"Because it was another casino manager, at least an assistant manager, this next one caught my eye. He worked at the Nevada Gold, his name was Rolland Thomas. The story said he appeared to have died from natural causes, but, as is often the case, there was never a follow-up story about a completion of the investigation."

"I remember this one extremely well. We discovered him in his apartment on his kitchen floor. The discovery was not pleasant, and I don't want to be too graphic."

"I'm asking the questions, I'll just have to deal with the answers."

"Well, he had vomited up everything in his stomach, as well as a lot of blood. He struck his head on the counter, causing a large contusion, but that was not the cause of death. The coroner did an autopsy, but it was only perfunctory. His results stated that he believed Mr. Thomas had a seizure which resulted in uncontrollable vomiting, diarrhea, and subsequent brain damage. All together, they were the basis for his demise."

"My instinct tells me you are not happy with his conclusion."

"No, I'm not."

"Can you tell me why?"

"Certainly. There's nothing secretive about this case. As far as the district attorney's office is concerned, it's closed. But even though ours is not a big city, our coroner is very busy. I felt then, and I feel now, that he didn't have the time or funds to perform an autopsy that was as expansive as it might have been. In his defense, he is on a fairly small budget, and some tests are very expensive. And unless there was reason to assume foul play, he simply made a judgment call."

"But you felt something was not quite right?"

"My gut said that there was more than the obvious. His medical records were excellent. He was close to obsessive about his regular check ups, and he was a health food nut. The only glitch in those records was not of his doing, and not because he had any acute or chronic diseases or maladies, he was in a car accident that left him with a limp."

"So, once again, you think someone else might have been involved?"

"Well, in my own mind I still can't rule it out. But I have no way to re-open the case and investigate it further."

Their food came, and they took a break from talk of death to eat and drink. The subject changed to simple small talk. David talked to her about how much he loved the Reno/Tahoe area, and asked her if she'd had much of a chance to explore it. She told him she hadn't. When she moved to Reno, she had to begin immediately preparing for her classes. She also taught in the summer, so she did not have a great deal of free time. She had, of course, been to see Lake Tahoe, as well as Truckee and Virginia City. She only had one day each time, so she didn't get to see as much as she would have liked.

David told her about some of the history of the area, and how much there was to experience. He explained how Truckee was originally built around a sawmill. It grew quickly, and before gambling was legal, if you wanted to take part in a card game, Truckee was the place to go. It was also the place to go where prostitutes were available. Some of the extremely small rooms they used are still standing at one end of the original town. The beginnings of the Truckee township are just west of the lumber yard, and underneath what are now boutiques and restaurants, tunnels exist so when a raid of the illegal gambling halls took place, the participants could escape unseen. The 'Capitol Building' still stands. It had formerly been the 'Capitol Saloon', with a huge wooden bar that was shipped by boat, unassembled, from Europe, around the Horn of Africa. On its top floor there is still a stage in the back where Mark Twain used to perform. Virginia City still has a couple of active silver mines, although little ore is taken from them, and they have underground tours daily. And every part of the seventy two mile shore of Lake Tahoe offers something different It would probably take a year to experience all of it. Then there are places like Rainbow, which is at the summit of I-80. The Rainbow Lodge is just south of the highway. It was originally a hunting lodge, but now was a rustic hotel, with a small, but excellent dining room. There is only one television in the entire place, and it is in the bar. When it was a hunting lodge, men were its sole patrons, and at the foot of the bar is still a trough where they would urinate. It leads out to the back of the lodge towards the woodpile. There, it would melt the snow, and make it easier to get to the wood and stoke the fireplace in the wintertime. The state government buildings in Carson City are worth visiting. Most have been remodeled, but some still have the grandeur of the old west on their walls and ceilings. He told her she would discover many more places to visit both in northern Nevada, and just across the border in California.

Hillary told him about her experience at the Stagecoach, and how she had felt being in the old casino. David could tell that she had become a Nevadan.

Their dishes were cleared and they got back to the reason for their meeting.

Hillary said: "I decided not to ask you about the robberies and cases of embezzlement I found, at least not today. So there are just three more investigations I would like to discuss, if you have the time."

David replied: "I cleared most of my afternoon so I wouldn't have to rush away, unless there was one of those pesky homicides."

Hillary smiled, and continued: "The next one I discovered was a story about five casino patrons who were found within a three day period, all deceased, and apparently all died from the same cause. The last story I read was about searching for a man in the casinos who might be a person of interest. There was no follow up article."

"These we know were homicides. What you read was about a picture that was taken from a surveillance camera of a man we have never found, and believe to be the suspect. The toxicology report showed the presence of Aluminum Phosphide in each victim's blood. It's a fumigant that if ingested by human beings can cause illness or even death. I believe it was placed in whatever each of the five was drinking. It would probably have a slight bitter taste, but if it was placed in alcohol, and if the victim was slightly intoxicated, he probably wouldn't have noticed."

"So you obviously showed the picture to people who worked and gambled in the casinos."

"Yes, of course."

"No one found him a familiar face?"

"No, in fact, I came to the conclusion that he must have been wearing some sort of disguise. If that's the case, I can't think of any way he could ever be identified."

"I can see how your job could be very frustrating at times."

"At times, it is."

"The recent case is about the shift supervisor at the Shangri La. It was reported that she died from carbon monoxide poisoning caused by a defective heater."

"This one is ongoing. I can't tell you a lot about it, with the exception that it's suspicious. I have someone checking out the heating system for me."

"You think it might have been tampered with?"

"I can't really say yes or no. But you probably have an insight about my thought process by now, and can decide for yourself where my investigation is going."

"Last one, and very recently in the paper. Another assistant shift manager by the name of Dale Fitzter was found with a broken larynx in Hazen. Nothing else was reported with the exception that foul play was suspected."

"Of course I know about this case, but I am not the lead inspector, still being involved with the Stryker investigation. I will most likely have some involvement in it at a later date."

"I really appreciate your input. I want my class to have accurate and timely information. I hope we can meet again sometime. I want to thank you, and hope we will have future conversations, if you have the time."

"I like the idea that you are focusing on things that happen in Reno. I've always thought that we live in an interesting area, and, unfortunately, there is always a dark side to every beautiful story. We'll talk again."

They said their goodbyes, shook hands, and went to their cars. Hillary was now very positive that because so much was left out of these stories, the majority of the articles would be examples of what *not* to do.

When Rafferty got to his car, he turned on his phone and had two voice messages. One was from his wife, and the other was from Sam Overton. He called Overton immediately.

He picked up on the third ring. Rafferty spoke first; "Mr. Overton? This is detective Rafferty returning your call". Overton said, "thanks, I have some information, or at least an opinion for you."

"Go ahead, I'm listening."

"I examined the heater we discussed, and although I didn't find any one thing to prove it was tampered with, in my opinion, someone rigged it so the exhaust would fail."

"You're pretty sure about it."

"in my years of experience, I would say I'm 99.99% positive."

"Thank you Mr. Overton, I'll be in touch."

Now for some personal contact with anyone who knew Ms. Stryker well.

Chapter 25

The Legend is a large casino with a large hotel. It was built on land that once had a grocery store and a very large parking lot. The day the foundation was poured, concrete trucks lined the highways throughout northern California, as well as northern Nevada. When it opened in the mid 90's, it employed about 1500 people. Skyways were attached on either side to allow customers from It's a Circus, and the Diablo to walk between the three casinos without having to walk outside on Virginia Street. So, while Legend created jobs, it eventually destroyed hundreds of jobs when smaller casinos on the street closed their doors. The day it was completed, many "old time" casino workers predicted it was the beginning of the end of downtown Reno.

Michael realized he should never have returned to work in a downtown casino. Downtown was on a slow but steady demise. Special events, designed to bring in millions of dollars to the community, such as "Hot August Nights" were targeted towards middle aged tourists with money to spend and fun to be had. Now it was an excuse for "gang bangers" from the Bay Area to come into town, trash the streets, and create problems for the casino security personnel and the police. But he had no place to go at present.

His relationship with Mitch wasn't getting any better. It was time to do something about it. He knew a lot about Mitch's habits. He knew that he was married to a dealer who worked south of downtown, had one ten year old daughter they must have had late in life, and that he drank coffee, black, all night long. He always went right home after work, now that Dale was no longer around. Word of mouth said he was a heavy drinker, but he must do it at home. One of these evenings when Michael got and EO, he just might have to follow him to be sure he went straight home, and didn't have a secret hangout.

CHAPTER 26

David Rafferty sat at his desk and thought about Hillary Fisk. She made him think more about what he had been doing for these three plus decades, and now there was this new information from Mr. Overton. He knew it wasn't that he didn't care as much anymore, or that he was not as detailed as he used to be, but he hadn't even considered that there might have been a connection to any of the casino related incidents he had investigated, until he had his lunch with her. The individual cases did not have a pattern related to cause of death, and no motive had been established. In addition, they had happened, in most cases, years apart. He was troubled but unsure of the path to which this all might lead. He would have to make the phone call this time. She was methodical enough that, between them, they just might produce an idea that could put some of this together.

Chapter 27

Michael got an EO on a slow Wednesday. When Mitch got off work at 1:30 in the morning, he was hiding behind some bushes outside the employee entrance. Mitch didn't go straight to the parking lot. Instead he turned left and walked down Sierra Street to the south. Michael stayed about fifty yards behind him so he wouldn't be seen. About three blocks later, Mitch stepped inside a little bar called the "Hideaway". Michael waited outside for about fifteen minutes. He had to have a look inside. He quietly opened the door, went in, and just stood there for a minute. The bar itself was about ten steps straight ahead. To the right there were six tables and four chairs at each. To the far right of the bar was a door that simply said, "restroom". He decided he should leave right away. There were only eight people in the entire place, five at the bar, and three sitting at one table.

James Turnage

He left, and thought about coming back an hour later, when Mitch would have been a little intoxicated. But he had no idea how long he might stay. Michael crossed the street, leaned against the side of a liquor store, and watched the door of the Hideaway.

About an hour and a half later, Mitch came out. He was a little unsteady on his feet, and walked back towards the Legend. Michael decided to go into the bar, and get a better look around. He walked up to the bar, ordered a scotch on the rocks. He sipped and studied his surroundings. What he hadn't seen the first time, was that just left of the bar were two small booths, big enough for only one person on each side.

At this time, Michael had Thursdays and Fridays off, Mitch, Monday and Tuesday. Michael decided that next week, on a Thursday, he would get to the Hideaway about 1:00 a.m., before Mitch arrived. He would take a seat in one of the booths, preferably the one closest to the bar. He would be sure Mitch did not see him. He would be patient, he would have his opportunity.

Chapter 28

David Rafferty hated one thing about his job. He detested being on the phone. It was a very necessary part of the job, but he nearly had to force himself to call people he didn't know, and ask, sometimes plead with them, for information. Phones were so impersonal.

Vanessa Stryker was very "social", but had few close friends. He decided to begin with the Games Manager at the Shangri La, the man who found her in her home. He was positive they had much more than a working relationship, after all, he had a key to the house. He didn't want to cause the man's wife any more grief than she was probably feeling already, so he decided to visit Jake Simpson without advance notice at work. Besides, it was one less phone call.

Rafferty concluded that if he arrived around two in the afternoon on a Monday, Mr. Simpson would most likely be in his office. And he was.

Rafferty walked right in and introduced himself, though they had met at Ms. Stryker's house on the day he had found her. Jake remembered him, but was obviously surprised to see him. Jake shook his hand, and offered Rafferty a seat on the opposite side of his desk. Rafferty sat, crossed his legs, and said nothing for several seconds. Jake finally asked, "so how can I help you, detective?"

Rafferty responded; "I have some questions. Some of them may be uncomfortable, but the death of Ms. Stryker appears to be more than an accident. She may have been the victim of a homicide".

Jake; "And what would make you think that"?

"I am certain that the heater in her home was tampered with, causing carbon monoxide to be released into the house, and resulting in her death."

"That's a very disturbing assumption. But why talk to me about it?"

"I need to know your relationship with the deceased. And I need to know why you had a key to her home."

Jake placed a hand on his chin, looked to the floor, obviously deciding what to say next. Finally, he rallied, pulling out all the bullshit he could, and said, "Vanessa and I were trying to make this casino the most successful in the Reno area. We met regularly to discuss ideas that would increase the customer base, both tourist and local".

Rafferty, the consummate investigator, let the statement hang in the air for a moment. Finally, he said; "Mr. Simpson, I don't believe you for a second. I'm not a rude man, but I'm not a fool, either. You had a key to her home. There was much more to your relationship than you're willing to tell me. If you like, we can go to the station and continue this conversation".

It took a while for Jake to think about everything. He finally spoke; "we don't need to go there. How much of this will be public information?"

"Whatever you tell me will be part of the official investigation. But, it will not be released to the press. I want the truth. I believe someone murdered Ms. Stryker, and I need to pin down as many of the details of her life as I can."

It took several seconds for Jake to respond. He finally decided that it was better for him to be truthful, than to become a murder suspect. He said; "Vanessa and I had been seeing each other for a few months. But I had nothing to do with her death, you have to believe that".

"I don't consider you a suspect, at least not now. But someone wanted her dead. Maybe it was an ex-husband, a former lover, or someone she had simply pissed off. What can you tell me about her past relationships?"

"We didn't talk a lot about those things. I know she was married once, but that was quite a few years ago, and he lives somewhere in Europe, France, I think. She had no children. I'm sure you know that she had one sister who lives in Georgia."

"Yes, she was notified about Ms. Stryker's death. Apparently, she was her only living relative. Did she ever talk about previous boyfriends or lovers?"

"I know she was seeing someone when she died, but I don't know who it might have been. Ours was just a sexual thing, she liked our relationship just the way it was."

"Did she ever mention where he lived, or where he worked?"

"All she ever said about him was that they met when she worked at Peyton Place. They were both games supervisors there, and left around the same time."

"Anything else you can think of that might help?"

"Nothing specific. She talked about the fact that because she was a woman, she had made several male enemies in the gaming industry. But she never mentioned anyone by name, or where they might have worked together."

"Thanks for your time, Mr. Simpson. If you think of anything else, even if you don't think it might be important, please call me." Rafferty gave him his card which contained his office number, cell phone, and pager numbers.

Jake shook his hand, saying, "I most certainly will".

Rafferty left Jake's office. He was well aware that there may be many more interviews before he solved this one, if he could solve it at all.

CHAPTER 29

When Michael arrived for his 8 p.m. dice shift on Saturday, he was in a hurry. He had trouble finding a reasonably clean shirt to wear, so he barely made it to work on time. His game was already full of players. He knew the day shift crew they were relieving would be happy to go home.

When he pushed the day shift dealer out, he had eight players on his end of the table. All of them were betting the pass line with full odds, and taking two come bets with full odds. It was not a difficult game to deal, just a lot of busy work, and no one was betting over ten dollars.

When he finally got his first break, he noticed Mitch wasn't in the pit. One of the senior box men was running it. He asked him where Mitch was, and got a one word answer, "sick".

In the break room, he asked one of the dealers from another table where Mitch was. He told him that he had called in the last three days. Michael thought to himself, "must be pretty damn sick".

Michael's game finally slowed down around 11:30. He was glad. There were no problem players, and the game was fairly smooth, but they were typical tourists from the northwest, and the dealers weren't receiving many tokes. Too much work for too little money.

When he got off at four in the morning, he decided to play the slots instead of going right home. In a small way, he was celebrating. It had been great not having to work with Mitch. Besides, he was drinking about a quart of scotch a night now, and sneaking drinks on his breaks. He didn't want to drink himself to sleep tonight. He went to one of the few small casinos that was still open. It was called the "Truckee River Casino". It had been in business as long as any other casino in Reno or Sparks. Located on a side street, about a half block off Virginia Street, it was mostly a local's spot. Many dealers, bartenders, and cocktail waitresses favored this little "hole in the wall", and that's why it was still open. They kept it very busy. Michael usually played poker machines, but tonight he wanted to try the very popular "Wheel of Fortune" machine. When certain combinations came up in the three windows, the player got to spin the wheel for an increase in the payoff of up to one hundred times.

He played the machine for a couple of hours, downed a half dozen scotches, and decided it was time to go home. The sun was coming up in the East. He cashed out his winnings which totaled 325 dollars. It had been a good night.

Chapter 30

Hillary Fisk was very happy with the material she had prepared for her class. She found a few talented and thorough reporters whose stories would be a great example for her class to learn from. Unfortunately, she only found one or two from each of them, they had obviously moved on to greener pastures. She had many badly written and incomplete examples by reporters who didn't last, or, sadly, were still writing for the newspaper.

She often thought about detective Rafferty. She couldn't stop analyzing their meeting, and how her gut feeling told her some of the stories they talked about might have a common thread. And the latest death of Dale Fitzter was certainly a murder. It was only the second death in her research that was caused by violent action. Although it was not Rafferty's case, she included it with the rest of her file. The follow up story, unusual as that was in Reno's newspaper, said that the murder weapon was some sort of cylindrical object, and that he had been struck with three times the force necessary to cause the fatal injury. It further stated that he was murdered somewhere else, and then transported to Hazen.

Hillary needed to talk to detective Rafferty again, but she hadn't completely formed the idea that had been floating around in her head. Maybe he was getting some answers that would clear up her many questions.

Chapter 31

Mitch didn't come to work on Sunday or Monday. On Tuesday, as Michael was getting ready for his shift, another dealer came up to him and said, "did you hear about Mitch?" Michael said, "I heard he was sick." The dealer responded, "he died last night. I heard it from one of the lady dealers who is close friends with his wife." Michael looked totally surprised, and asked, "what did he die from?" The other dealer; "He had been nauseas, was vomiting a lot, and had diarrhea. They think it was some sort of flu. Then on Sunday he became delirious, was having seizures, and that night went into a coma. He didn't last twenty-four hours after he lost consciousness." Michael just said, "wow".

In the paper the next morning, a story on the third page confirmed that "Mitch Carlson, swing shift dice manager at the Legend, died in his home last Sunday night.

The exact cause is unknown. An autopsy will be performed this week."

The only thought in Michael's head was, "my life has just gotten better."

CHAPTER 32

On the Thursday morning, three days after Mitch Carlson passed away, David Rafferty was called into the captain's office. Captain Murphy told him to have a seat. They exchanged pleasantries for several minutes, asking about families, discussing the relatively short time that Rafferty had left before retirement. Then Murphy got to the reason he wanted to see him.

"You probably read about the death of the dice manager at the Legend?"

"Yes, it appears as if he contracted some sort of virus."

"That's what everyone thought, but this morning I received a call from the coroner's office. The early findings suggest there might have been some other cause for his death. I know you are still working on the Stryker case, but I wondered if you would look into this one as well?"

"I'll find the time, but I do have interviews set up with some people Ms. Stryker worked with, and I'm still searching for the man she was romantically involved with."

"If you need help with some of the interviews, I'm sure we could find someone to assist you."

"Thanks, captain, but I need to do them myself. I've developed some ideas, and I need to make certain that all the right questions are asked."

"I understand. But if there is any way I can help, please let me know."

"I will. And I'll start this afternoon by making a visit to the coroner's office."

"Thanks, Dave. I'm not sure what I'll do *if* you actually retire."

"A little over twenty months to go."

Rafferty got a cup of coffee, returned to his desk, and thought about the two cases. He just might have to get involved in a third, the Fitzter case, as well. They both worked at the Legend, and to Rafferty, that just plain smelled.

At 3 p.m., Rafferty arrived at the coroner's office. The coroner himself was a man in his mid fifties, about 5 feet 9 inches tall, 220 pounds, with white hair, very thin on top. He had been Reno's coroner for over 20 years. He still worked too many hours, and when he wasn't working, he was reading publications related to his craft. His name was William Cohen. Rafferty liked and respected him.

Rafferty walked right into the examination room, he'd been there too many times before. Cohen was sitting at a small desk, going over some paperwork. He looked up, saw Rafferty, stood, shook his hand, and warmly said, "Dave, it's good to see you. I didn't know you were coming."

"Hello, Bill, I didn't know I was, until this morning. How's the family?"

"The kids are great, doing their own thing. As for my wife, she's trying to ruin my life. Just because my last exam showed my blood pressure was a little high, and I might be a little overweight, she limits me to one beer a day, and has taken away all my other favorite things, such as steak, bacon, sausage, cheese, and she now packs my lunch every day with only rabbit food, soy milk, and one sugar free cookie. Life's rough."

Rafferty laughed. "I understand. I was forced into much of that two years ago. You'll get used to some of it, but I still miss bacon, and I'm sure I always will. I admit that every once in a while I have a hamburger."

"I hear you're getting near retirement. How come you still work so hard?"

"I'm sure the bad guys out there figure I'm slowing down. I like surprises when they're not meant for me."

"So, what can I do for you?"

"The Captain asked me to take on the Carlson case. He said you have some suspicions as to the cause of death?"

"It's more of what I couldn't find. The autopsy is not complete, but I performed blood tests that showed nothing that said he had a viral condition serious enough to cause his symptoms, never mind death. I have ordered a complete toxicology report, but that might take a week, maybe more. Don't doubt me, I'll find out what the cause of death was, it just won't happen today."

"So, you're thinking some sort of poison?"

"I'm not prepared to define the cause of death, but I'm 100% sure it was not a 'flu virus'. Everything Mr. Carlson experienced happened too rapidly for a viral infection to have been the cause of death. Antibiotics would have, at the very least, slowed the process for a somewhat longer period of time."

"If I asked you to expedite it, when's the earliest the toxicology report could be completed?"

"It will take about a week, no matter how much pressure I put on the lab. It's not an all in one report. They have to rule out possibilities one by one."

"Okay. Thanks Bill, it was good to see you. We'll talk in a week."

They shook hands, and Rafferty left the room, headed to his car and his office.

Chapter 33

Michael could hardly believe his feelings at work. A dark cloud had been lifted from the dice pit. There was a lot of gossip about Mitch, but he wasn't interested in any of it. As far as he was concerned, a cancer had been removed from the casino.

The Legend did not appoint a new dice manager right away. There were several qualified box men who could perform those duties, and that may be why they were in no hurry. They most likely wanted to see who would take the initiative to absorb Mitch's duties. The dice pit was more relaxed. The most satisfying effect of Mitch's absence, was his number one crew now had to work like everyone else. Their table limit was reduced to a five dollar game like the others. They weren't happy about it, Michael was ecstatic.

In the employee's cafeteria, Michael was hearing more, and more complaints about Peg, and her increased harassment of certain "21" dealers. In Dale's absence, she had aligned herself with Carl, and his ideas as to the treatment of dealers who did not live up to his expectations. She spent more of her time "writing up" dealers, than taking care of her customers and her responsibilities. She was becoming a tumor as large as Dale had been. She was close to Dale's friend Mitch, and could become infected with the same virus. Wouldn't that be a pity?

Chapter 34

Hillary wanted to show her class shoddy journalistic practices, using the Reno paper as an example. Then she used examples of the very good ones as the exception to the rule. She had done a great deal of preparatory work, and her class was interested and receptive. But she was finding herself distracted. With the death of another Legend employee, the annoying feeling that something wasn't right was affecting every moment of her conscious thought. If there was one individual, who could in any form of the imagination, be responsible for some of these deaths over the years, he or she had to be discovered, caught and punished. If any more deaths could be stopped, they must be, and soon.

CHAPTER 35

David Rafferty was sitting at his desk. There were two piles of paper on it, one marked Stryker, and one marked Carlson. The Stryker file was a lot thicker. He had already interviewed six people that knew her well, and the only information he had learned of any value was a lead where he might find Jonathan Vickers, the man who was her significant other. He reportedly had taken a casino manager's job in Carson City.

Rafferty was troubled. Although at first glance it didn't appear these two cases were in any way connected, his gut was grumbling with doubt. And if you added in the Fitzter case, there was a tornado in there.

Sitting there, lost in deep thought, his phone rang. He answered it with, "Detective Rafferty".

The caller; "Hello, David, this is Hillary Fisk."

"Hi Hillary, good to hear your voice. What can I do for you?"

"This may sound silly to someone who is as experienced as you are investigating crimes, but the more I read, the more I think something isn't quite right about all these casino related deaths."

"Funny you should say that, I was just sitting here thinking about the same thing."

"Could we possibly get together again and talk about it?"

"I would love to, but it can't be right away, I have a very big case load, and I have lots to do, immediately, if not sooner."

"I understand. You tell me when and where, with the exception of Tuesdays and Thursdays when I have classes to teach."

"How about a week from Friday? I should have accomplished quite a bit by then, and, hopefully I'll be able to have my afternoon free. We could meet at the Gold and Silver again, say one in the afternoon?"

"Sounds great, I'll see you then."

Rafferty hung up, feeling a small satisfaction that someone else saw things his way.

Chapter 36

The Legend is as large as some casinos in Las Vegas. It has several pits containing dozens of table games. But, because Reno is supported mostly by weekend tourists, less than half of the tables available are open during the weekdays. Therefore, more than half the dealers are part time, working weekends and holidays, and sometimes special events, when more tables are open.

For reasons she alone understood, Peg was harder on these part time dealers than those who worked full time. She continually harassed them, making them look inept in front of the customers. Because many of these part timers were trying to become full time, there were never any complaints made about her actions to Human Resources. Those dealers just had to "suck it up" and go about their business.

Michael was witness to this, because when dice play was slow, his game, the late game with lesser talented dealers, was often closed, and he was sent to deal cards in the pits where the part timers generally worked. His being a dice dealer placed him on her list of those to harass. Admittedly dice dealers are not the most accomplished card dealers. Like everything else, if you don't do something every day, your skills are never perfected. But these pits were lower limits, dealing perfection was not the primary goal. Keeping customers in the casino, spending every dollar they had, that was the real objective.

With Dale no longer at the Legend, Peg was becoming tighter than ever with Carl, and therefore was given some of the duties Dale had performed. She loved the power. In the break room, many of the dealers were so angry with her they almost broke out in tears. The word "bitch" was frequently heard.

From listening to other dealers, he knew that she was married. But he also heard rumors that she was having an affair with a female dealer next door at the Diablo. Michael thought to himself, "we all have our sins, our little secrets." This might take a little time, and a lot of research and planning, but this parasite needed to be removed.

Chapter 37

With just a few phone calls, Rafferty located Jonathan Vickers. He was the Casino Manager at "Sierra Sam's", the largest casino in Carson City. He called him, and made an appointment for them to meet in two days, on a Thursday.

Rafferty arrived at Sierra Sam's at 11 a.m., his appointment was at 11:30. He wanted to look around, maybe have a cup of coffee, unwind, and check his notes after the 45 minute drive from the station. At 11:25, he went to the third floor and found Vickers' office. The door was open, he had no secretary, so he rapped on the wall. Vickers looked up, stood up, and walked from behind his desk to greet Rafferty.

He said, "Detective Rafferty?"

Rafferty replied, "yes, and you're Jonathan Vickers?"

"Yes I am. Won't you come in and have a seat?"

"Thank you."

"After I talked to you on the phone, I realized I might not be of much help to you, but I'll do my best to answer any questions you have."

"Good. First of all, I want to ask you why you didn't come forward when you heard about Ms. Stryker's death?"

"I actually heard about it on the evening news. I didn't know what to do. It was a terrible accident, and of course I was sad to hear about her death, but there was nothing I could do. Besides, I had just taken this position, and I didn't see any advantage to having my name in the papers."

"We know now that it wasn't an accident. Someone tampered with the heating system. So, I need you to think very carefully when you reply to my questions. I'm positive that whoever murdered her, knew her fairly well."

"So, I'm a suspect?"

"Right now, you're just someone who might be able to give me some answers, but to be completely honest, I haven't ruled you out."

"Okay, ask away."

"What is your description of your relationship with Ms. Stryker, and were you on good terms with her?"

"I don't think I was ever sure what our relationship was. We were more than just casual, but we weren't "in love". We never fought, we just shared a lot of time together. Now that I think about it, maybe we never had hard times because there wasn't enough emotion, enough passion between us."

"So there were no conflicts between the two of you at the time she died?"

"Nothing at all. We saw each other when we could. It was mostly about sex, and we enjoyed each other's company."

"Did she ever talk about having enemies, someone who might have wished her harm?"

"If she were here, she'd be the first one to tell you she was not the most liked person in the industry. She was defensive, ambitious, and, she was flirtatious, believing that was the only way for her to advance in her career. So I'm sure she stepped on the backs of some to achieve her goals, and they resented her for it."

"But did she ever mention anyone in particular?"

"Not by name. She casually told me one night about a pit boss she worked with who was extremely obvious in showing his animosity, but she said that he was leaving the casino, and she wouldn't have to put up with him any more."

"Anyone else. Anyone from her past she might have remembered as an unpleasant relationship?"

"As I said, there were probably quite a few, but she never mentioned any threats, or any serious altercations, if that's what you mean."

"Do you know Jake Simpson?"

"Yes, and I knew about their relationship, if that's what you're asking. It was fine with me. As I said, we had no commitment to each other. What we had was a mutual arrangement, we didn't make plans for the future."

"Do you think she might have had other arrangements with other men than only Mr. Simpson?"

"She might have, but I wasn't aware of any."

"If I have any more questions I'll be in touch."

They said their good-byes, and Rafferty was more troubled than ever by the lack of information he had obtained. He had to think of another strategy.

Chapter 38

Nine days after he talked to Bill Cohen, Rafferty received a call from the coroner. The lab had found the presence of a Toxalbumin in his blood cells. This toxic, sometimes fatal substance, comes from certain plants, that when given to the human organism in the proper dose and manner, can cause flu like symptoms, and even death. Someone had poisoned Mr. Carlson. That made two murders at the Legend. Now he had to get involved in the Fitzter case. Like most cops, Rafferty didn't believe in coincidence.

Chapter 39

Michael wanted to learn more about Peg. There was a problem. They shared the same nights off, and she was off duty at 1:30 in the morning, Michael at 4 a.m. He decided the thing to do was to request a change in his days off. That might take a couple of weeks, but he could wait. As long as he could take care of the problem, he could be patient.

Chapter 40

The first thing Rafferty did was call Mrs. Carlson. He asked to meet with her as soon as possible. She told him he could come over that afternoon around two.

The drive to the Carlson's home would take about five minutes. They lived in an older sections of downtown. Their home was off of California Street. It was a two storey structure with a large front porch. It was in good repair, and tastefully landscaped, and was probably built in the 1960's.

He knocked on the front door, and was promptly greeted by Mrs. Carlson. She was an attractive woman, maybe ten pounds overweight, with shoulder length blond hair, (although he didn't think that was her natural color), about five-feet five-inches tall. She asked him to come in. The living room was comfortably furnished with a couch, a love seat, and a leather recliner which faced a big screen television. There were lots of pictures on the walls, many of a young girl he assumed was their daughter.

Mrs. Carlson offered him water or coffee, he declined. Rafferty got right to the point of his visit.

"Mrs. Carlson, I'm sorry for your loss. What I have to tell you is not easy, but you have the right to know. This has not been in the paper yet, and unless someone asks me specific questions, it won't be, at least for a while. Your husband was the victim of a homicide."

"Oh my God! Are you sure?"

"Yes, I got a call from the coroner this morning. He was poisoned."

"Why? I can't imagine why anyone would do this." She put her hands to her face and began to sob.

Rafferty sat quietly while she absorbed this horrible revelation, and was forced to relive the pain of losing her husband. This was the part of his job he hated the most.

Mrs. Carlson recovered and said, "My husband was not an easy man. He didn't have many friends. But I can't think of any reason why someone would feel enough hate to kill him."

"It's been my experience, unfortunately, for some people it doesn't take much for them to find enough rage to commit homicide."

For a while, she said nothing, lost in unpleasant thought. "I'm sure you come in contact with too many people who find it easy to do bad things."

"Once in a while my job is a little depressing, but other times, when a case is resolved, it's very satisfying. It's not a career for everyone. Did your husband ever mention anyone in particular that he had problems with, or maybe feared?"

"The only one I remember was some years ago. That was before the Legend opened and we moved back to Reno. We were working in Biloxi, Mississippi, when someone we knew told us about the new casino being built in Reno. We were working at the "Mississippi Queen" at that time. He told me of a dealer who was from the gulf coast, unlike many of the dealers who came from Nevada or Atlantic City. There was a new dealer's school there, and this man was from the first class to graduate. His name was "Ronnie", or "Lonnie", or "Tommy", something like that. He was related to the casino owner, and Mitch was forced to put him on the dice game, even though he had no experience, and no talent. Mitch resented being forced to watch over this man, and they formed a mutual dislike for each other. He talked about it a lot. Maybe that was the primary reason he decided we should move back to Reno."

"I understand your husband came back here to work at the Legend, did you go to work there as well?"

"No, I knew lots of people in Reno. I deal all the games, but my specialty is roulette, and we had decided, because of his position, we shouldn't work in the same casino. If we would have, we wouldn't have been allowed to work the same shift."

"So he never mentioned anyone in particular at the Legend that he had a conflict with?"

"Not one individual. The only thing he said was that he had several dealers who he called "lumps", which meant they were not very good, and also had bad attitudes."

"Anyone in your personal life that he might have had a problem with?"

"Not anyone I could ever imagine would be that angry with him. He didn't get along with our neighbor on the south side of our house. They argued about water. When Ben, that's our neighbor, watered his back yard, it would run over into our yard and flood Mitch's vegetable garden. But that feud had gone on for years. He has, or had, two brothers. One lives in Washington state, near Seattle, and the other lives here. They weren't close, and there were no real problems between them."

"I'll talk to your neighbor anyway. As I said before, sometimes it's that one thing, something no one else might consider important, that makes a person act out. This is difficult, and please understand that I have to rule out all possibilities, but did he do drugs of any kind?"

"No, Mitch despised drugs, and those who used them. But he did drink."

"Beer, or hard liquor?"

"He was a 'Wild Turkey' man."

"Did he drink at home, or did he have a favorite bar?"

"He often went to a little bar downtown near the Legend called the Hideaway."

"So if I go there and ask some questions, the bartender would remember him?"

"I'm sure he would, that's the only place I'm aware of that he drank when he wasn't at home."

"One last thing. I know this is personal, but I have to cover every possibility. Did the two of you have money problems?"

"No, no way. We weren't rich, but we got a great loan on the house, and other than that we were bill free, not counting gas and electric, things like that."

"So, you would say you were comfortable?"

"You could call it that."

"Is there anything else you think might be important, no matter how trivial it may seem?"

"Nothing I can think of. I just can't believe all this has happened. I don't feel like any of it is real." Her eyes welled up again.

"Once again, I'm very sorry that I had to bring even worse news. Here's my card, it has all my contacts on it. If you think of anything, anything at all, please call me day or night."

"I will."

Rafferty walked out, she closed the door quietly behind him.

As he drove back to the station, he was very frustrated. He was as sure as he could be that there was more to all this than he was seeing. What was he missing? What could there be that links these cases together?

CHAPTER 41

When David Rafferty walked into the Gold and Silver on Friday afternoon, Hillary Fisk was waiting for him. He walked towards her table, she stood, and instead of shaking his hand, gave him a hug. David was a little uneasy about this. Mostly, because of his profession, the only hugs he got were from his wife, daughter, and grandchildren.

Just as last time, they decided to order right away, so their conversation would have as little interruption as possible. Their waitress came, and Hillary ordered vegetable pasta and iced tea. David had a turkey club on whole wheat, cottage cheese and tomatoes instead of French fries, and coffee. Their waitress left, and Hillary spoke first.

"Thanks for meeting me again. I have been very preoccupied with what we previously discussed, and now more has happened. Something just doesn't feel right to me."

"I've been feeling the same way. I've been getting headaches thinking about it. I can tell you now that the Stryker death was not an accident, and, I know you aren't aware of this yet, but the Carlson matter has been labeled a homicide, he was poisoned. My captain asked me to add it to my caseload. In addition, I have been meeting with Detective Bennet about the Fitzter murder. I was hoping he would have discovered something that might merge the two cases at the Legend, but so far, no luck."

"So Carlson is now a part of this. I know you're troubled by the same things I am. There seems to be no connection between all of it, but something tells me there is. I just don't see it."

"I've been looking at everything from one angle. I have to get my head turned around in another direction."

"Something I never asked you. I began my research at a period of about twelve years ago. Before that time, did you work many death cases related to casinos?"

"There were some. A dealer was shot, while she was working, by her estranged husband. A woman drove her Cadillac down the sidewalk next to the Goldmine, intentionally killing four people. I'm sure there were more, but I have to admit, those are the only two that stand out. I never thought about it before."

"So we're talking about a fifteen year, or less, time frame, does that make sense?"

"It does. What troubles me most is that all my interviews, everything else I've been looking at, none of it has produced anyone who might have had a motive. None of the victims were without enemies, but none of those enemies seems to have had a strong enough reason to commit murder. I've checked and cross checked every interview. It just doesn't add up."

Their lunch came, and just as before, they turned to small talk as they ate.

Hillary said; "I noticed you didn't have French fries today. Are you on a diet?"

"No, I'm supposed to be eating healthier, you know, high blood pressure, high cholesterol, all that stuff. When I'm not eating at home, I slide a little, but then I feel guilty. I have a great wife, and she's trying to keep me alive 'til I'm a hundred."

"Good for you, and good for her."

"So how's your class going?"

"Going well. I have a great group of students this year. They're enthusiastic, and ask a lot of good questions. Sometimes journalism is taken by those who just need to get credits out of the way. But I've already seen several in this group that could actually work in the industry."

"So you're still happy living in Reno?"

"Maybe more than ever. I've made a few good friends, and have learned much more about Reno, both past and present."

"That's great. When I retire, my wife, whose name is Jill by the way, and I plan to travel, but we'll keep our home here. I feel a real connection to this area, and always want to know I can come back home, not to mention our daughter and grandchildren living here."

They finished their meal, but neither spoke for a few minutes. They were both getting back to their thoughts, dark thoughts about murderers and their victims.

Rafferty spoke first; "I think we should make this a weekly thing. I don't like trying to accomplish things on the phone. I prefer face to face discussion. Ideas seem to come faster for me that way."

"Sounds great. A week will give each of us a chance to think on our own, and then we'll be able to exchange theories."

"That's how I see it. Other than what we've already discussed, nothing new, nothing else at all, comes to mind."

"Thanks again for meeting with me. I needed to talk to you, my head was spinning, and there was no one else who would understand all this."

"It's good to see you again, and I'll look forward to next Friday. If you need talk about any of this, please call me. If it's alright, I'll plan on doing the same."

"Of course. I never gave you my home number, which is actually my cell." She took out a piece of paper and a pen and wrote it down for him.

"Thanks, I guess I'll see you next week."

Hillary shook his hand good-bye. She remembered the uneasy way he reacted to her hug.

Chapter 42

When Michael checked his schedule for the upcoming week, his days off were now Tuesday and Wednesday. With Peg having Thursday and Friday off this would work well. The other thing that was different, was that without Mitch being there, Michael was now on the 7 o'clock crew. He would be working with better dealers, and have less chance of being sent to a "21" game.

When he got his first Tuesday off, he was outside the employee entrance at 1:15 in the morning, in the same spot he had found when he was waiting for Mitch. Around 1:40 in the morning, Peg came out. She walked to her right towards the Diablo. He kept his distance, there wasn't much cover to hide behind. Besides, he was pretty certain she was going into the casino.

She walked into the Diablo through a side door. He waited for about fifteen seconds, and went inside. He could see her red hair walking ahead of him towards one of the pits. Standing partially hidden behind a post, he saw her motion to a dark haired dealer. She continued down the aisle to a bar near the front of the casino. She ordered a glass of wine, and sat at a table facing the pit.

Most swing shift dealers get off at 2 a.m., in some casinos the dealers change their clothes, and leave the casino. One dealer, the one who Peg motioned to, walked straight to the bar and sat at the table Peg had chosen. They talked briefly, Peg finished most of her wine, and they stood up, ready to exit the casino. Michael followed them at a safe distance. They walked out of the Diablo, and went about a block down the street to McDougal's.

They sat at a table in the corner of a dimly lit bar on the second floor. Reno was known in its early days as the "Mississippi of the west". Open display of affection by same sex couples was not advisable. But from the far corner of the bar, Michael could see their expressions when they looked into each other's eyes. He decided he should leave the bar, he could be seen if they looked his way.

He went down the escalator to the main floor, positioning himself so that he could see them when they came down from the bar. He patiently waited for a little over an hour. They walked to a side door which was near Sierra Street, and took the back way towards the Legend. When they arrived at the employee's parking lot, they found a dark space behind a sign advertising a ninety-nine cent breakfast at the Nevada Gold, and kissed each other. Then Peg's friend walked towards her own employee parking area. Keeping his distance, Michael watched Peg walk into the lot where she got into a Ford Taurus, maybe a year or two old. He memorized the license number, and headed back home.

The next night, his second night off, he decided he needed to know more about Peg's friend. He figured the easiest way was to play cards on her game. He knew she wouldn't recognize him, they had never met, but he thought it was still a wise idea to change his appearance a little. He was sure that a fake mustache and beard, with a baseball cap, would be sufficient.

He walked down to the Diablo about 9 o'clock. She was in the same pit as the night before. There was only one player on her game. Michael walked up to it, saw is was a five dollar game, and took a seat. He put down two twenty dollar bills. She changed them for eight, red, five dollar chips. Her name tag said "Bev". He put a five dollar bet in the circle, and said, "how are you tonight, Bev?" She said, "I'm good, how about you?" "Great", replied Michael. In most Reno casinos, the employee's home town is on their name tag as well. Bev's said "Phoenix, Arizona."

Michael said, "I see you're from Phoenix."

Bev: "Yeah, actually I'm from Tempe, where the university is, but most people know Phoenix a lot better."

"Quite a different environment up here, isn't it?"

"Yeah, I like it a lot better, especially the weather. I was tired of the heat down south."

"Have you lived here long?"

"I only moved up here about six months ago. I worked in Las Vegas for over ten years, but I got tired of the hustle and bustle, as well as the weather."

The other player, who was well on his way to becoming completely intoxicated, must have gotten tired of the conversation. He slid of the chair, almost fell, and moved towards the bar Peg and Bev had briefly sat at the night before.

Michael didn't say much else, he'd found out enough right now. He played three more hands, said "good night", and went back home.

Chapter 43

Rafferty was not a night person, never had been. But, if he wanted to talk to the bartender who served Mitch at the Hideaway, he'd have to do it no earlier than eight in the evening. So, on Tuesday night he left his house about 8:15, and drove downtown. He found a place on the street to park about one-half block away from the bar.

He had never been much of a drinker, and never hung out in bars, so when he entered the Hideaway, he had to stand inside the door for a few seconds to adjust to the dim light, and take in the surroundings. He walked up to the bar, and took a stool to the far left, the same stool Mitch had sat at almost two weeks ago. The bartender didn't wear a name tag as they did in the casinos. Rafferty decided he would order a beer, and strike up a conversation. He was one of only five people in the place at this early hour. He drank abut half of the beer, and must have taken a longer time than most to consume it, because the bartender came back to him and asked if he wanted another. Rafferty pulled out his badge, and asked the bartender if he could ask him a few questions. He said, "sure, why not?" Rafferty asked, "what's your name?" He said "Vic". Rafferty said, "did you see the story about the dice manager from the Legend passing away?"

He said, "yeah, so why are you here? It said he had some sort of illness."

"So you knew him?"

"He came in here several nights a week after his shift."

"Was he always alone?"

"Sure. He would just sit here and have a few drinks. Not much of a conversationist."

"Did he ever talk to you about his job, or his home life?"

"No. He really never talked about much at all. When there was an event in town he might have said something about the people he had to deal with, but that was about it."

"Do you remember when you saw him last?"

"It was a week or two ago. And then I saw the story in the newspaper."

"Was there anything different that night?"

"No. Nothing that was unusual."

"Did you happen to notice anyone different, someone who stood out for some reason?"

"We have lots of people who come in here just because it's a bar."

"Just for the heck of it, do you recall anyone that night?"

"Hold on a minute." He left to take care of some other customers who needed refills. He came back a few minutes later. "I'm not sure, but I think it was that night. There was an odd looking man with a beard and mustache sitting at a booth over there." He pointed to his right to two small booths to the side of the bar. "The only reason I remember him was that those booths are seldom used, and when they are it's usually couples who want a little privacy."

"Would you recognize him if you saw him again?"

"I don't know. He wasn't unlike a thousand people I've seen before."

Rafferty gave him his card, and said, "if you think of anything, no matter how insignificant it might seem, please call me. And if this 'booth' person should come back, please call me right away."

Vic said, "sure".

Rafferty went home thinking, another dead end, maybe.

Chapter 44

Michael knew that if Peg and Bev wanted to have intimacy, they would have to go to wherever Bev lived. He had no idea what days off Bev had, so he figured he would have to follow her on a Wednesday.

When Wednesday came, he went to the Diablo forty five minutes before the swing dealers got off. From observing her when she met Peg, there probably wasn't an employee entrance they were required to enter and exit. He would have to follow her when she got pushed off her game.

Bev had the "early push", or the last break. She exited towards the back of the casino. Michael followed. Not wearing his false beard and mustache, he knew she wouldn't recognize him, so he stayed reasonably close. She went out the door that was farthest to the rear of the casino, stepped across the street, and went into a paid parking lot. Michael had parked behind the casino on the street. If he hurried, he could get to his car and move toward the lot where she parked. He made it just in time to see an older Dodge Neon exit the lot. He had to assume it was her. He followed her as she turned left on 4th Street, and headed west. She drove all the way to west McCarran Boulevard, turned left for about a quarter mile, and turned right onto Ridgecrest Avenue. She drove into an apartment complex, and parked in a reserved carport marked with the number 315. Michael parked in the visitor's parking area. He was sure that her numbered parking space related to her apartment number. He got out of his car to see where it was physically located. As he walked towards her space, he saw Peg's car parked in a visitors space one section down from where he was. He walked into the complex and saw that Bev's apartment was on the third floor at the front of the building. As he always told himself, planning and knowledge were the most important parts of his operations.

CHAPTER 45

The next Thursday Hillary had a hard time concentrating on her class. She was devoted to her students and giving them as much information as she could, but her mind was in a state of flux. Something was stirring around the perimeters of conscious thought. It wouldn't jump to the front of her brain, as she wished it would.

When her class was over, she made up her mind to find a way to vacate all thought for an hour or two. She decided the best way was to take a run around Virginia Lake. Virginia Lake is a man made lake almost a mile in circumference, in south central Reno. There are Canadian geese and ducks who reside in and around the lake, knowing many of its visitors gave them bird seed or bread crumbs. It's a comfortable area, both day and night, and very popular with the local residents. All around the lake is a speed limit of 15 miles an hour for cars, trucks, buses, and motorcycles, making it safe for children and joggers.

She left the classroom and headed south to her apartment. She changed into shorts and a tank top, running shoes, and filled her water bottle. She drove back north the less than ten minute drive, found a parking space on the curb, an began her run. After the second lap around the lake, she was more relaxed, more in control of her thoughts and emotions. She did one more lap, and headed for her car, home, and a shower.

She showered in water as hot as she could tolerate, dried off, put her hair up under the towel, and went to the kitchen to make something to eat. She decided on a little pasta with a mushroom sauce. She began sautéing the mushrooms in butter and garlic while the pasta was boiling. She had a bottle of Pinot Grigio chilling in the refrigerator, opened it, and poured herself a glass while the dinner was in progress. She put on a CD, a mix she had made of some of the old greats, such as Sarah Vaughan, Ella Fizgerald, Lena Horne, and Billie Holliday. She felt totally at peace.

When the pasta was ready, she turned off the CD player, and watched the evening news. That was probably a mistake, it ruined her relaxed state of mind. There was the inevitable follow up story about the now confirmed murder of Mitch Carlson. But it did serve to bring the idea that had been attempting to leap to the conscious part of her brain into full view. She was anxious to see David at lunch tomorrow.

CHAPTER 46

When Hillary Fisk arrived for her one o'clock lunch meeting with David Rafferty on Friday, she saw him getting out of his car just as she was heading for the entrance to the Gold and Silver. She waited for him to walk the twenty or so feet to where she was, greeting him with a warm handshake, and led him inside.

After they were seated, Hillary said: "Have you made any progress on either of your cases?"

Rafferty: "Not anything that makes me happy."

"Yesterday I had an idea. Tell me what you think."

"Okay."

"I think it makes sense, but it will require a lot of work on your part, since I'm not officially involved in any of this."

"That's okay. Most of police work is not very exciting. It's mostly tedious and time consuming, but produces more answers than all the dramatic events portrayed on television and in the movies."

"Okay, here goes. What if the personnel records of all the casinos where these questionable deaths have occurred, produced the name of one individual who worked at all of them, in a reasonable time frame related to the murders?"

David Rafferty was lost in contemplation for a while. Then he looked her in the eyes and said, "You know what, that might be an incredible idea. I've been racking my brain for an approach to find the cause and effect side of these cases. This angle makes sense, especially since there seems to be no motive for anyone I've interviewed to act in such an extreme way. Maybe we need to look at opportunity, and work from there."

"I'm so glad you see it that way. I couldn't bring forth my idea for a long time. It was hanging there somewhere in the back of my mind, but it just wouldn't show itself."

Their waitress came, who now knew them as regular customers. They ordered lunch. Hillary, who rarely ordered anything considered 'unhealthy', decided to have a BLT and French fries, with an iced tea. David, with guilt attached to his decision, asked for a Cobb salad, and iced tea as well.

Hillary couldn't wait to continue: "I am so positive that there is one individual who is connected in some way to all these cases. The apparent randomness, the time frame, it's bizarre and tells me there is someone who knows about all these deaths. Does that make sense?"

"In an unconventional way, it does."

"Is there any way I can help you get the records of employment?"

"I wish there was, but the requests will have to come from official police summons. I might have to get a court order from a judge. I hope that isn't necessary, it would force everything to take more time. We'll just have to deal with whatever happens."

The waitress brought their lunch, and they ate without saying much. Both of them were deep in thought, and a little satisfied that some action was taking place.

Rafferty broke the silence: "How's your sandwich?"

"It's great. As you've probably witnessed, I usually try to eat food that is healthy, but today I needed something else. I'll just have to run another lap tomorrow."

"I figured you were a runner, or something like that. You keep yourself in good shape. I used to run until about ten years ago when my knees began aching so badly after a run, I had to give it up. I walk, but it's not the same."

"I started running when I was in college with a couple of my girlfriends. Pretty soon I found that I preferred running alone. It's a way for me to unwind, clear my head, and of course it's great exercise."

"Same reasons I enjoyed it. I played a lot of basketball when I was much younger, we didn't have the greatest shoes, and the courts I played on were more often cement or asphalt, much harder on the joints than a forgiving wooden floor. So my knees paid the price later."

"So, back to the personnel records search. Where will you start?"

"Monday morning I'll begin with the Reno Queen. As you probably know, it's closed now, but I'm sure the records are stored somewhere. I'll have to contact the former owners, and find out where that might be."

"It looks like I've created a lot of extra work for you."

"Police work is what it is, and it's all I know. Believe it or not, even after all these years, there's not much about it I truly dislike."

"So, unless I hear from you before, shall we meet again next Friday?"

"Sounds good."

They said their good-byes, and walked to their cars.

Chapter 47

Hillary headed home, with a quick stop at the grocery store. Rafferty decided not to go back to the station. Instead he elected to go home early and surprise Jill with a dinner invitation. They hadn't been out for a while, and it looked like he was going to be pretty busy for quite some time. Maybe they'd go to their favorite place. It was called "Rapscallion's". It was noted for great seafood, but had added big, juicy steaks in the last few years. They also had a fine wine list.

Jill was surprised when he walked in the door in mid afternoon, and when he mentioned Rapscallion's, she was more surprised. She asked him, "what's the special occasion?" He said, "nothing. We haven't been out anywhere special for quite a while, and I thought you deserved a *real* date." Jill smiled, kissed him, and said, "I'll go and get ready."

While Jill was primping for their date, Rafferty called the restaurant to make sure there would be room for the two of them. After all, it was a Friday night. The hostess said she could squeeze them in if they could make it there by 6:30. Rafferty told her they'd be there.

They arrived about 6:20, their table was already available. Rapscallions had been in business for over 25 years. It was rich with old, polished wood. The booths were separted by stained glass partitions. The lighting was kept low, making the stark white tablecloths set with white china stand out. The waiters wore white jackets as well, completing the feeling of simple elegance. They were seated in a booth near the rear, semi-private, very pleasant. Jill wore her favorite dress. It was pink, with a scooped neckline, sleeveless, and reached just below her knees. She purchased the dress over ten years ago, and it still fit her well. She was a woman who believed in taking care of her clothes, and herself, and now she was getting her husband to join her by eating better. Rafferty leaned towards her and said, "you look very beautiful tonight." He was more in love with her now than when they married over 30 years ago.

Their waiter arrived, greeted them, gave them menus, and explained the specials. Tonight, in addition to their regular menu, they had fresh Dungeness Crab from the Oregon coast, trout from the rivers in Idaho, and Coho Salmon from the streams of Oregon, which had just arrived this morning. He then took their drink orders. Jill decided on glass of Clos du Bois Chardonnay, and Rafferty a glass of Rodney Strong Cabernet.

When their waiter left, Rafferty asked Jill, "we're not going to worry about my diet tonight, are we?" Jill smiled broadly, saying, "what diet?"

Their waiter came and Jill ordered the seared Sea Bass, with long grained brown rice with thinly slice shitake mushrooms and shallots, and asparagus spears sautéed in white wine, garlic, and butter. Rafferty had decided on the Crab, with garlic mashed potatoes, and brazed broccoli.

While they waited, and sipped their wine, Rafferty told his bride about Hillary Fisk. He remarked how intelligent she was, and how much he enjoyed their Friday discussions. Jill teased; "Should I be worried about her?" Rafferty playfully replied; "Well, I am pretty irresistible."

Dinner came. It was delicious, as they knew it would be. They talked the whole time they ate about their everyday lives, his work, their daughter, son-in-law, and the grandkids.

They left the restaurant, and drove north to the Truckee River. He found a parking place on the street. They walked along the river, holding hands, for about forty minutes, and decided it was time to go home. Rafferty thought to himself, "sometimes life is just plain wonderful."

CHAPTER 48

Peg Barrow was feeling pretty good about her life. She was on her way to achieving her goals at the Legend. Although Dale was her friend, and she missed him, with his demise, she had moved up the food chain. Her personal life was only getting better. Her husband of seventeen years was not interested in her anymore, and that was great. She no longer had to perform her wifely duties, because all he cared about was sports, and his fantasy teams. That, mixed with his alcohol consumption, insured that their bedroom was a place for sleep and nothing else. Bev had become the answer to all her physical and emotional needs. A couple of years ago her life was miserable. But things change, and for her, they were becoming everything she had hoped for.

Only one thing remained that was a little irritating. Her intentional close relationship with Carl had developed into a somewhat more than casual association with Larry

Columbo. She disliked him intensely. He was a drug addict, completely immoral, and an entirely committed womanizer. But he was the man with all the power. She would have to endure her encounters with him to ensure her ambitions. Carl's close, family like relationship with Larry, meant that she would have to join in certain activities she was not comfortable with.

She despised her job. With the exception of a few, she thought the dealers were greedy and without talent. But, it was her chosen profession, therefore she enjoyed making their pitiful lives as miserable as possible. She and Carl were totally aligned with their opinions about the dealers. He considered most of the dealers useless as well. When she reported a problem, he never doubted her, never investigated further. She could administer punishment to whomever she pleased, no questions asked, and always had his full support.

Chapter 49

Michael watched Peg very closely whenever he could. At work, he observed her spending more time with Carl than she had previously. Whenever Larry Columbo showed up, the three were inseparable. When he was able to follow her outside the casino he observed how she continued to keep her relationship with Bev very secretive. Most of the times she met Bev after work, they left in Bev's car and went to her apartment. Sometimes they just had a drink or two, and went their separate ways.

Michael's work was definitely better. The dice games were busier, and, because he was on an earlier shift, his crew was better. The money was still good. Now Michael could focus on the things that were important.

He had vacation time coming, and he needed to get away and clear his head, to think. Now that it was fall, he should be able to get time off if he requested it. A week would be nice, just to get away from the Legend. He put in his request for the first week of October. In a few days, the scheduler told him he was approved.

Chapter 50

Rafferty tracked down the former owners of the Reno Queen. They were an old Reno family who had also owned another small casino, and were partners in two others. They were two brothers, their last name was Williams, and they were in the phone book.

Rafferty made a call to the Keith Williams' home in mid morning on Monday following his Friday meeting with Hillary. It was answered on the second ring. A woman's voice said, "Williams residence". Rafferty said, "Good Morning, is this Mrs. Williams?" "Yes, it is, who's calling?"

"This is detective David Rafferty with the Reno Police Department."

"Is something wrong, detective?"

"No, nothing at all. I'm just looking for your husband. I'm hoping he'll have some information that might help me with something I'm working on. Is he available?"

"I'm afraid not. He left early this morning with his brother to look at some property in Mammoth Lakes. He won't be back until this evening."

"Would you give him my numbers, and ask him to call me at his convenience?"

"Surely. Might I tell him what it's about?"

"I just need some records from the Reno Queen."

"Alright, I'll tell him."

Rafferty gave her his office and cell numbers, and they said their good-byes.

He wanted to go to the Nevada Gold, personally, but if they refused his request, and he was forced to get a court order, he would have wasted time.

He called Human Resources, told the person who answered what he needed, and was put on hold. The next voice her heard was the Human Resources Manager. "This is Steven Bishop, how may I help you?"

"Good morning, this is detective David Rafferty with the Reno Police Department. I am working on a case that requires a list of your employees from about fifteen years ago."

"That's a lot of years, and hundreds of employees. And this is protected information which I can't release without an order signed by a judge."

"I don't need anything but names, no addresses, phone numbers, names only."

"I understand, but I can't do it without legal authorization."

"Rafferty said, I understand. I'll take care of it. I wouldn't want you to do something you were uncomfortable with. Thank you for your time, Mr. Bishop. I'll be talking to you soon."

"Have a good day detective."

Rafferty decided he'd better get busy. He would need to request a separate order for each property. He decided he should make a call to Hillary, letting her know that this idea of hers would take some time, but he was working on it.

Chapter 51

When Michael got off at 3 a.m. on Monday night, he felt a sense of relief. For nine days he would not have to enter the doors of the Legend. As did the Pot of Gold, the Legend gave vacation tokes, so if he needed money, he would come in at two in the morning, but he would only have to be there a few minutes, and he wouldn't have to be on the casino floor. The "toke room" was in the basement.

When he woke up just before noon on Tuesday morning, he made a list of things he would need on his vacation. He would have to purchase a few things he didn't have. He would need to make another trip to Sacramento. He'd go there tomorrow. Tonight, he would be outside the Legend when Peg got off work.

She walked out the same way she did previously, and went to the Diablo. She headed for the same bar and waited for Bev to get off. They walked out together, they found a spot to kiss good-bye, and went their separate ways. This was Michael's chance to find out where Peg lived. He had parked his car on a side street, in a spot where he could see Peg's Taurus. He had to quickly take a circuitous route to his car, so he wouldn't be seen.

He got to his own car just in time to see Peg drive hers out of the lot. She drove east to Center Street, turned left, and got on I-80. She stayed to the right and proceeded to the lane that would allow her to transfer to 395 north. She drove for about a mile, and exited on north McCarran. She turned right, and continued on McCarran until it intersected with Pyramid Highway. She turned left, drove for about five miles to Spanish Springs, where Michael had stopped to get something to eat and drink when he was returning from Pyramid Lake. She turned left on Eagle Canyon Road, went through two roundabouts, and, when she reached Spanish Springs High School, turned right on a street named Mercedes, She parked on the curb in front of the fifth house on the right. The house was dark. Maybe her husband wasn't home yet. Michael wondered what he did for a living? He could probably find out from another dealer at work. He watched her unlock the front door, close it, and a light came on in the front window.

Satisfied with what he had learned, he returned home. He had a lot to think about. It was always in the planning.

The next morning, he left for Sacramento about nine. He arrived in less than three hours. He hadn't stopped this time. After he purchased what he needed, he found an IHOP, and had a quick breakfast of bacon, eggs, and pancakes. He drove right back to Reno, and was home just after 3:30.

Although he was tired, Michael left his apartment Thursday at 1 a.m. to see what Peg was up to after work. She would be off the next two days, so he had to learn all that he could learn.

As she had before, she went to the Diablo. She walked right to the game Bev was dealing, waved at her, and did something different. She turned around and headed for the back door. She almost ran into him. He had to quickly move behind a row of slot machines to avoid being seen. He stayed where he was until Bev was pushed off her game. She immediately headed towards the same door. Michael hurried behind her. When she stepped outside, Peg's car was waiting at the curb. Bev jumped in, and they took off. Michael couldn't be certain where they were going, he could only guess.

He went to his car and decided to drive to Peg's house. Because when they went to Bev's apartment, she usually drove, he was playing a hunch. When he got to her house on Mercedes, the Taurus was parked in front. His first thought was that Peg's husband must work graveyard. Then he considered the possibility that he just wouldn't be coming home tonight. Very interesting.

He knew now that he had to learn more about Peg's husband. He wasn't due back to work for a week. The answer came to him right away. He would go in Friday morning at 2 a.m. to get his tokes. There were plenty of dealers he would see who had an extreme dislike for Peg. He was sure to get some information from one of them.

Chapter 52

By Thursday morning, Rafferty had all his requests for the information he needed from the casinos ready to be taken to the judge. On Tuesday, he had received a call back from Keith Williams. He said the files were stored in a warehouse, but a court order would be needed for Rafferty to have access to them. Some of the more recent cases meant that only a few year's records would be needed, but the whole process would be mind numbing, and take quite a while.

He had a great relationship with several judges, but he knew judge Sylvia Weinburg the best. She was a fair, and conscientious judge, but, as long as all the *I's* were dotted and the *T's* were crossed, she believed the police should be allowed to do their job. Rafferty called her law clerk just before 9 a.m., and asked if the judge could see him sometime that day. He was put on hold. A few minutes later, the clerk came back on the phone, telling him she could spare a few minutes when the lunch recess began around 12:30. He said he'd be there.

Rafferty believed in being extra courteous to judges. He arrived at 12:15, just in case the recess was early, and he could get out of the judge's way quickly so she could enjoy her lunch. Her law clerk took him to the judges chambers. Judge Weinburg walked in about 12:25. He stood and shook her outstretched hand. She told him to take a seat. Judge Sylvia Weinburg was 55 years old, about 5 feet 7 inches tall, but carried herself as a woman of 35, and therefore appeared much taller than she actually was. She sat behind a one hundred year old oak desk, and, as she always did, got right to the matter at hand.

Rafferty said, "Thanks for seeing me so soon, judge, you know I appreciate it."

Judge Weinburg replied, "I've know you a long time, I figured it must be important."

"I appreciate it. It *is* important to me. I think I've accidentally discovered a series of very serious crimes committed over quite a long period of time."

"Could you give me a brief story line?"

"I'll be as brief as possible. I've been investigating two murders, both casino employees. Detective Bennet is working on another case, also casino related. One of mine is from the Shangri La, one from the Legend. Detective Bennet's is also from the Legend. A professor from the university has been researching crimes involving casinos, and she, and I, both believe that someone has been committing murder for years. We want to see the employment records from the casinos involved for those time periods. We believe we will find a single name that will be on all those lists."

"Interesting. So, were all the murders committed in the same manner?"

"No, and that's why no one thought there was a link between them. I don't believe in coincidence. There are too many, and all of them were never solved. I will only be asking for names, at least right now. I need no other personal information."

"I have no problem with that. You will have plenty to keep you busy for a while. I'll sign the orders this afternoon. You can pick them up in the morning."

"Thanks, judge. I appreciate your swift response. And, you're right, I won't have much idle time."

"Good day, detective. Nice to see you again."

"Same goes for me, judge."

Rafferty walked out of the courthouse and back to his car thinking, "I hope I get all of this done before I retire."

Chapter 53

Michael had a lot of time on his hands. He had nothing happening in his life other than work. There was much to plan, much to do, and these were the only things that were important.

He had learned a great deal about Peg and her habits. He needed to acquire more information about Carl, and even Larry Columbo. That might be difficult. He and Columbo did not travel in the same circles. And Carl was not someone he had developed any kind of relationship with. He knew Carl liked him, at least for his abilities on the dice game. He would have to find a way and get closer to him.

He had talked to a couple of the part time female dealers about Peg's husband when he picked up some of his tokes. Veronica had known Peg in two other casinos as well, where she was also disliked. Peg had been married about ten years. Her husband worked for the railroad, and was sometimes gone for several days. Veronica had never met him, never seen him in one of the casinos where Peg worked. The only personal thing she knew about him was that he was several years older than Peg.

Michael had three more days before he had to return to work. He spent a lot of his time diagramming Peg and Bev's routine. He had easily found out her husband's schedule. Amtrak didn't vary from its regular routes.

When Michael went back to work on Thursday, the dice pit only had three games. A roulette game had been moved into the empty space created by its removal. He looked at the main "21" pit. There it was, right in the middle of the front side. His first thought was, "that's the dumbest fucking thing I've ever seen." Dice games are noisy and having one in the pit would ruin the quiet conversation on the card games. In addition, it is common for dice to fly off the table. The edges are sharp, and can actually cut someone. And what would happen if a die hit someone in the eye? He knew this had to be Carl's idea. He just wasn't very bright. Which gave him an idea.

The next time Carl came into the dice pit Michael decided to put his plan into action. When he got pushed out for a break, he walked up to Carl, and said, "moving the dice game was your idea, wasn't it?" Carl said, "yes it was".

Michael: "Very creative."

Carl: "I hoped being in the pit would encourage more players, maybe some new players, to try their luck."

"I'm sure it'll work"

"I think it will."

Michael headed down to the break room positive Carl had believed the bullshit he had just handed him.

Two breaks later, Michael was sitting by himself in the break room, when Carl came in. He ordered some food, saw Michael, and sat down with him. Carl started talking about how he'd been losing weight. Michael told him he noticed. He said he had been on the "Atkin's" diet. All he had been eating was protein. He had just ordered a steak. He continued talking about diets, and food. Michael pretended to care, but was thinking that he was the most boring man in the world. Several minutes later, it was time for him to go back to his game. He wanted to run, not walk.

CHAPTER 54

Hillary was still spending a lot of time ruminating about what she now thought of as hers and Rafferty's cases. She was one hundred percent sure that if there was one killer, he, or she, had to be a pit supervisor or a dealer. It all fit together. With the exception of the five "regulars" who were poisoned, all the deceased worked on or around the table games, and the five had all been seen playing on dice games. She would call Rafferty and ask if he was thinking the same way.

She wondered what type of person could commit all these murders. She read a couple of online articles from FBI profilers. They didn't give her much insight. Serial killers seldom have distinct qualities that make them obvious suspects. There were only a few characteristics that all of them shared. They are almost always men, and once they are discovered, most had been members of dysfunctional families, and were likely to be anti-social". She saw how difficult David's job could be.

The next morning, before she had time to call David, her phone rang. It was him. He had received the records from the Reno Queen, and would start copying personnel records that afternoon. She told him about her assumption that they were looking for a pit supervisor or dealer, and he told her he had come to the same conclusion. This would help a little, eliminating records from other departments. He told her he hoped to have all the records from all the casinos by the end of the week.

Chapter 55

Whenever Carl was around, on the casino floor, or in the employee's cafeteria, Michael made sure he talked to him or at least said hello. After about a week, Carl started hanging around Michael when he worked, and even walked with him to and from the break room. Michael had to force himself to pay attention to what he was saying. Carl's ego was bigger than the casino itself, and Michael was subtly inflating it even more.

Because of the hours Michael worked, he ate his dinner on his third break, somewhere around ten or eleven in the evening. About ten days after he began his plan to get closer to Carl, he was sitting alone in the employee's dining room when Carl came up and asked if he could join him. Michael said "sure", certain he sounded very pleased. Carl talked about the job, his diet, the same old stuff for about five minutes. Then he said, "some of us get together once in a while to unwind and have a little fun, would you be interested in joining us?" Michael kept what he felt was a big smile to a small grin, and said, "sure". This was more than Michael had hoped for.

Chapter 56

Late in the same afternoon, Rafferty received the files from the Nevada Gold. He looked over the content, and saw that their files were much larger than the Reno Queen. He knew that the Nevada Gold was a casino that hired many more people in a year than most, but he hadn't anticipated how many more. He put them aside, and went home. He would tackle them first thing in the morning.

Chapter 57

Rafferty finished both of the casino's files in one day. Only three names had worked at them both around the time of the murders. There was a female games supervisor, Talia Rosen, a male supervisor, Walter Grayson, and a dealer, Michael Whitten. The files from the Shangri La were to arrive tomorrow, and the Legend's the following day.

That afternoon he decided to call Hillary. It was Wednesday, and they were going to meet on Friday, but he wanted her to be up to date on his progress. She answered on the third ring.

"Hello, this is Hillary Fisk."

"Hi Hillary, it's me, David. How are you?"

"I'm fine. I was just thinking about our Friday lunch."

"I'm looking forward to it, but I thought I'd get you up to speed ahead of time, I'm getting the last of the files that day, and am anxious to get to them, so our lunch will be brief."

"Why don't you tell me what you've discovered so far, and we skip lunch? If you'd like to, you could even call me on the weekend."

"Maybe that's a good idea. Here's what I know so far. I've finished the first two casinos, and have three names, two men and one woman. To be frank with you, I don't believe it's a woman, but I can't rule her out. Tomorrow I get the third set of files, and, as I was saying, the last on Friday."

"You've made quick progress! Why don't we plan a Wednesday lunch next week? Do you think you'll have them all done by then?"

"I should. If I don't think that will happen. I'll call you Monday, and we'll plan another time."

"Sounds great. I wish there was some way I could help you."

"Me too. But, with these files under the control of a court order, and the rules of privacy, that's not possible."

"Okay. See you Wednesday."

"Bye."

Rafferty always felt better after a conversation with his young cohort. She was bright, and had a zeal that he could easily relate to.

CHAPTER 58

The next Saturday night Michael worked, Carl stopped him as he was leaving the pit on his break. He told him that next Thursday would be the night for his group's little party. It would be held in one of the penthouse suites on the top floor of the Legend. Carl would make sure Michael had the night off. The party would start about nine.

When Carl left, Michael was excited about next Thursday. He wondered who would be there. He was sure that Larry Columbo, and Peg would be there, but who else was in their group?

Everything was ready. He had planned well. Now it was simply the where and when he could take action. He was sure it wouldn't be long until he could empty some of the blackness growing inside of him.

CHAPTER 59

When Michael woke up Thursday morning, he found he had forgotten something. Other than his suits he had purchased when he was a pit boss at the Shangri La, he didn't own any clothes other than levis, sweat pants, and shorts. He would have to purchase a pair of slacks, some sort of shirt, and dress shoes.

He didn't want to spend the money, but he decided he had to go to the mall where he would find "Macy's". They had two stores in the mall, one primarily offering women's apparell, and the other offering men's.

He shopped for about fifteen minutes, and came to the unsettling conclusion that he would have to spend over one hundred and fifty dollars. He selected a pair of grey slacks, and a long sleeve shirt that was grey with thin vertical black, red, and dark grey stripes. In the shoe department, he found a pair of black loafers. When the cashier rang it all up, he had spent one hundred and seventy five dollars, not including tax.

He started getting ready for the party about 8:30 that evening. He planned to get there around 9:15. Although it was a short walk, he thought he should take his car and park it behind the Legend. You never knew what might happen.

At twelve minutes after nine he got in the elevator, pressed the top button, and rode up to the penthouse floor. There were four, and Carl had told Michael it would be in number three. He swung the brass knocker, and a few seconds later Carl opened the door. He invited him in, shook his hand, and said, "I'm glad you could make it, Michael". He led him over to meet their host, Larry Columbo. Larry was about 6 feet 5 inches tall, dark hair and dark eyes, definitely Italian in descent. Michael immediately felt Larry possessed an arrogance and an aire of superiority which would make him unpleasant to be around. They exchanged greetings, and then Carl led him to a table filled with seafood, terryiaki steaks on a stick, meatballs made from ground Kobe beef, rumaki with bacon slices thicker than he had ever seen, pastries, and almost anything else he might desire. Then he took him to the bar, where a bartender offered everything from beer, wine, twelve year old scotch, rare bourbons, Grey Goose and Kettle One vodka, and Padrino and Cabo Wabo tequila. Then Carl left him on his own. Surveying the room, he saw Peg in a far corner, talking with three female dealers from his shift, Christine, Debra, and Sandra. In another corner he saw a dice dealer he worked with whose name was Danny. He didn't know anyone else by name, but he recognized a few pit bosses from day shift and graveyard, as well as a few dealers. There were about 25 people in all.

Michael ordered a Johnnie Walker Black on the rocks, went to the food table and filled a plate with shrimp scampi, a couple of terryiaki steak skewers, and some pastries filled with a raspberry cream. He decided to be as invisible as possible, at least for now, so he introduced himself to the day shift people, all the while observing Peg, Larry, and Carl. They remembered him from his short time on the day shift dice crew, but none ever got to know him, not even his name.

After ten minutes of small talk, mostly about the casino, Michael was totally bored. He made his getaway by announcing that he had to use the "little boy's room". He washed his face and hands, and prepared to rejoin the group. Danny was talking with Christine, Debra, and Sandra. Michael walked over to them, figuring he might hear some gossip that would be of use to him later. Peg had joined Larry and Carl, becoming the familiar "gruesome threesome".

Michael had never talked to the women before, he knew their names because they were all high limit dealers, and on the toke committee. Danny introduced them. Christine spoke first; "How come we haven't talked before?"

Michael said; "I guess we just never had the opportunity. So, tell me, how long have these parties been going on?"

"I guess it's been about a year. We've been having them once a month."

"Is it always the same people?"

"You're the first addition to our group in a very long time. We lost a couple. Dale had been a part of it, and Mitch too. No one even knows about them unless they've been invited."

"So, is it just for fun, or is there an agenda as well?"

"I'm not sure what you mean by 'agenda'."

"I was wondering if this was something like a think tank."

"Oh. No, not officially, but we do get into discussions about the casino."

"That's good. Sometimes things need to be changed. I'm glad Larry and Carl want our input."

"We're all trusted by them. They don't feel the same about any of the other people in the pit."

Michael excused himself to get another drink.

The rest of the night was mostly light conversation. He talked, or actually listened, to Larry and Carl ramble on about upcoming events which included a chance for them to leer at scantily clad young girls in one, and "biker chicks" in the other some of whom wore only halter tops, and chaps with nothing more than a thong underneath them. Peg joined them for a few minutes, but said little. Michael was gaining a new respect for actors. This wasn't easy for him. He wasn't social in the slightest, he was a true loner, and proud of it. But, he was making it work.

Mercifully, the party broke up around 2:30 in the morning. Larry, Carl, and Christine, as well as a few from the other shifts, were pretty drunk. He had observed them gulping down one drink after another. He had also seen Larry, Carl, Peg, Christine and Danny disappear into another room for short periods of time. He was certain they were doing drugs of some sort. Everyone has a vice or two.

As he said his good-byes to Larry and Carl, Carl said, "we decided to do this again in a couple of weeks. We usually do it once a month, but lots of things are coming up in the casino, and we thought we should have a little fun when we could". Michael said, "great, thanks again for the invitation". Two weeks would be just fine.

CHAPTER 60

At one o'clock on Friday afternoon, Rafferty had all the files he needed. He was beginning to feel his age, exhausted after the tedious job of going through hundreds of files. As he began reading through the files from the Shangri La, he was not pleased. They were not well organized. Whoever put them in the box did not care if they were even in chronological order. When he got the files from the Legend, they were almost as bad. Rafferty had to put them in proper order before he could begin his search. He finished around 4 o'clock on Friday afternoon. He'd had enough. He was going home to his bride, a comfortable chair, and maybe a vodka martini. He might have to work on Saturday, but for today, he was done. His brain was fried.

Before he left for the day, he called Hillary to update her on his progress. There was no answer on her office phone. He called her cell, got her voicemail, recorded a brief message, and left for home to be with his bride.

He had called Jill to let her know he would be home a little early. She told him he sounded tired on the phone. He admitted he was. When he got home, she greeted him with the vodka martini he had wished for. She handed him his drink, smiled, and kissed him. He inhaled the wonderful aroma of garlic in the kitchen. She saw him react, and said, "we're having one of your favorites, roasted garlic chicken with wild rice and asparagus." His day was rough, but his night was going to be wonderful.

Chapter 61

Rafferty decided not to go in on Saturday to review the files. He was mentally tired to the point that he couldn't organize his thoughts. Monday morning, he arrived at 7 a.m., "Peets" coffee in hand, ready to tackle the boxes next to, and the pile on, his desk. He finished the files from the Shangri La around noon. He decided he should have something to eat, so he left the station and walked west towards the downtown casinos. Two blocks away was a small Vietnamese restaurant. He had a chicken and vegetable dish he had never heard of, with rice and tea. It was good, not great, but he was satisfied. He walked back to the station, and got ready to tackle the last of the files, those from the Legend.

He worked until 6 o'clock, and still had about a six inch stack to go. He would finish them tomorrow morning, and put together his summary.

CHAPTER 62

Michael found it hard to concentrate on his work Monday. Thankfully, he wasn't very busy. It was only a week from Thursday until the next party. He was glad he had the next two days off. He would be spending all of his time with the final planning and preparation for what he believed would be his best day ever.

He didn't even mind that he had to spend more money on another shirt to wear to the party. He could get away with the same slacks and shoes, but he definitely couldn't wear the same shirt. He went back to Macy's and purchased a beautiful, and expensive, red silk shirt. It cost him 95 dollars, but it felt great against his skin, and he was about to accomplish something fantastic, he should feel good.

Chapter 63

Tuesday morning Rafferty was at his desk finishing up a task he almost wished he hadn't started. He worked quickly, and just after 11 a.m., he finished the last of the files. It took only a few minutes to put the results together. Only two men had worked at all four casinos. They were a games supervisor by the name of Walter Grayson, and a dealer, who had also been a supervisor at the Shangri La, by the name of Michael Whitten.

Rafferty made a simple inquiry to the state agency that issued work cards to all employees who worked in the pits, the Nevada Gaming Commission. He discovered both were single men. Grayson was forty four years old, and had been born in Carson City. Whitten was forty five, and had moved to Nevada in the mid eighties, obtaining his first gaming license in 1986. Next, Rafferty had to find out what shifts they worked, within a precise time period when they had been at each casino. He was optimistic the Human Resources departments would give him this information without another court order. Hopefully, they would accept the current document as a license to divulge additional, and minor, information.

He called Hillary to confirm their lunch tomorrow. He got her voice mail that told him she was in class today. He left a message telling her if things worked out, that by the end of the day, he would have one of the men more suspect than the other.

Chapter 64

When Hillary got back to her office, and listened to the message from David, she had an idea. She would call her friend, the General Manager of the Stagecoach, Larry Hall.

He answered on the second ring; "This is Larry Hall."

"Hi Mr. Hall, it's Hillary Fisk from the university."

"Hi Hillary, and remember, it's Larry. What can I do for you?"

"I don't know if you'll want to, but I need a small favor."

"I'll be happy to help you if I can."

"I need some information about a couple of casino employees. I don't know if either of them ever worked at the Stagecoach, so I'd be asking you to get information from other casinos. I thought that someone in your position would receive less reluctance than someone not in the industry."

"What kind of information? There are certain things that will not be released even to me."

"I need to know what shifts they worked during certain time periods."

"That shouldn't be too difficult. How many casinos, and how many people are we talking about?

"There are just two men, and four casinos, though I'm more interested in two of them, the Shangri La, and the Legend."

"I know people in HR in both. I think they would be willing to give me what I ask. The information is not extraordinary."

"I appreciate this Larry, it will really help."

"This isn't about your class, is it?"

"No, it's something else. Something that may be much more important."

"I'll see what I can do. Give me the particulars, and I'll call you in a couple of days."

Hillary thanked him, gave him the two names, and an approximate time period for the two casinos.

CHAPTER 65

Hillary was very anxious. She arrived for her lunch with David almost twenty minutes early. She took a table, and ordered a glass of iced tea, and waited for David's arrival.

He walked in five minutes early himself. Hillary made eye contact right away, waved, and he walked to the table. She got up, was going to shake his hand, and he surprised her, he gave her a short and gentle hug. They sat, exchanged greetings, and looked over the menus to order right away, as usual.

As soon as the waitress took their order, Hillary couldn't wait any longer to tell him what she'd done.

"I've got some news, and I hope it will help. Remember a while back when I told you I met the General Manager of the Stagecoach?"

"Yes I do."

"Well, I called and asked him to find out the shifts our two men worked. He felt confident he could get the information from the Shangri La, and the Legend."

"That's great. I feel we're so close, every bit of information will help us. When will he get back to you?"

"He said in a couple of days, I''m hoping by this weekend."

"The sooner the better. The casinos have been reluctant to give me any more information than what was specifically spelled out in the orders from the court. So, how have you been?"

"Good. But I have to admit I've been feeling restless, and not of much use to you."

"Most of this was your idea to begin with. And, you couldn't help me with the files. The help from your friend could be a breakthrough."

Their lunches came, and they talked about more personal things. David told Hillary about Jill, how and when they met while undergrads at UNR, what a great person she was, and about their daughter and their grandchildren.

Hillary told him about how she had been in love only once, in her senior year of college. But, then she had decided to go onto grad school, and he was offered a teaching job at a high school in Arizona. He was in debt with several student loans, and needed to get to work. They considered a long distance romance, but they proved that never works.

When their dishes were cleared, they felt they might as well leave. Hillary said she would call him the second she heard from Larry.

They hugged, gently, once again, and said their good-byes.

Chapter 66

Peg sat alone in her backyard deep in thought. Her husband was on a train, doing his job, and Bev was visiting her sister in southern California. She didn't know how much more she could take. She loathed Larry, and had learned to dislike Carl intensely. She had no problem with their attitudes about work and the casino, but personally they were extremely unpleasant to be around. She was "in the click", and sure that her efforts would produce the result she so wanted, to be a shift manager at the Legend.

The worst was that in less than a week she would have to endure another one of their little parties. She didn't mind most of the people, but she didn't really consider any of them friends. She enjoyed the good food, and the choice of the finest alcohol, but she wasn't really into the drugs. They didn't make her feel good, just a little sick to her stomach, and therefore a little dizzy. She took as little as possible, just enough to make sure Larry and Carl believed she was one of them.

She would have enjoyed these evenings a lot more if she could have Bev along to keep her company. Of course, that was impossible. If they knew she preferred women over men, they would certainly shun her. She would be in a worse position than she was before she made her new "friends". She would have to attend the party, of course. But she wouldn't do any more drugs with them. She might just refuse, or maybe she could fake it.

Chapter 67

Monday morning Hillary received her call from Larry Hall. She was going through some of her student's papers about nine o'clock. She answered on the first ring.

"This is Hillary Fisk."

"Good morning Hillary, it's Larry. Sorry I haven't gotten back to you sooner, we've been very busy here, and it seemed like I was constantly putting out fires."

"That's okay, Larry, I sincerely appreciate any information you could get for me."

"It was really not difficult at all. I got a call back from my friend at the Legend on Thursday, and my other friend from the Shangri La on Friday. They were more than happy to give me the little information I needed."

Hillary wrote everything down, word for word, thanked him extensively, and said good-bye.

She phoned David immediately. He, too, answered on the first ring.

"Good morning, this is Detective Rafferty. How may I help you?"

"Good morning, David. It's Hillary. I just got off the phone with Larry, and he gave me the answers to my questions. Could we meet in a couple of hours for lunch? I'd prefer to give you everything in person."

"Sure, how about our usual place around eleven thirty?"

"Sounds perfect, see you then."

At 11:25, both Hillary and David pulled into the parking lot. They walked into the Gold and Silver together. They were now known as "regular patrons", so the waitress took them to a booth in a corner, so they could talk in private. When they were seated, she took their order immediately. They both decided to have a chef's salad and iced tea.

When she left, Hillary pulled out the paper that contained Larry's information.

"Both Walter Grayson, and Michael Whitten worked swing shift at the Shangri La around the time Vanessa Stryker was murdered. They were both games supervisors. Grayson was there until a year after she was killed. Whitten resigned just before she died. Grayson worked at the Legend as a supervisor for less than a year. He was on graveyard. Whitten started there over four years ago on Day shift, transferred to swing, and is still there. He is a dice dealer."

David let this sink in for a few minutes. When he finally spoke, he said; "What you've told me tends to point to Michael Whitten, but we can't be sure until I do some investigation into their personal history. It will be easier now that I can label them both as suspects."

"That's exactly what I thought you'd say.

Their salads came. They took a couple of bites, and David spoke; "When this is all done, soon, I hope, why don't you come over and have dinner with Jill and me?"

"I'd love to meet her. Sounds like a great idea."

They chatted about Reno, the surrounding area that both believed had the greatest weather in the world. She told him more about her classes, the great students she had, and her growing love for the "greatest little university" in the world. He told her about his education at UNR, and how he played on the basketball team. He wasn't a star, but those were times he'd never forget.

They finished, left together, hugged each other near their cars, both filled with excitement and anxiety that their detective work was coming to an end.

Chapter 68

Tuesday morning, Rafferty got to his office just after 7:30. He wanted to get to judge Weinburg's office before court convened at nine. He got his paperwork together, separate requests for each man, and walked to the courthouse.

He got there before 8:30. He took the elevator to the sixth floor. Her outer office door was open. Her clerk was at his desk. Rafferty asked him if he could have a few minutes of the judge's time. He went in to ask her. He stepped right back out, and said, "Come right in, detective". Sylvia Weinburg greeted him, not yet in her robe. She wore a pale blue suit, black pumps, very little make-up or jewelry. As always, she was all business. She told him to have a seat on the sofa, and she sat on the opposite end.

Judge Weinburg said; "You must have gotten some results from the orders I signed for you weeks ago."

"I did, judge. And once again, thank you very much. I now have two suspects related to several murders. I need to have permission to search more deeply into their backgrounds so I can narrow it down to one."

"I see. And what brought you to the conclusion one of your suspects is a murderer?"

"Mostly the opportunity. Each of them was working for the casinos at or around the time the murders were committed. I believe the motive will be more defined as I investigate further."

"I'll be honest with you, detective, if I didn't know you so well, and if you hadn't always been one hundred percent honest with me, I might not consider signing any more papers, based on the slim evidence you have at this time. But, I also believe that the instincts of a good detective, mixed with solid police work can produce results the district attorney would eagerly accept. I know from the DA's office that cases you were involved in, produced a conviction rate of over ninety percent. So, I'll read these over on my lunch break. Unless you hear from me to the contrary, you can pick them up after 4:30 this afternoon."

"Thanks again, judge. I won't abuse your trust."

Rafferty picked up his papers precisely at 4:30. He knew where he could locate Whitten, so his search would begin for Grayson's present employment, and his residence.

Wednesday morning, he started with his last known employment, the Legend. He went to human resources, and showed the manager his documents. His name was Fred Alcott. He asked him if he'd wait a minute. They had been updating their system, and most of their employee records were now on disc. Five minutes later, he returned. He had printed out the year's record for Rafferty. Rafferty thanked Alcott, and returned to his office.

He first looked for his address. He lived in an apartment across from Meadowood Mall, aptly named, the "Meadowood Apartments". He found a phone number listed. He dialed it, but only received a message on an answer phone, telling him, "you've reached Walter Grayson, leave a message at the beep". He read on. His graveyard shift supervisor, Greg Sherwood, had put notes in his file. Grayson had been a good employee, and had given two weeks notice. He had been offered a positon as assistant shift manager on graveyard at Peyton Place. Rafferty took a chance and called their human resources office. He identified himself as detective Rafferty of the RPD, and asked to speak to the manager. A few seconds later a woman's voice came on the line and said, "this is Marjorie Helms, manager of human resources. How may I help you?"

"Good Morning Ms. Helms, this is detective David Rafferty with the RPD. I need your help. Is this a good time?"

"It depends, what can I do for you?"

"I only have one question, I need to know if someone is still in the employ of Peyton Place. I have an idea. Let me give you the number of the RPD switchboard. If you'll call and ask to be transferred to me, you'll at least know that this call is legitimate."

"You're sure that's all the information you need?"

"Yes, for now. If I need more, I'll bring the necessary documentation to you."

"Okay. I'll call right back."

Three minutes later, his desk phone buzzed. "Hello, Ms. Helms?"

"Detective Rafferty?"

"Yes, thank you for cooperating with me. I sincerely appreciate it."

"If that is all you need, there shouldn't be a problem."

"I simply need to know if a Walter Grayson is still working for you. The information I have is that he is on the graveyard shift."

"Yes, I know Mr. Grayson. He's the assistant shift manager, and a fine man."

"Thank you, that's all I needed to know at this time. Thank you again Ms. Helms. Have a fine day."

"You too, detective."

Rafferty would attempt to reach him by phone a few more times. If that didn't work, he might have to get up in the middle of the night, and take a drive over to Peyton Place. He knew that casino employees who worked graveyard often slept odd hours with the blinds closed, and the phones turned off.

Rafferty had a sudden thought. He put a call into Jake Simpson at the Shangri La. He was told that Mr. Simpson was out of his office, could he be given a message? Rafferty left his number. About forty five minutes later his phone rang. It was Jake Simpson. He said; "Hello, detecitve Rafferty. This is Jake Simpson. What can I do for you?"

"Thanks for calling back, Mr. Simpson. I need some information about a couple of people who worked for you."

"I'll be happy to help, if I can."

"Thanks. Do you remember a Walter Grayson?"

"Sure, he was a supervisor on swing."

"What can you tell me about him, professionally and personally?"

"Well, professionally, he was good at his job. He was efficient, reliable, and somewhat subdued, almost emotionless, as he performed his duties. Personally, I didn't know him that well. We didn't work together for a long time, and swing shift is so busy that few of us get to know each other outside of work."

"What was his relationship with Ms. Stryker?"

"I'm not sure what you mean. She was his boss."

"I mean, did they get along? Were there conflicts between them personally, or in the performance of his job?"

"He was very quiet, and he kept to himself a lot, so I can't really answer that."

"Okay, what about a Michael Whitten?"

"I knew Michael fairly well. I hired him both here and at the Pot of Gold in Sparks."

"What can you tell me about him?"

"Michael's a very good dice dealer. I'm not sure he liked being a supervisor."

"Any information about his personal life?"

"It seems strange, now that you ask, but I never saw him hang out with anyone after work. He never talked about family, a girlfriend, hobbies, nothing at all."

"What about he and Ms. Stryker?"

"The best way to describe it was 'uncomfortable'."

"Can you elaborate?"

"Well, I have good reason to believe they disliked each other."

"And why do you feel that way?"

"She gave him a write up for something, and I'm sure Michael never forgave her for it. But, even before that, they seemed to avoid each other."

"Anything else?"

"No, like I said, thinking about him now, I didn't know who he was at all."

"Thanks for your time, Mr. Simpson. If I think of anything else, I'll call you."

"Have a good day, detective."

Rafferty thought he had two strange men, loners, whose lives he had to look into. They were always the most difficult.

He had tried to call Walter Grayson at one in the afternoon, and again at three. As he was about to leave for home just before five, he gave it one more try. A groggy sounding voice said, "this is Walter."

"Mr. Grayson, my name is David Rafferty. I'm a detective for the Reno Police Department. I need to talk to you. Is this a good time?"

"I just woke up. What's this about?"

"We need to meet. When's a good time?"

"If you'll give me a reason for calling me, maybe I could find some time."

"All I can tell you over the phone is that it's about some things that happened at the casinos where you worked."

"Hmmm. I don't work tonight. I guess we could talk in an hour or so."

"That's fine. Would you like me to come to your apartment, or would you prefer to meet somewhere?"

"I've been sleeping most of the day. I need something to eat. Why don't we meet at "Chili's" on McCarran and South Virginia about seven?"

"Sounds fine. You'll know me. I'll have on a dark grey suit and blue tie. I'm around six feet tall, with grey hair."

"If I get there after you, I'm just over six feet tall, about a hundred and eighty pounds. I'll be wearing levis, and I guess a red and white striped polo shirt."

"Thanks, Mr. Grayson, see you then."

CHAPTER 69

As Michael was getting ready for work Wednesday evening, he was feeling something he seldom experienced, contentment. Tomorrow night would be a dream come true for him. He wasn't the slightest bit nervous. He would have trouble *not* showing his excitement. He was in complete control of the situation. He knew it was always in the planning, not acting out because of emotions. He was going to make changes that would affect his life, and those of many others. Too bad the others would never know what he had done for them.

Chapter 70

Rafferty arrived at Chili's right at 6 o'clock. He went inside, looked over the crowd, and spotted who he thought was Walter Grayson, immediately. Grayson looked up, saw him, and motioned for him to come over. They made the customary introductions, and sat. Grayson already had a beer. Their waiter came, and Rafferty ordered a lemonade, then changed his mind. The acid would keep him from sleeping later. He asked for ice water instead.

When the waiter brought his water, he asked if they were ready to order. Rafferty said he would have a small dinner salad, oil and vinegar on the side. Grayson, who was obviously very hungry, ordered a bacon, mushroom, cheesburger, with onion rings.

The waiter left, and Grayson spoke first; "What's this all about, detective?"

"I'm investigating some events at several casinos, and you were employed by all of them. First, let me ask you some questions of a more personal nature, if that's all right."

"I guess so."

"How old are you?"

"I'm forty four."

"Are you married?"

"I was, but that ended over five years ago."

"Do you have children?"

"One. She's nine years old."

"Lives with you, or her mother?"

"Her mother. They live in Las Vegas."

"Do you see her often?"

"No, its pretty far away. Whenever I can, I fly down there and spend a couple of days with her."

"Is your ex in the casino business?"

"Yes, she's a dealer."

"So, is she working at a casino in Vegas?"

"Yeah. She's a dealer at Luxor."

"What's your relationship with her?"

"We're divorced. She took my kid. What do you think?"

"I understand."

"How do you feel about women in general?"

"Where's this going, detective?"

"I'm just trying to get to know you better."

"Can we just cut to the chase?"

"Okay. At present, the Reno Police Department is investigating the homicides of three individuals. One from the Shangri La, and two from the Legend. You were a supervisor at both places. We need to know what you can tell us."

"I read about the two at the Legend. I didn't really know either one of them. We were on different shifts. Who was it at the Shangri La?"

"Vanessa Stryker."

"I thought that was an accident. Wasn't it something to do with her heater?"

"That's what we thought at first, but it was obviously tampered with."

"Wow!"

"How well did you know her?"

"She was my boss."

"I know that. I mean, did you get along well? Did you have any sort of personal relationship?"

"We both did our jobs. I believe we were both professionals. Personally, we had a drink or two after work at the bar, but that didn't happen very often, and it wasn't planned, it was just by chance. We both just happened to be there at the same time."

"Was there a physical attraction between the two of you?"

Grayson chuckled. "That's funny."

"Why is that funny?"

"She was the only one that I ever told, at least at the Shangri La. I'm gay."

"Is that what caused your divorce?"

"Yeah. I couldn't play the role any longer. I knew it was a mistake when we married, but I was afraid. My ex, Barbara, and I had been friends all through high school. We went to different colleges for a couple of years, she at UNR, and I went to USF. We both dropped out, and got reacquainted in the casinos. One thing led to another, and we got married. I was more afraid of coming out than of living a lie. Now, she's bitter, not that I can blame her. Life is what it is. I just try to get by one day at a time."

"I'm truly sorry, Mr. Grayson. Life can be tough. One last thing. Can you think of anyone who might have wished Ms. Stryker harm?"

"Not really. I mean, she wasn't real well liked, but no one who would want to take her life."

"Thanks, Mr. Grayson, if you think of anything else, please call me. And If I have any more questions, I'll be in touch."

Rafferty put a ten dollar bill on the table, handed him his card, and told him he was sorry for taking up his time, said good-bye, and left.

He doubted that Grayson was a murderer who would take his misery out on others. So, he was pretty sure he was down to Whitten. He'd work on him tomorrow. But, he was a good detective. He would check Grayson's story.

He thought about calling Hillary, but it was a little late, and he knew she had an 8:30 class in the morning. Maybe he'd try to get hold of her before her class started.

Chapter 71

Michael woke up at nine on Thursday morning. He just couldn't sleep. He gave into his emotions, got up, showered and shaved, and thought he would take a drive. That almost always helped him relax.

It was a nice day, already sixty degrees by 10:30 in the morning. There was a lake he always wanted to see just north and a little west of Reno. It was called "Frenchman's". He had heard it was popular, especially with fishermen.

He stopped and bought some snacks at a "7/11" near the university, and connected with 395 north towards "Hallelujah" junction. He turned west on California highway 70 to Chilcoot, and then north onto Frenchman's Lake Road.

It took him a little over 45 minutes. Once he had turned onto Frenchman's Lake Road, he had a view of awesome rock formations alongside. Then it opened up to see a rather large lake, surrounded by thousands of evergreens. It appeared peaceful, and un-crowded. He would find a place to park, and take a walk.

It wasn't Lake Tahoe, but then nothing else is. But it was quite pretty, and serene. There were several boats out on the lake, but none were racing around wildly as they had on Pyramid, and too often did the same on Lake Tahoe. They all appeared to be fishing.

After he found a suitable parking space, Michael walked along the shore. Fifteen minutes later, he got the urge to wade into the inviting water. He took his shoes and socks off, rolled up his pants legs, and stepped into the blue liquid. The bottom was very muddy. The water was cold, but not as cold as Lake Tahoe, whose waters remained frigid even in the middle of August. He only stood there a few minutes, turned around and found a place to sit. It was as quiet here as it had been in the redwoods. He felt very alone, and it felt good. Tonight he would have to pretend to be social once more.

He spent a couple of hours trekking around the shore, and through the woods. He decided it was time to head back home.

He got back to his apartment around 2:30. When he unlocked his door he saw his phone was blinking. There must be a message, but he never had one before. No one knew his phone number. He hardly ever used his phone at all. He made up his mind to just delete it. It was most likely a wrong number.

Chapter 72

Rafferty had been at Legend's human resources office at 8:30 on Thursday morning. He showed the manager his court signed documents, and was given a copy of Michael Whitten's personell file.

When he was back at his desk, and reading the file, he saw the information he needed, and an interesting fact that he had no "emergency contact" information. Because he worked swing shift, he would wait to call him until about ten. He read the entire file. There wasn't much else, it was fairly basic. Performance reviews were slightly above average. Nothing stood out about him, pro or con.

He placed a call to Hillary's office. He knew she would be in the classroom, but he wanted to leave her a message. He told her he was pretty sure it was Whitten they were looking for, and that he was going to make an attempt to talk to him that very day.

Rafferty made his first call to Mr. Whitten about 10:30. On the sixth ring, an automated voice on an answer machine told him to leave a message. He didn't. At one o'clock, after he had grabbed a tuna sandwich for lunch, he called again. Same irritating message. He'd try once more. If he didn't get a response, he'd go see Mr. Whitten at work. According to his file, he worked Thursday evenings.

CHAPTER 73

When Hillary finished her Thursday class, and returned to her office, the first thing she did was check her messages. There were two. One was from another faculty member who "wished to talk with her, at her convenience", and the other was from David. She listened to David's, and called him right away.

"This is detective Rafferty."

"Hi, David, it's Hillary."

"Hello, Hillary. I guess you got my message?"

"Yes, thank you. Tell me what made you decide it wasn't Grayson?"

He told her about their conversation, and his sexual preference. He also told her he wouldn't totally eliminate him until he checked out everything he was told.

"I see. So you believe there's a good chance Whitten is our man?"

"I do, but there's still much to learn about him. Before I'm able to take any more legal steps, I need a motive for at least one case, and some sort of evidence, or a witness."

"You said you were going to try and talk to him as soon as possible?"

"That's the plan. I've been calling him all day, but, no luck. His address is near the university. I thought about dropping by on my way home tonight. Or my other option is to make a visit to the Legend this evening when he's working."

"Which do you think is best?"

"I'll probably guarantee results by going to see him at work."

"Makes sense. Will you call me after?"

"It may be late."

"That's okay, I'll be waiting."

Chapter 74

Michael had everything ready by 8 o'clock. He showered and shaved and made sure his clothes looked appropriate. He would leave for the party sometime after nine. He didn't want to make an entrance, he hoped to just blend in. He knew he wouldn't need his car this time, so he would take the short walk to the side door of the Legend.

Chapter 75

Rafferty parked at the Legend about 8:30 in the evening. He was on the fifth floor of the parking structure, so he punched the button marked "casino level" on the elevator, exited, and followed the signs to the table games area. He saw the dice pit in the back section of the floor. There were two games open. He wondered which one was Whitten's. He didn't see anyone who resembled the picture that was faxed to him from Gaming Control. Maybe he was on a break.

He walked up to the game on the left, asked the box man if he could have a word with him. He told him he was looking for Michael Whitten. The box man told him he had the night off. Rafferty thanked him, and walked back towards the elevators. He was disappointed, he had his schedule. He must have taken an extra day off. When he got back to his car, he called Hillary, and told her the bad news.

On the drive home to Jill, David thought about what he would do the next day. First, he'd make an early call to Whitten's home. Then, he'd get down to some old fashioned police work. He still had to confirm Grayson's information, and he wanted to talk to some of the people Whitten had worked with in other casinos. He might start at the Nevada Gold. Several others should know him there, he had worked there twice. He suddenly remembered that Jake had told him he hired Whitten at the Pot of Gold. Nothing had happened there, that he knew of, but maybe there was someone who could provide some information.

CHAPTER 76

Michael arrived just before 9:30 at the party. It was in the same penthouse suite. He knocked, and this time the door was answered by Peg. He was a little surprised, but hoped he didn't show it. She was congenial, but not warm. They had never had a good relationship at work. But, because he was Carl's guest, she had to be pleasant. He went inside and saw the same people as before, with an addition of some he had not.

There were three women he had seen in the break room but didn't know. He tried to place them in their uniforms. One was blonde, maybe five feet nine inches tall. She wore a short sleeveless dress, electric blue in color. She was pretty with very long legs, displaying an obviously "paid for busom", and was drinking out of a martini glass. He was pretty sure she was a cocktail waitress on his shift, but didn't work the dice pit. Another was a red head. She was a little older, maybe late thirties. She was also very pretty, wearing tight pants and a top that was tight enough to reveal perfect cleavage. When she turned to the side, her pants showed an above average derriere. She worked in one of the restaurants. The third was a dealer, maybe forty five. She was attractive, conservative in attire. Michael had seen her on the "21" tables, but never would have thought her to be a part of a group such as this.

Once again, after receiving a black label on the rocks from the bartender. Michael attempted to be invisible. And for about ten minutes, he was.

He watched Larry move over to the leggy cocktail waitress. He talked to her for a few minutes, and then they disappeared into one of the other rooms, which Michael assumed was a bedroom. A few minutes more, and Carl moved towards the food server. A minute later, Christine joined them. The three disappeared to another room. Not to be left out, the slightly older dealer joined Peg in a seemingly innocent huddle. Michael wondered. Did Larry and Carl know about Peg's sexual preference?

Michael figured this was a good time. When he was sure no one was watching him, he went into the small room he had seen Larry, Carl, Peg, Christine, and Danny go into at the last party. He was sure no one saw him. Everyone was engaged in their own form of debauchery. The room was an ante room for the penthouse's master bedroom. He looked around and saw several covered containers. One he knew immediately was pot, with several packages of papers next to it. There was a covered bowl with a powder he was sure was cocaine. There were pills of several different colored capsules, and several bottles of Cabo Wabo tequilla. This was where it would all happen for the select few.

Michael completed his plan, which took no more than three or four minutes, and rejoined the party.

Within the next thirty or forty five minutes, the partiers returned from the bedrooms. Then, for about an hour or two, everyone ate, drank and laughed, even Michael, who pretended to find them all humorous.

Just after one in the morning, Larry, Carl, Christine, and Peg, went into the ante-room. Michael, whose composure was usually in his complete control, had to hide the elation he was feeling. He knew what they were doing inside the small room. Although he had no personal knowledge of who or what Christine was, he felt no remorse for her. Whatever she decided to do tonight, simply confirmed she was part of this evil clique.

When they all came out, Michael noticed some of their eyes were slightly dilated. Everything was happening as he had planned it.

This time the party didn't end until after three in the morning. Almost everyone was totally incapacitated in some way. Michael stayed in a corner as he observed everyone else make their exit. When he finally made his, only Larry and Carl were still there. When he said good night, he told them, "I hope you enjoyed your party". He then walked home, knowing he would sleep well.

CHAPTER 77

Rafferty arrived at the station just after seven on Friday morning. He took his notes out of his briefcase, and was ready to call Michael Whitten, when he had an epiphany. Whitten's personal history, and everything he had read in his files, told him he would not answer his phone calls. He made the decision that after lunch he would go to his residence.

Meanwhile, Rafferty went through Whitten's files in more detail, trying to apply his years of experience and intuition into a theory about his profile. He called the Gaming Commission, and asked if they would fax over a better picture of him. Maybe they could blow up the picture attached to his file. They said he would have it in about thirty minutes.

Time quickly passed, and all of a sudden it was two in the afternoon. He finally got the picture of Whitten. He was an average looking man. The only distinctive thing about him was the lack of a smile, the complete blank expression on his face.

Less than ten minutes later, Rafferty was called into Captain Murphy's office. He sat and immediately saw the very sober expression on his boss's face.

Murhpy took a deep breath and said; "Thirty minutes ago, we got a call from a maid who works for Larry Columbo, the General Manager of the Legend casino. She found him in his bedroom, she was certain he was dead. We sent a squad car to his residence. When they arrived, they called in immediately and requested the coroner's staff be alerted. They were needed at the crime scene as soon as possible. We haven't received confirmation that the coroner and his forensic team have arrived, but I want you over there right now. When you have a cause of death, and a why, a who, or any reason to believe foul play, I want you to call me immediately. Of course the press is not to be given any information until we decide to brief them."

"Got it boss. I'm on my way."

Mr. Columbo lived in Washoe Valley, on Franktown Road, on an estate that was over three acres. The house was almost eight thousand square feet. He lived alone, but had regular maid service, landscape service, and a trainer who cared for the five horses in his stable. When Rafferty arrived, there were hundreds of yards of yellow tape surrounding the house, intended to keep away sight seers, and the press. He parked his car in the driveway, and approached a uniformed officer designated to turn away unwanted visitors.

Rafferty walked quickly towards the main entrance to the house. Once inside, another uniform told him the crime scene was upstairs, the third room on the right. He walked up the winding staircaise, and down the hall.

Another uniform and two technicians were standing outside the room he was headed for. He went inside, put on a pair of latex gloves, and found his friend Bill Cohen in the room, next to the bed. This would be a high profile case, and Bill obviously decided he should be the one to perform the initial examination.

Rafferty walked up to his old friend. He asked him what his opinion of the scene was.

Cohen said; "Right now, I'm not sure. There are no signs of obvious foul play, but the deceased apparently was not able to call for help, and whatever the cause, the result was violent, as you can see by the residue on the sheets and the carpet. I'll do an autopsy immediately, and have the results in 24 hours."

"Thanks, Bill, I appreciate it. I'll try and control the media. I know they'll be all over this one."

"No doubt."

Rafferty was about to leave, when his phone buzzed. The caller ID showed it was his boss, Captain Murphy. He said; "Rafferty here."

"David, it's me, Murphy. I just received another call, another unexplained death. This time it's the Games Manager at the Legend, a man by the name of Carl Fowler. His wife called 911 a couple of hours ago. By the time they got him to the emergency room, he was convulsing, and died fifteen minutes later. Wait a minute, I'm getting another call."

Rafferty held for about three minutes. Murphy came back on, "a dealer from the Legend just arrived at emergency with the same symptoms. They don't know if she'll make it. I think you'd better get to Saint Mary's right now."

"On my way."

He arrived at Saint Mary's emergency room fifteen minutes later. He identified himself to the staff. The doctor in charge of the Legend dealer's treatment told him they were working on her, but it didn't look good.

Rafferty; "What's her name?"

"Her ID says Christine Kelley."

"Thanks. Let me know as soon as you can if I can talk to her."

"Okay, detective, I will."

Rafferty knew the routine all too well. When a patient, a victim, was in emergency, or intensive care, it could be a long time until he might be allowed access to the individual. At least fifty percent of the time, the patient/victim, would lose his or her battle for life before he could talk to them at all.

He was sitting there for over an hour, when the doctor came out to see him.

The doctor said; "I don't know if she'll make it, but we have her stabilized for now. Her vital signs are weak, and her respiration is labored. If she regains consciousness, and can speak, I'll let you know."

Rafferty thanked him, gave him his card, and decided there was nothing else he could do right now.

CHAPTER 78

Orin Delano, an orderly at Saint Mary's, had made quite a bit of side money giving information to Selena Velasquez, a reporter for channel 3, one of the local television stations. He had heard about the two employees of the Legend who had come into the emergency room, one dead, one hanging onto life. He took a break and called her. He told her of the situation, and within fifteen minutes, a camera crew and the reporter were at the hospital.

When the ensuing commotion began, a representitive for the hospital intercepted them, telling all concerned that no information pertaining to the treatment of any individual at this hospital would be given to anyone without the need, and the right, to know.

Selena Velasquez knew this would be the response. She just wanted any kind of statement and some film. With cameraman in tow, she headed for the police station. By this time, the other two local stations had heard about the event at the hospital, and were set up at the station as well.

Less than ten minutes after the media had bombarded the police station, Captain Reynolds, a spokesman for RPD, came out to meet the crowd. He made a short statement; "Within the last few hours, we have confirmed deaths of two downtown casino executives. A third employee of the same casino is in very serious condition. We will have a press conference later this evening, and an update on the third person involved in this incident. At this time, there is no confirmed cause of death for the two executives. We hope to have more information for you at the press conference. Thank you."

With that, he turned around, and went back inside the station, reporters yelling questions to his back.

Selena Velasquez had her story for the five o'clock news. She was the only one who knew they worked at the Legend. Her story line began, "deaths of multiple Legend employees, a mystery".

CHAPTER 79

Peg Barrow was working in the main pit at the Legend on Friday evening when Debra, another regular guest at the party, called her over as she was returning from her break. She told her she had been watching the news in the break room, and the lead story was that two executives who worked for the Legend casino, were pronounced dead from unkown causes. In addition, a female dealer was in critical condition. Her prognosis was not favorable.

Peg said absolutely nothing. She was in shock. Her first thought was for herself. Her hopes for being a shift supervisor were not going to happen. When she calmed down, she came to a swift conclusion. This had to be related to last night. She could be one of them. She started to shake uncontrollably. "Get it together, Peg."

Debra had come to the same conclusion. Something had gone wrong at the party last night. She was scared to death. It seemed like everything that happened was like most of the parties they had. No one seemed different. Nothing was out of the ordinary. She kept asking herself, what made it different for them? It finally came to her, "it could have been me".

Chapter 80

The RPD was in turmoil. Something unreal had happened, but until the cause of death was confirmed, there could be no assumptions, no suspicions. Rafferty felt like everything he was working on was spinning uncontrollably. If this had to do with Whitten and his investigation, how? The answer was in the time line. When, what, how, and why had all this happened? He couldn't begin until the coroner had discovered a cause of death, and the approximate time it happened.

Less than four hours after the doctor told him about Christine Kelley's condition, she lost her battle for life.

That made the total number of deaths at the Legend five. He was too slow in solving these murders. He felt he had failed.

Chapter 81

Peg knew she had to talk to the police. There was no doubt in her mind something had happened to them while they were at the party. What else could it be? She would make the call on her next break.

Chapter 82

Hillary had gone for a run. She got back about 5:15. She took a yogurt out of the refrigerator, sat on her couch, and turned on the news. She liked channel three, mostly because of their more accurate weather predictions. Selena Velasquez was finishing her story about suspicious deaths of casino employees. She expected the news conference from the RPD, would take place in about thirty minutes.

Hillary sat and stared at the television, her mouth agape. Her first thought was to call David, but she knew he was probably very busy right now. She had missed most of the story, but her gut told her they were from the Legend. She couldn't just sit, she had to do something, but what? After she watched the news conference, maybe something would come to her.

She paced the floor for the next twenty minutes. She thought about all the work David had been doing, and knew him well enough to know that right now he was very unhappy, even a little depressed.

Finally the screen showed the microphones set up in front of the police station. A few minutes later, a man in full dress uniform stepped up to the dais. He began; "Good evening ladies and gentlemen. For those of you who don't know me, I'm Lieutenant Mark Woodbine, media liason for the RPD. As you know, two men from the Legend casino have lost their lives. And just before I stepped up to the microphones, we received confirmation that a third person, a female dealer, also lost hers. The names are being withheld until all family members have been notified. All three had very similar symptoms, but, as of this moment, the coroner has not been able to determine a cause of death. We will let you know the results of laboratory tests which will confirm whether this was due to natural causes, or the result of foul play, as soon as we receive them. Our first task will be to attempt to determine if they shared something in common within the last few days. Anyone with any information about the three individuals should call the Reno Police Department, or secret witness. The numbers will be on your screen. That is all I have for now. I will not take questions at this time, everything we know at the moment has been given to you. Thank you." With that said, he turned and walked back into the station, followed by the clamorous voices of the media.

Hillary was in a complete state of shock. It took her a couple of minutes to feel the tears running down her face.

She came back to present time when the phone rang. It was David. She couldn't believe he took the time to call her.

"Hi Hillary. I'm sure you've heard the news."

"Hi David. I just finished watching the press conference."

"I didn't get to see it, too busy."

"How are you? I've been thinking about you ever since I saw the news. What are you feeling?"

"I won't lie. It's been tough. I can't help thinking I should have done something sooner. There's no proof right now that this was related to our search, but, as you know, I don't believe in coincidence."

"Is there any way I can help? Anything at all?"

"There's not much *I* can do right now. We need a lot more information. What we're hoping is that someone will call us with knowledge that will give us some direction. So far, we haven't found any clues at the residences of the victims, so, until something changes, we just wait."

"That's got to be hard. Thanks for taking the time to call me. Of course I was shocked, but then I became worried about you. Have you talked to Jill?"

"I called her just before I called you. She and I have been through a lot together. She understands. She also understands it never gets any easier."

They said their good-byes. David headed back to the station. Hillary paced the floor. She wouldn't sleep tonight.

Chapter 83

The hour following the news conference produced hundreds of telephone calls to the RPD. The switchboard operator transferred calls to every detective and ranking officer on duty, as quickly as possible. The usual number of crank calls surfaced more quickly than any containing information of some value. Four different detectives received calls from individuals who claimed to have been at a party the night before with the deceased. Rafferty had taken one call himself that gave him certainty that this was the lead he was hoping for.

A games supervisor from the Legend, by the name of Peg Barrow, told him about the previous night's party, and how she knew each of the deceased quite well. Rafferty asked her if they could get together as soon as possible. She told him she was at work. Rafferty said he would be right over.

Chapter 84

When Michael arrived for his seven o'clock dice shift, he felt pretty good about himself. But, when he looked towards the main pit and saw Peg standing there, he was shocked and confused. He was sure he had seen her go into the "drug" room with the other three. He had watched the news, and was positive the other three were no longer of this world. What happened with her? How had she survived?

Once he calmed down and had time to think clearly, he came to the conclusion that it didn't matter. She, too, would soon be somewhere else than here.

Chapter 85

Rafferty parked in the Legend parking garage less than ten minutes after he got off the phone with Peg Barrow. He took the elevator down to the casino floor, asked the first dealer he saw to direct him to Ms. Barrow. He saw her not fifteen yards away. Her red hair made her stand out. He walked up to where she was, motioned her over, identified himself, and asked her if she could go somewhere with him and talk. Peg went to the podium in the pit, picked up the phone, made a short call. Then she walked over to one of the other supervisors, told him something, and walked back towards Rafferty. She moved outside, and quietly said, "there's a lounge around the corner, we can talk there".

They found a table as far away from the bar as possible, and sat.

Rafferty; "Thanks for your call, Ms. Barrow."

"I had to call you. It's too much of a conincidence that we were all at the same party."

"First of all, where was the party held?"

"In one of the penthouses upstairs."

"There's more than one?"

"There are four up there. We were in number three."

"What I would like from you, if you are able, is a complete list of everyone that was there."

"I can do that. There were a few there whose names I don't know, but it really is just a few."

"Any ideas, a hunch, as to what might have happened?"

"No, nothing. I was working when I got the news. I'm still in shock."

"Understandable. How soon could you give me that list?"

"I could probably do it on my next break. I'd do it right now, but I'm not thinking very clearly."

"That's fine. I totally understand. When is your next break? I'll come back about the time it ends, and pick it up from you, if that's okay."

"It should be just before nine. I get a half an hour, so if you're back here at 9:15, or a little later, I'll meet you right here."

"Thank you. That'll work just fine."

Peg went back to work, Rafferty went to find the shift manager.

About five minutes later, a well dressed gentleman of about fifty five years walked up to him. He reached out his hand, and said, "detective Rafferty?"

"Yes. Are you the shift manager?"

"The name's Ron Grankowski. How may I help you?"

"I'm sure you've heard the news tonight."

"Yes. And like everyone else, I still can't believe it. Must have been some horrible accident."

"We're not sure what it was, yet. What we do now know, is that they were all at a party last night. This party took place right here at the Legend in penthouse number three. I need to have that room untouched. While I was waiting for you, I called for a couple of uniforms to post guard. I would like to see it right now, if that's possible."

"A party, what sort of party. I have no knowledge of anything like that happening here."

"It appears very few knew about it. Can I see the room?"

"Of course. Let me call up to the hotel manager. He'll have someone escort you up there immediately."

Ron made a call, and led Rafferty up to the hotel desk. The manager, an Hispanic man by the name Roberto Contrearas, introduced himself. He asked Ron, "is this okay? Should we see a search warrant?"

Rafferty; "Mr. Contrearas, if you think I need a search warrant, I can get one. Right now, all I want is to physically see the room. We need to know what happened up there last night."

Ron; "You can go with him, if you'd like, Roberto, I think a walk through would not be a problem."

"Okay, let me get the key."

Rafferty knew that Mr. Contrearas had to know the room was being used on the previous night. There could be no chance of a conflict between the party, and possible use by a "high roller".

Rafferty thanked Ron. Contrearas came back, and the two of them headed for the elevators.

When they arrived at the penthouse level, as Rafferty walked out of the elevator, he was thinking, "one floor, and only four rooms. I don't make enough money".

Contrearas unlocked the door, they were immediately hit by the stench of cigarette smoke and alcohol. The room had obviously not been cleaned yet. Rafferty took that as a lucky break. Walking inside, he noticed full ashtrays, drink glasses, and partially eaten plates of food on almost every flat surface. He turned to Contrearas, and said, "we need to leave here right now. I'm going to call the lab people, and let them begin their investigation". As he was saying this, two uniformed officers arrived at the door. Rafferty told them that no one, including the two of them, was allowed to enter the room.

Rafferty walked to the elevator with Contrearas. He informed him that as of right now, this was a crime scene, and a full forensic team would be here shortly. He suggested Contrearas advise his superiors. Contrearas got onto the elevator, Rafferty pulled out his cell and called the station. As was everyone else, Captain Murphy was at his desk. He took Rafferty's call, and ordered a team out immediately. He called the coroner's office, suspecting Bill Cohen would want to be in complete control of the situation.

Everyone arrived within 45 minutes. Rafferty had to excuse himself shortly after they arrived. It was just after nine, and he wanted to be ready for Ms. Barrow when she came back from her break.

Chapter 86

Michael couldn't help but see all the commotion. It seemed there were policemen everywhere. He was concerned, but not worried. There was no way that he could be suspected of anything. Hardly anyone even knew who he was.

CHAPTER 87

Rafferty got downstairs to the lounge about ten minutes after nine. A couple of minutes later Peg walked up to him, and handed him a piece of paper. She said, "this is the list. The only three names I don't have are three women who were additional guests. They work here, and if need be, I can find out who they were."

"Thanks, Ms. Barrow. If I need more information, I'll be in touch."

Rafferty looked at the paper. He noticed the names of the deceased right away, and as he looked down the paper, one name jumped out at him, Michael Whitten. His face flushed with surprise, although he would've been more shocked if his name was not on the list. Just then, his phone rang.

"David? This is Bill Cohen. I think you need to see this right away."

"I'll be right up."

He got on the elevator, and was back at the penthouse within three minutes. Bill greeted him a few feet inside the entrance. He led him to a small room off the living quarters. Rafferty didn't need to be told what he was looking at. Drugs, and lots of them.

"Can we get these to the lab asap, for immediate analysis?"

"That's the plan."

"Call me as soon as you know anything."

Rafferty walked around the penthouse, careful not to get in the way, or disturb anything in the rooms. He saw that three of the bedrooms had been used in some fashion. Sex and drugs go together, so no surprise there. The fourth bedroom, the master suite appeared untouched. Maybe the drugs in the ante room made this room off limits. He wondered what Whitten had done at the party. Was he into drugs, or kinky sex. What role did he play in a crowd that contained the upper crust of the casino? And, if he did have a part in all of this, what was his motive? And, why all these people at once? Lots of questions. He would find the answers. At least he hoped he would.

Fifteen minutes later, he walked outside of the penthouse, and to the end of the hallway. He called Hillary.

"Hello."

"It's David. I have to be brief, but all of this evenings news apparently took place at a party last night, right here at the Legend. And, guess who was on the list of partygoers?"

"You've got to be kidding. But you wouldn't kid about something like this."

"Right, and right again. We found lots of drugs and booze. The lab is working on the drugs right now."

"Thanks, David. I don't believe I'll be sleeping tonight, so call me whenever you feel like it."

"I will."

They hung up, and David returned to the penthouse, not sure of what he could do until he had at least one shred of hard evidence.

Chapter 88

Peg couldn't tell the detective she had been doing drugs with the three who had died. In fact, she didn't, she faked it. The drugs must have been bad, or laced with something. She was entirely positive about the cause of their deaths. There were only four of them in the room that night.

She started to shake. If she was into drugs, she would not be alive. She would have been number four. There were often as many as six people in that room, but the others were into other things that night. There was heavy drinking, and there were a few more sexual encounters than usual. She needed to see Bev. She needed to talk to someone who would understand. But Bev was working next door. All she could do was leave a message on her phone, asking if they could meet after work.

Chapter 89

As networks will do, the story about the three Legend employees was repeated continuously. There was nothing new to report, but that didn't stop them from talking about it incessantly. Speculation was abundant.

Selena Velasquez knew lots of people in her city. She had friends in almost every government office, and many of the local businesses, including the casinos. She was at the Legend on Friday evening when the police and lab technicians arrived. She had been talking to a couple of bartenders she knew. If you want information, bars were the place to go. It often came from the cocktail waitresses, who traveled throughout the casino doing their job. Everything eventually filtered back to the bar, and therefore the bartender.

When the group arrived at the elevators, Selena asked the bartender, John, "what's going on"? He told her that there had been a party in one of the penthouse's the night before, and the three who died were all guests.

Selena went back to her office at the television station. She had a scoop for the ten o'clock news.

Chapter 90

It was a long night for everyone involved. The technicians worked as quickly as possible, but were taking extreme care not to compromise any evidence, or overlook even the smallest detail. Rafferty could have, and probably should have, gone home to get a few hours sleep. He couldn't get his feet to move towards the elevators. If anything, even a small piece of evidence, was discovered, he had to be there. He knew it would be morning, probably after sunrise, before the first lab tests would be released. The autopsies would take longer.

Meanwhile, Hillary was spending the night going over her notes. She didn't expect to find anything new, but it gave her something to do, and a way to feel involved.

The techicians finished around 5:30 in the morning. Rafferty posted two uniforms at the door. No one was to enter the room. The techs might want to return. He went downstairs, found the graveyard shift manager, and made sure coffee and some food would be taken to the uniforms on the penthouse level.

As he decided to head to the parking lot, his phone buzzed. "Rafferty".

"Hi David, it's Bill."

"Hi, Bill. I didn't expect to hear from you for several more hours."

"I got a call from my lab people. They were analyzing the drugs for the presence of any unusual substance. Mixed in the cocaine was another powdered substance. It was the same that I found in Mitch Carlson's autopsy. It's a Toxalbumin. The specific genesis has not been established, but, when inhaled, it is often fatal. It can be lethal in other forms as well. The percentage of the poison was ten times greater than what I discovered investigating Carlson's death. There were other substances in the marijuana, and some of the capsules contained questionable contents. They haven't been identified as of yet. I should be finished with tissue and blood sample tests from the victims, insuring they had taken the drugs, by mid-afternoon."

"So it was murder. I know I don't have to say it, but for now let's make sure this is between you, me, and the lab."

"Definitely."

Rafferty had no doubt that Hillary was awake. He called her as he was walking to his car. He wasn't sure the phone even rang, she picked it up so quickly.

"Hello, David?"

"Good morning, Hillary. Did you get any sleep?"

"No, not really. You sound exhausted."

"I am. But I have some news, news only you, myself, the coroner, and the lab people can know about. The drugs at the party contained some sort of poison, or poisons."

"So it was Whitten?"

"Seems like it."

"What are you going to do?"

"First, I'm going home to kiss my wife, and get a couple of hours sleep. Then breakfast. Then I'll go back to the station, and start calling the names on the party list I got from Ms. Barrow. I'll start with her, and go down the list. I have to interview everyone, if for no other reason than to eliminate each person as a suspect, one by one."

CHAPTER 91

Bill Cohen couldn't wait to finish the first portion of his autopsy. He had started with Mr. Columbo, then Mr. Fowler, and finally Ms. Kelley. He had taken blood samples from each, and tissue from their livers, and finally urine samples. While they were being analyzed, he looked at their hearts and lungs. There was a great deal of trauma in the major organs. This was no surprise. At Mr. Columbo's home, in his bedroom, their was fluid everywhere, obviously expelled from his body with great force. Death had not been easy.

Somewhere around one in the afternoon, as he had been working on Ms. Kelley, he got the call from the lab.

The Toxalbumin was from a plant named Jatropha curcas. It was first discovered in Portugal, but can be grown in many places, even in a desert environment. It is toxic in many forms, in relatively small amounts, especially when inhaled. There was enough of the substance in the cocaine alone to kill a hundred men.

The other substance found in the marijuana, and in some of the pills, was Aluminum Phosphide. This was a fumigant used mostly in India. It was also the most widely used substance in the area for those who wished to commit suicide. The Toxalbumin was also present in some of the pills. As with the Toxalbumin, there was an excessive amount of the fumigant present in everything.

Bill had but one thought, someone wanted these people to die, and die quickly enough that they had no hope of getting medical attention.

He was tired, and his mind was a little slow, but the name of the fumigant sounded very familiar. He knew he had encountered it before. Then it struck him. He went to his files, which were all on computer, and therefore crossfiled in several different ways. He typed in "Aluminum Phosphide", and in less than thirty seconds, the case of the five men who had frequented the local casinos popped up. He now remembered it well. That was a very hectic time in his career, but he now recalled how they had all died within three days, and all with similar symptoms. And all five had the fumigant in their toxicology reports.

He called David, immediately.

Rafferty was at his desk, making phone calls. He had lined up interviews with six of the partygoers. His phone rang, he picked it up right away. It was the coroner, his friend, Bill Cohen. Bill told him the lab results from the analysis of the drugs was complete. He told him about what they found. He said the test results from the victims would be available very soon. He then reminded him of the five victims they had investigated some years previous.

Rafferty asked him if these lethal substances were easy to obtain. Bill told him he believed they would be. Rafferty thanked him and hung up. This was one of those times when the probability of one person being the guilty party was very high. Now it was time to prove it.

He moved Whitten's name right after Ms. Barrow's on his list of those to be interviewed.

Chapter 92

Peg had spent Friday night at Bev's apartment. At ten, the following morning, her cell phone rang. She picked it up, but she didn't recognize the number on the caller ID. She knew who it was. The only person who had this number, who she didn't know well, was the detective. She decided to answer it.

She said, "Hello".

"Is this Ms. Barrow?"

"Yes. Who's calling?"

"This is detective Rafferty, we talked last night."

"Sure. What can I do for you.?"

"Can you come to the police station around three o'clock this afternoon? I have some questions which I believe you may be able to answer."

"Should I bring an attorney?"

"If you think you need one. I just think you are the best person to give me information I need about Thursday night's party."

"Okay, I suppose I could. But I have to be at work by 5:30.

"I don't think it will take very long."

"All right, I'll be there."

Peg was nervous. She'd have to tell him about the drugs. She doubted he would believe she hadn't taken any herself. But, if she had, wouldn't she be in the morgue right now?

Chapter 93

Peg Barrow arrived at his desk exactly at three. He took her to one of the interrogation rooms so they could have privacy. They sat, he offered her coffee or a bottle of water. She declined.

Rafferty spoke first; "Thank you for coming in Ms. Barrow. To protect you and me, this conversation will be recorded. This won't take long. First of all, was this a one time thing?

"If you're talking about the party, no, they've been happening about once a month for almost a year."

"Did the guests at the party change, or were they mostly the same each time?"

"We were always the same group."

"We found lots of drugs at the party. Did everyone take part in them?"

"No, that was a select group."

"Were you part of that group?"

"Yes, but I didn't actually take any, I faked it."

"Why would you fake it?"

"I needed to have Larry and Carl think I was part of their inner circle. I had ambitions."

"You're talking about Mr. Columbo, and Mr. Fowler?"

"Yes, they were the General Manager, and the Games Manager."

"Who else was invited to share the drugs?"

"Christine, who was the third who died, and a Dealer named Danny, and I don't even know his last name. Once in a while, a woman who Larry or Carl wanted to be with, might be invited, but that was not the usual."

"So, mostly only the five of you. Was Danny with you?"

"No. He was preoccupied with one of the girls."

"Did anyone else ever go into the room where the drugs were?"

"Not that I know of, I mean, there could have been people going in there at other times. It was a big place."

"You said it was always the same people, but was there anyone who was new to the group?"

"There were the three women whose names I didn't know, and there was a new dealer who had only been to the last two parties."

"What was his or her name?"

"His name is Michael Whitten."

"How well do you know him?"

"Not well, he is, or he was, Carl's friend."

"Anything else you can think of?"

"Not right now."

"You have my numbers."

She left, and Rafferty believed everything she had said. He had checked with some other casino employees who knew her, and had confirmed her ambitions, and no one was aware of her having used drugs.

Rafferty didn't even bother to attempt a call to Whitten. He must have seen the lab crew at the Legend. The elevators that lead to the penthouses are in plain sight of the dice pit. Besides, everything was on the news, not to mention casinos being incredible rumor mills. He was certain he wouldn't answer his phone. He'd have to make a visit Saturday night to the Legend.

He parked in the garage around 9 o'clock. He would first find Ron Grankowski, the swing shift manager. He would ask for Michael Whitten to be taken off of the game, and escorted to any office or room available.

He had to wait about ten minutes for Mr. Gronkowski to arrive. He had been occupied with a complaint from one of their bigger customers. He walked right up to Rafferty, hand extended, and said, "detective, nice to see you again. Is there something more I could do for you?" Rafferty explained that Whitten had been one of the guests at the party, but he had been unable to reach him. He told Gronkowski what he needed, and in turn, was told that he would be more than happy to assist. The owners of the casino had instructed him to give full cooperation to the police department.

Gronskowski said they could use his office, located on the basement level. He escorted Rafferty there, as he told one of the security guards to bring Whitten down immediately.

Michael knew exactly what it was all about when he was taken off his game. He was on the party's guest list. But there was no way they could link him to anything else. He was sure of that.

He walked into Ron's office, and saw what he expected. Sitting behind Ron's desk was a man who was obviously a policeman. Ron was standing beside him.

Ron said; "Have a seat, Michael. This is detective Rafferty with the Reno Police Department. He has a few questions to ask you about the party Thursday night."

"Okay."

"I'll leave you and the detective alone. If you need me, I won't be far."

He left, closed the door behind him, and Rafferty said; "I need to inform you that this conversation will be recorded. Is that a problem for you?"

"I don't believe so."

Rafferty took his pocket recorder out and set it on the desk. "Mr Whitten, will you state your full name?"

"My name is Michael Whitten, no middle name."

"Were you a guest at a party on the premises of the Legend casino and hotel last Thursday evening?"

"Yes, I was."

"Who was in attendance at the party, besides yourself?"

"I didn't know everyone. There were the three in the paper, a pit boss named Peg, two other dealers by the names of Sandra and Debra, a dice dealer named Danny, and the rest I knew by face, not by name."

"Had you been to any other parties at this location?"

"Just one, a couple of weeks ago."

"What did everyone do at these parties?"

"The usual. We drank, there was lots of food, we were having a good time."

"Were there drugs as well?"

"Not to my knowledge."

"Did you suspect anyone was doing drugs?"

"There were several rooms in the penthouse. I'm sure it was possible."

"But you have no personal knowledge of someone using an illegal substance?"

"No."

"Including yourself?"

"I don't do drugs."

"How well did you know the victims?"

"I only knew Carl, and not really that well."

"So why do you think you were invited to the party?"

"Probably because Carl liked me. He thought I was a good dealer."

"So, were these the best and brightest of the gaming staff?"

"Not necessarily. The party was by invitation only, and I couldn't guess why some got invited, and some didn't. As I said, this was only my second time."

"Did you see anything out of the ordinary that might lead you to have suspicions as to the cause of death of these specific three people?"

"I saw nothing unusual at all. It was a party."

With that, Rafferty gave him his card, and told him, "call if you can think of anything else."

When Whitten left, Rafferty was left with nothing. He actually expected this would be the result. His next step was to talk to anyone who knew him. He needed a reason to allow him to obtain a search warrant for Whitten's residence. He hoped someone else at the party had seen something, anything at all.

Chapter 94

Selena Velasquez was a bulldog. She hounded every person she knew in the casinos, the police department, the DA's office, and the Coroner's office, until she got some information no one else had. Mid Saturday afternoon, it paid off. A well paid source, who worked in the laboratory that supported the Coroner's office, called her with some valuable information. The three deaths were now labeled homicides.

She was so exited, she could barely type the story into her word processor fast enough.

When the news aired, hers was the lead story. "Legend Employees, Victims of Homicide."

She read the story as she herself had written it: "Larry Columbo, Carl Fowler, and Christine Kelley, all employed by the Legend casino, in downtown Reno, were poisoned while attending a party on Thursday evening, in a penthouse located at the hotel inside the Legend. They had all ingested drugs that were laced with substances that caused them to lose their lives. Their deaths were traumatic, and none of them ever had an opportunity to speak to authorities before they lost their battle for life. There are no suspects at this time. All those who attended the party are being interviewed by the RPD. We will keep you informed as we receive updates from spokespersons for the authorities."

Chapter 95

Rafferty's Monday would be filled with interviews of the partygoers. He had called Hillary Sunday and told her about the interview with Whitten. They had agreed to meet for a brief lunch the following day.

Around eight, Monday morning, he was called into Captain Murphy's office.

"Good morning, David."

"Good morning, boss. What's up?"

"I know you were out late Saturday night, so I'm sure you didn't see the late news."

"No I didn't, but I read the paper yesterday. We have a leak somewhere."

"We believe we know where the leak is, but not who, as of now."

"I'll just have to deal with it. We need to reveal to the press that everyone who attended the party is a suspect at this time."

"You know they're going to try and get to you, especially Ms. Velasquez."

"Do you think I should make a public statement?"

"No. I don't want everyone in the city to know what you look like. There will be enough of that as it is. Unless you want to be a celebrity."

"Only to my grandchildren."

Rafferty returned to his desk. His first appointment for the day was with Danny, the dice dealer who was also at the party. His last name was Patterson. He was off on Monday and Tuesday, so they decided to meet early on Monday so Danny could do other things on his days off.

Patterson arrived promptly, Rafferty got up and met him halfway into the squad room. He directed him to the same interrogation room he had used with Ms. Barrow. He offered Patterson a seat, and then offered him coffee.

"Actually, that would be nice. I didn't get off until 2 a.m., and I'm a bit groggy."

Rafferty returned with two cups of black coffee, and packets of cream and sugar. They both drank it black. He informed him, as he had Whitten, that the conversation would be recorded.

"Thanks for coming in Mr. Patterson. Technically, everyone who was at the party is a suspect, but this interview will not be of an accusatory nature. I just need some information. I'm trying to put the pieces together."

"I'll help if I can."

"I'll dispense with information I already have. I was given a list of all those at the party. I know when and how long these parties have been taking place. What I'm hoping to get from you are more specifics."

"Okay."

"As I'm sure you've seen or read, all three of the deceased had taken drugs. I know only certain people were invited to participate, and you were one of them. Don't be nervous, I'm not going to ask you about your drug use, nor am I looking to put you in a position that might involve legal action. This is purely about three cases of murder. Understood?"

"Yes, I've got it."

"Why weren't you with the four others who went into the ante room?"

"I was interested in one of the day shift dealers who was there. We'd been flirting back and forth for a couple of months, and this seemed to be the right time to take it further."

"So why didn't you excuse yourself, join the others, and then return to her afterwards?"

"Well, to be quite honest, I had hopes for something more than just conversation that night. If I take drugs, I'm not always able to perform."

"I see. What is the lady's name, I may have to verify what you just told me."

"Her name is Cynthia Woods. I've talked to her already, and I think she's expecting a call from you."

"What do you know about Ms. Barrow?"

"Peg? Not a whole lot. I did see her go with Larry, Carl, and Christine, but I saw her at work. How did she survive?"

"That's what I was going to ask you. She claims she faked doing drugs."

"She may have. In fact, one time, for sure, I saw her move a straw to the side of her nose when she was doing coke. But I just figured she was so high already that her hand was unsteady."

"Did you see anyone go into the room before or after the four in question?"

"Not that I remember. Shortly after they went in, Cynthia and I found and open room. We were together for over a half an hour."

"Thanks, Mr. Patterson. If you think of anything else, even something that seems very insignificant, please call me."

Rafferty gave him his card, and they shook hands good-bye.

His next appointment was at eleven. Sandra Spencer, also a swing shift dealer, had been a regular at the parties since they started. He wondered why she wasn't part of the select invitees to participate in the expensive stuff.

She arrived a few minutes after eleven. Rafferty greeted her in the same spot he had met Patterson. They went into the same room. She sat, and Rafferty offered her coffee or water. She said, "a bottle of water would be nice".

When Rafferty returned, he sat across from her, and informed her that the conversation was going to be recorded.

"Ms. Spencer, first of all, thank you for coming. I will answer a couple of your questions, before you can ask them. This is part of a homicide investigation. I believe someone at the party on Thursday evening intentionally murdered Mr. Columbo, Mr. Fowler, and Ms. Kelley. As of right now, everyone who attended that evening is a suspect. Now, don't be nervous. What I'm looking for is what everyone and anyone saw or heard."

"Okay, but I'm still nervous. I've never been accused of doing anything illegal."

"And you're not now, either. This is a discovery interview."

"Okay."

"I know what went on in the ante room to the master bedroom. I know those who had been invited. One thing I'm curious about. You had been at these parties from the very beginning. Why weren't you one of the invitees?"

"I don't do drugs. I don't approve of them. They actually scare me."

"Do you drink alcohol?"

"When I arrive at the party, I get a glass of white wine. It lasts me the entire time I'm there."

"Did you see anything unusual that night. Did you see anyone else enter that particular room?"

"Not that I can remember. Besides, everyone seemed to be pairing up, or into something I wasn't interested in. I left about eleven, and went home."

"All right, Ms. Spencer. Here's my card. If you think of anything else, please call me day or night."

"I will, detective."

She left, and Rafferty got ready to depart for his lunch date.

They had agreed to meet at noon. He still had about twenty minutes. His next appointment was at 2 p.m., with a day shift games supervisor by the name of Zachary Taylor. Interesting name. The family must be into military history, or the presidents of the United States.

Rafferty arrived at the Gold and Silver a few minutes before noon. Hillary was waiting for him. He walked to the booth she was in, she stood, and they hugged. When they sat down, their waitress came right over. They told her they didn't have a lot of time, so she took their order. They both liked the idea of soup and salad. The soup of the day was French onion, and they had their choice of salad. They both decided on the Caesar, and iced tea.

When she left, Rafferty spoke first; "It's good to see you, Hillary. Things have been happening so quickly that it seems we haven't talked in person in weeks."

"I know. I'm still in a little shock over everything. But you have all the news. Please, go ahead."

He recounted everything from Saturday night through the two interviews he had today. He told her how all he needed was one witness who saw Michael in that room, or one person who overheard something. He doubted he could obtain any physical evidence until he had reason for a search warrant.

Hillary said; "I think I like my job a lot better than yours. It sounds so frustrating."

"You know, when I was a young detective, and I became frustrated, I imagined it would ease with age and experience. I was wrong. It never gets any easier, especially in this case when I'm 99% sure I know who the perp is."

"Something will happen soon, David. You know it will."

"I hope so, I've hit the wall. I'm so tired I could sleep on my feet."

Their food came. While they ate, there was little conversation. Hillary wished there was something she could do. She knew there was really nothing at all.

After they finished their lunch, Hillary asked if he would like to take a walk. There wasn't much to see in the area they were in, but it wasn't even one o'clock yet, and David's next meeting wasn't until two.

They walked east on fourth street, back towards the casinos. They detoured down a residential street. They hadn't said much, until Rafferty finally spoke. "You know, this is the strangest case I think I've ever been involved in. I still haven't the slightest idea as to what might be his motive. According to his files, he's a totally unremarkable man. He's never been in any kind of trouble that I'm aware of. I can't even find a parking ticket."

"Weren't there others like him? Ted Bundy comes to mind."

"True. And if that's true, I wonder how many more are out there? If you hadn't become curious, I'm not sure he would be a suspect, even now."

They walked for about thirty minutes, and ended up back at their cars. They hugged good-bye, and Rafferty went back to the station to get ready for his 2 p.m. meeting.

Chapter 96

Michael watched every story about the party on every network. He read every word printed in the paper. He couldn't get enough.

Naturally, every person at the party was being scrutinized. It was very unlikely someone else could have poisoned them. Just to be sure he was safe, he should box up some of the stuff he had in his apartment. He could rent the smallest space in a storage unit for almost nothing. He'd have to do that on his next day off.

He wasn't really worried. There was no evidence left in the penthouse that could link him to the deaths. He had been very careful. He had planned well. Everyone was better off without the three. Peg would be the fourth. That would be his focus now.

Chapter 97

Mr. Taylor arrived at the squad room right on time. They went into the interrogation room. Rafferty offered him coffee or water, he declined. Rafferty then told him the conversation would be recorded.

"That's not a problem."

"Mr. Taylor, how long have you been a guest at these parties?"

"From what I was told, I became a regular at the third."

"Who invited you?"

"It was Mr. Columbo. I had worked for him in another casino before the Legend opened. I guess we knew each other for almost ten years."

"Did you know the other guests well?"

"Some of them, but not all."

"Did you know about the drug use in the room leading to the master bedroom?"

"I was never in there, but I knew what was going on."

"You were never invited to join in?"

"Once, a long time ago, but I declined. It's not really my thing. I'm not an angel, but I prefer good booze."

"Other than the three deceased, and Ms. Barrow, did you see anyone else go into that room?"

"I didn't see anyone else go in, but I saw someone come out."

"About what time was that?"

"It wasn't long after the party started, maybe ten, ten thirty."

"And who was it you saw?"

"It was the new guy, a dealer on swing shift. I knew him a little on days, before he transferred."

"What is his name?"

"Michael, but I don't recall the last name."

"Could it be Whitten?"

"That's it. I remember now from the pit assignment sheet."

"From what you're saying, you didn't know him well?"

"No. He always kept to himself, not very social."

"Can you think of anyone at the party that had a reason to wish harm to any of the three victims?"

"Not really. I mean, no one likes everyone. But this was a small group. No one was there without an invitation. I never heard anyone talking badly about anyone else who attended."

"Thanks, Mr. Taylor. Here's my card. If you think of anything else, feel free to call me, anytime."

Mr. Taylor left, and Rafferty now had reason to get his search warrant. He had one more meeting scheduled for today at four. It was with Debra Manning, another dealer on swing shift. He would take his paperwork to the judge early Tuesday morning.

Rafferty was positive his four o'clock interview was not going to produce anything new, but being a good detective is in the details, following through with a plan. So, when Ms. Manning arrived at four, he followed the same procedures. After she was seated, and he brought her a bottle of water, and informed her that the conversation was going to be recorded, he began.

"Thank you for coming Ms. Manning. I have been interviewing other guests from Thursday night's party, and many of the questions I had, have been answered. What I will be asking you will be specifics from your experience, your point of view. Is that all right with you?"

"I guess so."

"Did you see anything unusual at this particular gathering?"

"I don't think so. It's always the same group, so everyone pretty much does the same things."

"And what about the room where a few took part in drug use?"

"They were always the same people as well."

"Did you see anyone go into, or come out of that room, who was not usually included?"

"No, but I did see Peg go in early by herself, and come out a few minutes later."

"You're referring to Ms. Barrow?"

"Yes."

"No one else?"

"No. The rest of the party was as it always was. People were doing their thing, mostly drinking, eating, and, of course, some sex."

"Can you think of anything else out of the ordinary?"

"Nothing."

"Thank you Ms. Manning. I'm going to give you my numbers so you can call me if you think of anything else."

With card in hand, she left. Rafferty was thinking, "I guess I'll have to have another talk with Ms. Barrow".

Chapter 98

Peg was very upset. She hadn't lied to detective Rafferty, but she had omitted a detail. She hoped that no one had seen her go into that room earlier in the evening.

CHAPTER 99

Rafferty had to go to the Legend Monday night. He needed to talk to Ms. Barrow before Ms. Manning talked to her. He would be there at six.

When he arrived, he asked the first supervisor he saw to page Ron Grankowski. A few minutes later, Mr. Gronkowski strolled up to him. They exchanged greetings, and Rafferty told him that he needed to have a few minutes with Ms. Barrow. Gronkowski said he could use his office again. Rafferty went to the basement, and waited in his office. Five minutes later, Ms. Barrow arrived.

"Good evening, Ms. Barrow. Once again, I need you to know that this conversation is being recorded."

"Okay."

"During my interviews with the guests from the party, a new development has come to my attention. I was informed that you made a visit to the room where the drugs were early in the evening, long before the four of you went in together. Is that correct?"

For a few seconds, Peg looked down at her hands. She finally spoke; "Yes, I did, but it's not what you think."

"Then tell me, Ms. Barrow."

"I went in early to take the contents out of some of the capsules. I made sure the yellow ones were empty, so I could swallow them and appear to be part of what was going on."

"And why didn't you tell me before?"

"When you interviewed me, I assumed something had been added to the stuff in that room. I was afraid you would think that I had been the one."

"So why should I believe that you weren't?"

"I'm not that kind of person. I couldn't kill anyone."

"Some people I've talked to, some who have known you for a long time, said you could be ruthless to get what you wanted. How badly did you want Mr. Fowler's job?"

"That's not it! I hoped he would make me a shift manager."

"I'm supposed to believe that?"

"It's the truth. I couldn't kill anyone."

"We'll see about that. For now, don't make any plans to leave the area, and you might want to find an attorney. You can go back to work."

Peg left on shaky legs. Rafferty knew he had scared the shit out of her. That was his intention. He still believed Whitten was his man, but he didn't like being lied to.

At 8 o'clock on Tuesday morning, Rafferty was at the courthouse. He walked into judge Weinburg's office at five minutes after eight. He had the tape recordings, and a request for a search warrant in hand. Her clerk didn't even greet him, he immediately went into the judge's chambers, and opened the door for him. Judge Weinburg seemed to have been expecting him.

"Good morning, detective. It seems we have become early morning friends. I'm pretty sure I know what this is about, there's been nothing else on the television, or in the papers. So, what can I do for you?"

"Good morning, judge. I have a suspect in the case of the three murdered Legend employees. He may be linked to the others I had you assist me with previously. I have the necessary request for a search warrant, and I have a recording of a statement by a witness giving me reason for my suspicion. Would you like me to play it for you?"

"Go ahead, detective."

Rafferty played Mr. Taylor's statement. He then informed the judge of the coroner's findings, and why the search warrant was necessary, and as soon as possible.

Judge Weinburg took the papers from Rafferty, and signed them immediately. He thanked her, and hurried back to the station. He would need several forensic technicians, and a couple of uniforms to secure Whitten's residence.

Chapter 100

Monday night, Michael got an EO around 10:30. Tuesday, being his first day off, he decided he would get up early and take a drive up to Lake Tahoe. He was in a great mood. He had slept well for three nights in a row, unusual for him.

He threw a jacket in his car, and left before 8:30. He got onto 395 south on a cloudless morning. His drive would be casual, the work traffic was mostly finished by this time. He would go to Sand Harbor. He still missed the Pacific Ocean, but Tahoe was as close as he could get to it.

Chapter 101

Rafferty and his team arrived at Whitten's apartment at 9:30. He knocked on the door, but got no answer. He walked around the other side of the building, and found another door. He knocked, and was greeted by a woman in her sixties. He showed her his credentials, and introduced himself.

"I'm detective Rafferty of the Reno Police Department. And, who might you be, ma'am?"

"I'm Virginia Milsap."

"We were trying to talk to Michael Whitten. Do you know him?"

"Yes, of course. He rents the other apartment from me."

"We need to get inside his apartment, and no one appears to be home. We have a search warrant." He showed her his papers.

"But, what's he done? He's been an ideal tenant. He's quiet, never has anyone over, he just keeps to himself."

"I'm not at liberty to disclose why we need to search inside. Can you help us?"

"I guess so."

Ms. Milsap went inside her apartment, came out with a ring of keys, and walked with Rafferty back around the building. She reluctantly opened the door to Whitten's apartment, all the while informing Rafferty that whatever they're looking for, they wouldn't find it. Mr. Whitten was the best person she ever had in that apartment.

Rafferty thanked her, and before he and the techs entered the apartment, they put on gloves and placed booties over their shoes. Entering the main room, he first noticed how sparsely furnished it was. There were no pictures on the walls, no collectables sitting on tables. It was purely functional. The main focal point of the room was a television with a VCR, and stacks of tapes neatly arranged in cardboard boxes. He walked into the small kitchen, where he found only one thing on the counter, a small microwave. Opening cupboards, he found two plates, two glasses, and a couple of microwaveable containers. His silverware consisted of two forks, two spoons, and a knife. There were dozens of plastic utensils, still wrapped in cellophane. In another drawer, he found one utility knife. There were no pots and pans, no cookware of any sort. He opened the refrigerator and found a bottle that apparently was filled with water, some take out boxes of partially eaten food, and a bottle of soy sauce. The cabinet next to the refrigerator contained a box of wheat crackers, and two bottles of inexpensive scotch, one only two thirds full.

Obviously, Whitten never planned to have company. Rafferty had investigated men who he considerd "loners" before, but no one quite like this.

He went into the bedroom. There was only one thing in there, a futon mattress on the floor. A single blanket was tossed aside. There were no sheets. A single pillow lay eskew at one end of the mattress. The adjacent bathroom had a razor, shaving cream, a toothbrush and toothpaste, a cheap bottle of aftershave, a comb and a plastic brush. The medicine cabinet had a bottle of aspirin, deodorant, and a bottle with no label. In the shower was a bar of soap. There was no shampoo, Rafferty guessed he used soap to wash his hair.

All this took Rafferty about ten minutes. He walked outside so he would be out of the tech's way. He sat on a small stone wall, and waited.

Fifteen minutes later, one of techs stepped outside. He called to Rafferty, "I think you'd better see this." Rafferty followed him inside. He was taken to the bedroom.

"I found a couple of loose boards inside the closet. I haven't taken out what I found, yet, I thought you'd want to see it."

In a space about a foot square, and maybe eight inches deep, were plastic bags. There appeared to be four of them. He couldn't be sure, but he thought he knew what was in them. "Carefully remove them, mark them, and personally take them to the coroner's office. Make sure Bill Cohen gets these himself. He'll know what to do."

Chapter 102

Michael had enjoyed his morning. He stayed in the Tahoe area for over three hours, had lunch at the Black Bear Diner, and was ready to go home. He had some packing to do.

He drove along highway 28, which follows Lake Tahoe's shore. It was the long way home, but such a beautiful drive was worth the extra time it would take. He drove through small communities such as King's Beach, Carnelian Bay, and Tahoe City. Not far past the Squaw Valley Ski Resort, he connected with highway 89, which took him to U.S. 80 east. Once he was on Interstate 80, it was a short forty minute trip. He took the exit for Virginia Street around three in the afternoon. When he turned off of Virginia, he could see the corner of his apartment building. There were too many cars there. Fifty yards closer, he saw two of them were police cars. He drove past. When he had put at least a half dozen blocks between himself and his apartment, he pulled to the side of the road. How was it possible he had become a suspect? How could it have happened so fast?

It came to him almost immediately. Somehow Peg had survived. She must have seen him go into the room earlier in the evening. She hadn't taken any drugs. And she must have told the police. She was gonna pay for this. Because he failed to remove her from her useless existence, he was now in danger.

He was close to Bev's apartment. He would go there first and look for Peg's car.

The drive took him just over ten minutes. He saw Bev's Neon in her parking space, but no sign of Peg's Taurus. He'd have to drive to Spanish Springs and see if she was there.

Michael, who planned his entire life so carfully, was unsure about not only what to do next, but about his entire future. He knew what they would find in his apartment. He should have taken care of it all before he took his drive. He was so sure they wouldn't connect him to Thursday night's events. And certainly not so soon.

The drive to Peg's house gave him about twenty five minutes to think. If he found her car there, what would he do next? How would he know if her husband was home?

When he turned onto her street, he stopped at the corner. Her car was parked in front of her house. Now what? He had to go somewhere and think. But where? He couldn't go home. Where could he find a quiet place to solve this puzzle? Then he remembered the first time he had been in this area. He would drive out to Pyramid Lake.

CHAPTER 103

Before Rafferty left Whitten's apartment, he had observed the techs bagging and marking several pieces of material to be taken to the lab. In the same closet where they found the plastic bags, that were already with the coroner, they found an aluminum baseball bat wrapped in a towel as far back on the closet's shelf as it could be. They also found wigs, false mustaches, and beards. They determined that the unmarked bottle in the medicine cabinet was spirit gum, used to attach his disguises. With the exception of the "Death Wish" series of movies, and several other revenge movies, the tapes were not labeled in any manner. There were only colored dots, some red, green, yellow, and black. It was decided both boxes of cassettes should be taken as well. There was also a video camera, and several tapes. Underneath the one chair in the living room, facing the television, they found a binder. In it were dozens of pages about various subjects, and all were apparently copied from library books. There was information about poisons, physical anatomy, automobile repair, heating and air conditioning, martial arts, and lots of information about forensic science.

The apartment was small, so the techs were finished before four in the afternoon. Everything they collected was at the lab by 4:30, and Rafferty was back at his desk. He hadn't been there ten minutes when his desk phone rang. It was Bill Cohen.

"Rafferty."

"Hi David, it's Bill. I knew you'd want to know right away. The plastic bags you sent me had the Toxalbumin and the fumigant in them. He's the guy."

"I was pretty sure. Thanks, Bill."

Rafferty went right into Captain Murphy's office. He gave him a summary of the day's events. Murphy made a call to the DA's office, and an arrest warrant was issued for Michael Whitten.

When He got back to his desk, he called Hillary at home. He knew she often went for a run after work, but at least he would leave a message.

She answered on the second ring.

"Hello."

"Hi, Hillary, it's David."

"I've been so anxious. I've been sitting here, hoping I might hear from you."

He filled her in on what they'd found, and an arrest warrant had been issued for Whitten.

"I hope they find him soon. Because you still don't have a motive, I'm thinking about his physical violence. No one else needs to suffer."

"I agree. We have no idea where he might be. We have an unmarked car, with two officers, across the street from his apartment. We're hoping he comes home this evening, and there'll be a quick and easy end to this."

"I hope so too. Thanks for calling, David. I'm glad you're safe, and this is all coming to an end."

"Get some sleep, Hillary. I'll talk to you soon."

Rafferty thought he might sleep well tonight too.

Chapter 104

When Michael got to Pyramid Lake, he parked and stared out at the huge body of water. For several minutes his mind went blank. Then he began to get angry. It was all *her* fault. It was always the women in his life who were the source of his greatest misery. The men that got in his way all acted like women, they were petty and conspiring. It all started with his mother, then Catherine. All of his troubles in Reno started with that bitch, Lydia. Then there was Vanessa, and now Peg.

He had to disappear. He wouldn't go to jail, and with what they must have found in his apartment, he most certainly would. He'd made a mistake, a big one, and now he was the one being hunted. Peg should have died with the rest of them. Maybe he should head south, go to Mexico. He could get lost there. Or maybe north to Canada, they had gambling there. He could change his name, and find a job.

But before he went anywhere, he had to finish what he had started. Peg had to go, but how, and when? He thought about everything for several hours. It was getting dark, and that would make it easier for him to move around. There was less chance he'd be recognized.

He knew how he could get to Peg, the same way he did when he had followed her to her rendevouz with Bev. It was always in the planning.

Chapter 105

The next day Rafferty and two other detectives began examining the items they took from Whitten's apartment. The lab had released almost everything, having taken samples from many items. They had found minute traces of blood, and a few skin cells on the aluminum bat. They cut hairs off the beard and mustache, looking for traces of saliva.

The first thing they did was to look at some of the videos, the ones without labels. Because there were more unmarked ones, than those that were labeled, and more of those had black dots on them than the other colors, they began with those.

When the picture came on the screen, the three men were sickened. The movie showed a man and a woman, both their faces covered. The woman was in shackles, both hands and feet, and they were spread a couple of feet apart. There was duct tape over her mouth. She was wearing nothing but underwear. The man was in jeans, and no shirt. He was striking her repeatedly with a leather whip. On a table behind the man, were other implements which included knives of different sizes and shapes, clubs wrapped with thick cloth or rope, what appeared to be a branding iron, and something that had what looked like fishhooks attached to it. Rafferty's first thought was that Whitten was into S and M. But there was going to be no sex in this film.

The three men watched the man torture her with various instruments for about ten minutes. Rafferty stood up and turned off the machine. He couldn't watch any more. He now knew that each of the tapes had to be viewed, but it wouldn't be by him. Violent acts he had seen, too many of them. But the cruelty he had just watched was far beyond anything he had previously witnessed, and never wanted to again.

He left the other two detectives to watch at least part of all the tapes, and report back to him later in the day. He would go through the binder they had found.

Most pages were filled with information pertaining to the fragility of the human body, whether it be from physical attack, or destruction of internal organs. There were handwritten notes on many of the pages, as well as phone numbers with area codes located in California. There were several pages about heating units and air conditioners, and notes on those pages about the effects of carbon monoxide poisoning. In the back were pages written in some sort of shorthand, or code. RPD had some good people in their lab who might be able to decipher these pages. If not, there was always the FBI. The last page was a list of names, most were crossed off. Rafferty recognized nearly every one of them.

Rafferty talked to the people in the lab about the aluminum bat. He told them to be sure and compare the samples they had removed with tissue taken from Dale Fitzter. And, if they still had access to samples from Lydia Stone, who was killed years ago outside the Stagecoach, they should check those as well.

Late in the afternoon, the two detectives who had been watching the tapes came to Rafferty's desk. They told him they had only watched ten to fifteen minutes of each tape. Just like Rafferty, they couldn't take much more than that. They had figured out Whitten's color coding system. The black dots were the worst, the most violent. Yellow dots were sex tapes where the women engaged in rough sex. Green were all mild S and M, and the red were more hardcore, mostly with two men and one woman, and she was not enjoying it. Most of these tapes were obviously homemade.

One of the detectives laid a tape on Rafferty's desk. "Then we found this one. There's no colored dot at all. It's a "snuff" film. There is a woman in bondage, who is mutilated, and then bludgeoned to death."

"What?"

"Yep, it's a recording of a murder."

"What kind of a sick man have we discovered here?"

"I'm no shrink, but I'd say he is very angry, especially at women."

"So, we're beginning to see some kind of motive here. The revenge films, and now these, all in someway portraying women being treated violently."

Rafferty thanked them, and then apologized for making them watch such horrible things.

Chapter 106

When Peg got off work at 1:30 in on Thursday morning, she was exhausted. She was looking forward to her two days off like never before. She and Bev had plans to sleep in late, have a casual breakfast, and maybe take a drive up to the lake, and find a nice spot on the shore to have dinner around sundown. As she was leaving the building, someone jumped out from behind the wall. It was Michael Whitten. He was glaring at her, eyes filled with hate. In his right hand was a tire iron. He growled at her, "you bitch. This is all your fault. I should have ended your miserable life weeks ago." Peg started to back up, hoping to get back inside. Michael moved towards her, raising the weapon over his head. He wasn't going to let her get away this time.

"Reno police! Drop the weapon. Lay face down on the ground, NOW."

Michael looked over his shoulder, saw two men with guns in their hands. He dropped the weapon, and started to lower himself to the ground. Suddenly he sprinted forward, lunging for his target. The two policemen rushed to grab him just as he was about to jump on Peg who had fallen down as she tried to escape Michael's reach. They put handcuffs on him, and read him his Miranda rights. As one of the officers walked Whitten back to their car, the other helped Peg up and explained what had just happened.

"We were across the street in our car, when we saw him position himself behind the wall. It was too dark to see who it was, but we were pretty sure. I'm glad you told detective Rafferty that you realized Whitten had possibly targeted you at the party. It looks like you were 100% correct. Are you all right? Would you like someone to drive you home?"

"I'll be okay. I'm on my way next door to meet someone for a drink. I can really use one now."

She thanked him, said good night, and went to meet with Bev.

Chapter 107

When Whitten arrived at the jail, he was fingerprinted, and had his mug shot taken. He was taken to a cell, and locked up for the night. He hadn't said one word to the two policemen, or anyone else. He was thinking, "when I get out of here, I'm gonna have to do something special to her. This is all her fault".

Chapter 108

Whitten was examined for three solid days. He was given four to five hours between sessions. He never broke. He constantly stared at the table. He drank water, barely nibbled at any food he was given. The RPD had brought in psychaitrists, but even they received no response. He seemed to exist in another world.

CHAPTER 109

On Saturday evening, a week and a half after Whitten had been captured, David and Jill Rafferty had Hillary Fisk over for dinner. The Rafferty's son-in-law, daughter, and grandchildren joined them.

Jill had made Lasanga with meat sauce, served with loaves of garlic bread, and a green salad. There was Chianti for the adults, and sodas for the kids. This was a celebration. They ate, talked about their personal lives, and laughed for a couple of hours. The kids finally got tired. David and Jill's daughter, Maria, helped clear the table, and put the dishes in the dishwasher. She then helped John, her husband, get the kids ready to go home. There were lots of hugs good-bye, and promises to get together soon again. Maria told Hillary she knew someone she might like to meet.

Just after nine, David, Jill and Hillary were alone. David brought out a bottle of his favorite Brandy, and they went into their cozy living room.

Hillary began; "What a wonderful evening, thank you both. You have a wonderful family."

Jill; "You're very welcome. It's a pleasure getting to know you, and, yes, we think John, Maria, and the kids are great. Although, we might be a little prejudiced."

David; "It seems like I've known you forever. It's as though we have a second daughter."

"You feel like family to me, too, although we became friends in a strange way."

"True, not everyone begins a relationship investigating murder."

Jill; "Well, I think you two did an incredible job together. To think this went on for so many years, and no one had any idea."

"Hillary deserves the credit for that. It all started with her."

Hillary asked; "So, what's the future for Mr. Whitten?"

"He's not going to trial, at least not right away. His evaluations suggested that he has severe mental problems, and only understands part of what is happening to him."

Hillary; "Was the lab able to connect him with all the cases you and I suspected him of committing?"

"Not yet, and I'm sure they never will. The last three are, of course, iron clad. There were traces of tissue and blood on the aluminum bat that matched those of Dale Fitzter, and we may be able to place Whitten at the bar where Carlson was, a few days before his death. There is no way to prove the murder of Lydia Williams was committed by him. There was no evidence on the bat that would connect it to her death. We looked at the films of the man we believed killed the five men who were locals, and the hair, and facial hair, appear to match those we found in his apartment, but there is no way to prove that he was the one wearing them in court. The body of Rolland Thomas definitely contained the fumigant we know was fatal for the others, but we have no way of proving Whitten was involved. We've been interviewing people he worked with, and have determined he had difficult relationships with all of the victims. In the case of Ms. Williams, and Mr. Thomas, the word 'hate' was used. But this has only helped us understand more about his motives, and how disturbed he was. And in the case of Ms. Stryker, we know her heating system was intentionally damaged, but no one saw him, and there was no physical evidence at the house to link anything to him."

Jill; "Wow, it's amazing he was finally caught. How long was he this crazy, this angry, angry enough to committ murder?"

"We believe it may have gone as far back as his late teenage years. We've found records dating back to just after he was out of high school. His mother was found dead in the apartment she and Whitten shared. She had suffocated. How she had suffocated was never determined, she was found face down on her bed. There were no signs of foul play. The only thing they discovered in the lab was an alcohol level almost three times higher than that which would determine someone was intoxicated. When it happened, Whitten was just a few months shy of eighteen. She had a small life insurance policy of 20,000 dollars. After a couple of months, the courts decided he could have the money at eighteen, and live without assistance, if he so chose. He did.

We also discovered he was married once, but not for long. His wife supposedly left him while they were spending a weekend in Palm Springs. She never came back from their trip. Her parents, who live in Kansas City, Missouri, hired an investigator, but he found nothing. What we found was a video camera, and some tapes. There is nothing specific on them. The little there was on two tapes, was innocuous. There were scenes taken in a desert, somewhere. There was a few minutes of what appears to be the Pacific Ocean, somewhere around Los Angeles. There were short clips of what appear to be Lake Tahoe, Pyramid Lake, and areas east of Sparks. No one has been able to determine why he took the videos, and if they had any relation to his psyche, or the deaths we were investigating."

Hillary; "It appears his hatred for women began a long time ago."

"An FBI profiler has been working on his case for about four days now. He says that there are similarities between Whitten and several other serial killers. What's unusual about him, is the number of years involved. Most serial killers cannot resist increasing the frequency, and the number of their episodes. This happened for him only at the end, and it appears to have been a case of opportunity. Then, again, maybe his anger had reached a point where he no longer was a careful as he had been. We'll never know the answers to all of it."

Chapter 110

Sitting alone in his cell, Michael decided that this wasn't so bad. As long as he kept them thinking he was crazy, he wouldn't have to have a roommate, or in this case a cellmate. He had plenty of time by himself to find a way out of this. He didn't have to worry about food, and he didn't have to go to work. The only thing he really missed were his videos. He was sure the cops were enjoying them now.

He wondered what Peg was doing. He had all the time in the world to plan what he would do to her when he got out.

THE END

"Michael Whitten looked out at the Pacific Ocean. He was alone, as always. He had just come back from a vacation in Reno, Nevada. He liked it so much, he decided to move there. He wanted to start a new life, have a better life.

Little did he know that he would start a new career, and then slip right back into old patterns.

What he had planned when he decided to move to 'the Biggest Little City', would not happen. His life would follow a course decided by fate, and poor decisions. But, none of it would be his fault."

Acknowledgements

I'm an avid reader. I have always admired the abilities and imagination of the authors whose books I read. I never thought I could write an entire novel. When I was forced into early retirement because of a disastrous turn in our Nation's economy, I had plenty of time to at least give it a try.

Every great author I have seen interviewed gave one excellent piece of advice, write about what you know. I worked for the casinos in Reno and Sparks for about twenty years. I know a lot about them. Because I am mentally sick and somewhat demented, Michael Whitten was created.

Aluminum Phosphide and Toxalbumin are real. Aluminum Phosphide is a favorite form of suicide on the Indian continent. The Toxalbumin I referred to was specifically Jatropha curcas. It is a plant and can cause death. I used my "author's privilege" to allow them to be slightly more poisonous than they actually are. Both can cause the type of death I described, but would have to be given in the proper form and dosage.

Because they could be obtained easily, they were the poison of choice for my anti-Hero.

I thank my beautiful, bright, and intelligent bride, Sandy, for her encouragment. She helped me edit, but she did something else she seldom does that meant more to me than I could say, she read it. She doesn't read fiction novels, but she read mine, and was a kind and honest critic.

Lastly, I want to thank you for reading my story. I understand now how many authors must have felt about their first attempts. I have been excited and nervous. I know now what is meant by "writer's block". It simply means that you don't like what you've written. It becomes a do-over. I hope you enjoyed the story half as much as I enjoyed writing it.

I did it!!!

About the Author

He currently writes articles for a Las Vegas based newspaper. An avid reader of novels, retirement gave him to opportunity to attempt one himself. His favorite authors offered advice to all novice writers to writed about what they knew best. So here it is, his first novel based on the Reno/Sparks casino industry.

He has accomplished what most people would love to do—write, actually finish, and publish a novel. Few accomplish this goal, but the author has. I wish him every succes with his future writing!